KT-563-301

NEVER WORLD WAKE

MARISHA PESSL

■SCHOLASTIC

Scholastic Children's Books
An imprint of Scholastic Ltd
Euston House, 24 Eversholt Street, London, NW1 1DB, UK
Registered office: Westfield Road, Southam, Warwickshire, CV47 0RA
SCHOLASTIC and associated logos are trademarks and/or
registered trademarks of Scholastic Inc.

First published in the US by Penguin Random House, 2018
First published in the UK by Scholastic Ltd, 2018

Text copyright © Marisha Pessl, 2018

The right of Marisha Pessl to be identified as the
author of this work has been asserted by her.

ISBN 978 1407 18795 2
A CIP catalogue record for this book
is available from the British Library.

All rights reserved.
This book is sold subject to the condition that it shall not,
by way of trade or otherwise, be lent, hired out or otherwise circulated in
any form of binding or cover other than that in which it is published. No
part of this publication may be reproduced, stored in a retrieval system,
or transmitted in any form or by any means (electronic, mechanical,
photocopying, recording or otherwise) without prior
written permission of Scholastic Limited.

Printed by CPI Group (UK) Ltd, Croydon, CR0 4YY
Papers used by Scholastic Children's Books are made
from wood grown in sustainable forests.

3 5 7 9 10 8 6 4 2

This is a work of fiction. Names, characters, places, incidents
and dialogues are products of the author's imagination or are used
fictiously. Any resemblance to actual people, living or dead,
events or locales is entirely coincidental.

www.scholastic.co.uk

For David

Sometimes there are no answers,

Sometimes you find love,

Sometimes the dark has teeth,

Sometimes it hides doves.

The one thing you can expect in life,

As you step down its twisted road,

Is that you will be speechless.

Then? Ask someone who knows.

—J. C. Gossamer Madwick,
   The Dark House at Elsewhere Bend

PART 1

CHAPTER 1

I hadn't spoken to Whitley Lansing—or any of them—in over a
year.

When her text arrived after my last final, it felt inevitable,
like a comet tearing through the night sky, hinting of fate.

Too long. WTF. #notcool. Sorry. My Tourette's again. How
was your freshman year? Amazing? Awful?

Seriously. We miss you.

Breaking the silence bc the gang is heading to Wincroft for
my bday. The Linda will be in Mallorca & ESS Burt is getting
married in St. Bart's for the 3rd time. (Vegan yogi.) So it's
ours for the weekend. Like yesteryear.

Can you come? What do you say Bumblebee?

Carpe noctem.

Seize the night.

She was the only girl I knew who surveyed everybody like a leather-clad Dior model and rattled off Latin like it was her native language.

"How was your exam?" my mom asked when she picked me up.

"I confused Socrates with Plato and ran out of time during the essay," I said, pulling on my seat belt.

"I'm sure you did great." She smiled, a careful look. "Anything else we need to do?"

I shook my head.

My dad and I had already cleared out my dorm room. I'd returned my textbooks to the student union to get the 30 percent off for next year. My roommate had been a girl from New Haven named Casey who'd gone home to see her boyfriend every weekend. I'd barely seen her since orientation.

The end of my freshman year at Emerson College had just come and gone with the indifferent silence usually reserved for a going-out-of-business sale at a mini-mall.

"Something dark's a-brewin'," Jim would have told me.

——

I had no plans all summer, except to work alongside my parents at the Captain's Crow.

The Captain's Crow—the Crow, it's called by locals—is the seaside café and ice cream parlor my family owns in Watch Hill, Rhode Island, the tiny coastal village where I grew up.

Watch Hill, Rhode Island. Population: You Know Everyone.

My great-grandfather Burn Hartley opened the parlor in 1885, when Watch Hill was little more than a craggy hamlet where whaling captains came to shake off their sea legs and hold their children for the first time before taking off again for the Atlantic's Great Unknowns. Burn's framed pencil portrait hangs over the entrance, revealing him to have the mad glare of some dead genius writer, or a world explorer who never came home from the Arctic. The truth is, though, he could barely read, preferred familiar faces to strange ones and dry land to the sea. All he ever did was run our little dockside restaurant his whole life, and perfect the recipe for the best clam chowder in the world.

All summer I scooped ice cream for tan teenagers in flip-flops and pastel sweaters. They came and went in big skittish groups like schools of fish. I made cheeseburgers and tuna melts, coleslaw and milk shakes. I swept away sand dusting the black-and-white-checkered floor. I threw out napkins, ketchup packets, salt packets, over-21 wristbands, Del's Frozen Lemonade cups, deep-sea fishing party boat brochures. I put lost cell phones beside the register so they could be easily found when the panic-stricken owners came barging inside: "I lost my . . . Oh . . . thank you, you're the best!" I cleaned up the torn blue tickets from the 1893 saltwater carousel, located just a few doors down by the beach, which featured faded faceless mermaids to ride, not horses. Watch Hill's greatest claim to fame was that Eleanor Roosevelt had been photographed riding a redhead with a turquoise tail sidesaddle. (It was a town joke how put out she looked in the shot, how uncomfortable and buried alive under her plate-tectonic layers of ruffled skirt.)

I cleaned the barbecue sauce off the garbage cans, the melted Wreck Rummage off the tables (Wreck Rummage was every kid's favorite ice cream flavor, a mash-up of cookie dough, walnuts, cake batter, and dark chocolate nuggets). I Cloroxed and Fantasticked and Mr. Cleaned the windows and counters and doorknobs. I dusted the brine off the mussels and the clams, polishing every one like a gemstone dealer obsessively inspecting emeralds. Most days I rose at five and went with my dad to pick out the day's seafood when the fishing boats came in, inspecting crab legs and fluke, oysters and bass, running my hands over their tapping legs and claws, barnacles and iridescent bellies. I composed song lyrics for a soundtrack to a made-up movie called *Lola Anderson's Highway Robbery,* drawing words, rhymes, faces, and hands on napkins and take-out menus, tossing them in the trash before anyone saw them. I attended grief support group for adolescents at the North Stonington Community Center. There was only one other kid in attendance, a silent boy named Turks whose dad had died from ALS. After two meetings he never returned, leaving me alone with the counselor, a jittery woman named Deb who wore pantsuits and wielded a three-inch-thick book called *Grief Management for Young People.*

" 'The purpose of this exercise is to construct a positive meaning around the lost relationship,' " she read from chapter seven, handing me a Goodbye Letter worksheet. " 'On this page, write a note to your lost loved one, detailing fond memories, hopes, and any final questions.' "

Slapping a chewed pen that read TABEEGO ISLAND RESORTS on my desk, she left. I could hear her on the phone out in the hall, arguing with someone named Barry, asking him why he didn't come home last night.

I drew a screeching hawk on the Goodbye Letter, with lyrics to a made-up Japanese animated film about a forgotten thought called *Lost in a Head*.

Then I slipped out the fire exit and never went back.

I taught Sleepy Sam (giant yawn of a teenager from England visiting his American dad) how to make clam cakes and the perfect grilled cheese. *Grill on medium, butter, four minutes a side, six slices of Vermont sharp cheddar, two of fontina*. For July Fourth, he invited me to a party at a friend of a friend's. To his shock, I actually showed. I stood by a floor lamp with a warm beer, listening to talk about guitar lessons and Zach Galifianakis, trying to find the right moment to escape.

"*That*, by the way, is Bee," said Sleepy Sam. "She does actually speak, I swear."

I didn't mention Whitley's text to anyone, though it was always in the back of my mind.

———

It was the brand-new way-too-extravagant dress I'd bought but never taken out of the bag. I just left it there in the back of my closet, folded in tissue paper with the receipt, the tags still on, with intention of returning it.

Yet there was still the remote possibility I'd find the courage to put it on.

I knew the weekend of her birthday like I knew my own: August 30.

It was a Friday. The big event of the day had been the appearance of a stray dog wandering Main Street. It had no tags and the haunted look of a prisoner of war. He was gray, shaggy, and startled with every attempt to pet him. A honk sent him skidding into the garbage cans behind the Captain's Crow.

"See that yellow salt-bed mud on his back paws? That's from the west side of Nickybogg Creek," announced Officer Locke, thrilled to have a mystery on his hands, his first of the year.

That stray dog had been the talk all that day—what to do with him, where he'd been—and it was only much later that I found my mind going back to that dog drifting into town out of the blue. I wondered if he was some kind of sign, a warning that something terrible was coming, that I should not take the much-exalted and mysterious Road Less Traveled, but the one well trod, wide-open, and brightly lit, the road I knew.

By then it was too late. The sun had set. Sleepy Sam was gone. I'd overturned the café chairs and put them on the tables. I'd hauled out the trash. And anyway, that flew in the face of human nature. No one ever heeded a warning sign when it came.

My mom and dad assumed I was joining them at the Dreamland Theater in Westerly for the screwball comedy classics marathon, like I did every Friday.

"Actually, I made plans tonight," I said.

My dad was thrilled. "Really, Bumble? That's great."

"I'm driving up to Wincroft."

They fell silent. My mom had just flipped the Closed sign in the window, and she turned, wrapping her cardigan around herself, shivering even though it was seventy-five degrees out.

"How long have you known about this?" she asked.

"Not long. I'll be careful. I'll be back by midnight. They're up there for Whitley's birthday. I think it'll be good for me to see them."

"That's a long way to drive in the dark," said my dad.

My mom looked like I'd been given a prognosis of six weeks left to live. Sometimes when she got really upset, she chewed an imaginary piece of gum. She was doing that now.

"Part of the grieving process is confronting the past," I said.

"That's not the point. I—"

"It's all right, Victoria." My dad put a hand on her shoulder.

"But Dr. Quentin said not to put yourself in stressful situations that—"

"We've established that Dr. Quentin is an idiot," I said.

"Dr. Quentin is indeed an idiot," said my dad with a regretful nod. "The fact that his name is one-half of a state prison should have been a red flag."

"You know I don't like it when you two gang up on me," said my mom.

At that moment, someone—some red-faced weekender in seersucker shorts who'd had too many stouts at O'Malligan's—tried to open the door.

"We're closed," my mom snapped.

——

That was how I came to be driving my dad's ancient green Dodge RAM with the emphysema muffler fifty miles up the Rhode Island coastline.

Wincroft.

The name sounded like something out of a windswept novel filled with ghosts and madmen. The mansion was a sprawling collection of red brick, turrets, gardens, and crow gargoyles, built in the 1930s by a Great White Hunter who'd supposedly called Hemingway and Lawrence of Arabia his friends. He had traveled the world killing beautiful creatures, and thus Wincroft, his seaside estate, had never been lived in more than a few weeks in sixty years. When Whitley's weird ex-second-stepdad, Burt—commonly called E.S.S. Burt—bought it in foreclosure in the 1980s, he gut renovated the interiors in an unfortunate style Whitley called "if Madonna threw up all over Cyndi Lauper."

Still, it wasn't unusual to open a chest of drawers in the attic, or a musty steamer trunk, and find photographs of strangers gripping rifles and wearing fox furs or some weird piece of taxidermy—a ferret, red frog, or rodent of unknown species. This gave every visit to Wincroft the mysterious feel of being on an archaeological expedition, as if all around us, inside the floors, walls, and ceiling, some lost civilization was waiting to be unearthed.

"We are our junk," said Jim once, pulling a taxidermy lizard out of a shoe box.

Leaving the interstate, the road to get there turned corkscrewed and dizzying, as if trying to shake you. The coast of Rhode Island—not the infamously uptight Newport part, with the stiff cliffs and colossal mansions smugly staring down at the tiny sailboats salting the harbor, but the rest of it—was rough and tumbledown, laid-back and sunburnt. It was an old homeless beachcomber in a washed-out T-shirt who couldn't remember where he'd slept the night before. The grasses were wiry and wasted, the roads salty and cracked, sprouting faded signs and faulty traffic lights. Bridges elbowed their way out of the marshes before collapsing, exhausted, on the other side of the road.

I still had their phone numbers, but I didn't want to call. I didn't even know if they'd be there. All these months later their plans could have changed. Maybe I'd knock and Whitley wouldn't answer, but her ex-second-stepdad, Burt, would, E.S.S. Burt with his too-long, curly gray hair; Burt, who a million years ago had written an Oscar-nominated song for a tragic love story starring Ryan O'Neill. Or maybe they would all be there. Maybe I wanted to see the looks on their faces when they first saw me, looks they hadn't rehearsed.

Then again, if they didn't know I was coming, I could still turn around. I could still go join my parents at the Dreamland for *His Girl Friday*, afterward head to the Shakedown for crab cakes and oysters, saying hi to the owner, Artie, pretending I didn't hear him whisper to my dad when I went to the bathroom, "Bee's really come around," like I was a wounded racehorse they'd decided not to euthanize. Not that it was Artie's fault. It was the natural reaction when people found out what had happened: my boyfriend, Jim, had died senior year.

Sudden Death of the Love of Your Life wasn't supposed to happen to you as a teenager. If it did, though, it was helpful if it was due to one of the Top Three Understandable Reasons for Dying as a Kid: A. Car accident. B. Cancer. C. Suicide. That way, after you selected the applicable choice, the nearest adult could promptly steer your attention to the range of movies (many starring Timothy Hutton) and self-help books to help you Deal.

But when your boyfriend's death remains unsolved, and you're left staring into a black hole of guilt and the unknown?

There's no movie or self-help book in the world to help you with that.

Except maybe *The Exorcist*.

If I was a no-show tonight, my old friends would come and go from Wincroft, and that would be that. Not showing up would be the final push of that old toy sailboat from my childhood, the one shove that would really send it drifting out toward the middle of the lake, far from the shoreline, forever out of reach.

Then I'd never find out what happened to Jim.

I kept driving.

The twisting road seemed to urge me onward, yellowed beech trees streaking past; a bridge; the sudden, startling view of a harbor where tall white sailboats crowded like a herd of feasting unicorns before vanishing. I couldn't believe how easily I remembered the way: left at the Exxon, right on Elm, right at the stop sign where you diced with Death, run-down trailers with strung-up laundry and flat tires in the yard. Then the trees fell away in deference to the most beautiful kiss of sky and sea, always streaked orange and pink at dusk.

And there it was. The wrought-iron gate emblazoned with the *W*.

It was open. The lamps were lit.

I made the turn and floored it, oak branches flying past like ribbons come loose from a ponytail, wind howling through the open windows. Another curve and I saw the mansion, the windows golden and alive, all hulking red brick and slate, crow gargoyles perched forever on the roof.

As I pulled up I almost laughed aloud at the four cars parked there, side by side. I didn't recognize any of them—except for Martha's Honda Accord with the bumper sticker HONK FOR GENERAL RELATIVITY. If pressed I could, with little trouble, match the other cars with their respective owners.

I had changed so much. From the look of these cars, they had not.

I checked my appearance in the rearview mirror, feeling immediate horror: messy ponytail, chapped lips, shiny forehead. I looked like I'd just run a marathon and come in last. I blotted my face on the roll of paper towels my dad kept in the door, pinched my cheeks, tucked the loose strands of dark brown hair behind my ears. Then I was sprinting up the stone steps and rapping the brass lion knocker.

Nothing happened.

I rang the doorbell, once, twice, three times, all in one crazy, deranged movement, because I knew if I hesitated at all I'd lose my nerve. I'd sink, like some lost boot caught inside a lobster trap, straight back to the bottom of the sea.

The door opened.

Kipling stood there. He was wearing a chin-length pink wig, blue polo shirt, Bermuda shorts, flip-flops. He was extremely tan and chewing a red drink stirrer, though it fell out of his mouth when he saw me.

"Good Lord, strike me down dead," he said in his cotton-plantation drawl.

CHAPTER 2

Grand entrances don't happen in real life. Not the way you want.

What you want is something between a Colombian telenovela (screaming, faces agog, running mascara) and a Meryl Streep Oscar™ Moment (crackling dialogue, hugs, the whole world coming together to sing in harmony).

Instead, they're awkward.

My sudden appearance at Wincroft was a poorly aimed torpedo. I had misfired, and now I was drifting aimlessly, explosive, but without a target. Standing in the foyer under the chandelier in my jean cutoffs, sneakers, Wreck Rummage–stained T-shirt, faced with their freshly showered, glam selves, I felt ridiculous. I shouldn't have come.

They were heading to a sold-out punk rock concert at the Able Seaman in Newport, the beachfront dive bar where we'd spent many a weekend senior year with fake IDs and weekend passes, so they were greeting me, but also getting ready to go. So there was an awful feeling of distraction and poorly dubbed conversation.

First Kip hugged me. Then he surveyed me politely, as if he were on an art museum tour and I were the tiny, underwhelming painting some guide was blathering on and on about.

Whitley came running over.

"Oh, my God, Beatrice." She air-kissed me. "You actually came. Wow."

She was even more jarringly beautiful than I remembered: thigh-high stiletto jean boots, oversized sweatshirt with a sequin mouth on the front, black fringe cutoffs, perfume of gardenia and leather. I was at once hit with the magazine ad that was her presence and also finding it impossible to believe she used to be my best friend. Countless nights at Darrow-Harker School in Warwick, Rhode Island—home of the Crusaders—we sat up illegally after curfew, cheeks polka-dotted with zit cream, wool socks on our feet. I had told her things I hadn't told anyone. Now that seemed like an out-of-place scene cut from some other movie.

"How are you, Bee?" she asked, squeezing my hands.

"Good."

"This is the *best* surprise. I mean, I could—I'm— Oh, *shoot*. The patio cushions need to be brought in. It's supposed to rain, right?"

And then she was racing away, long blond hair carouseling her back. "Kip was right," she called out as she vanished into the kitchen. "He said you'd show up out of the blue like some presumed-dead character in a movie starring, like, Jake Gyllenhaal, but we told him he was nuts. I thought you'd rather die than see any of us again. Now I owe him, like, fifty dollars—"

"One hundred dollars," interrupted Kip, holding up a finger. "Do not try to renege. Ghosting on debts is one of your worst qualities, Lansing."

"What? Oh, wait. We have to give Gandalf his Prozac or he'll pee everywhere."

"Gandalf is depressed," Kip explained to me with a prim nod. "He also suffers from multiple personalities. He's a Great Dane who thinks he's a lapdog."

"I know Gandalf," I reminded him weakly.

"Beatrice."

Cannon was jogging barefoot down the staircase, Puma sneakers in hand. At the bottom he stopped, surveying me with a warm smile.

"I can't believe it. Sister Bee in the flesh. How's God?"

"Funny."

He looked different too. He was still sporting his signature gray hacker's hoodie, but it was no longer misshapen and dusted with orange Cheez-Its powder after wearing it two weeks straight in the arctic subterranean computer room at Darrow. It was cashmere. Cannon had become semifamous when, sophomore year, he discovered a bug in Apple's OS X operating system: when you accidentally tapped certain keys, your screen froze, and your desktop turned into the surreal winter scene of Apple's Blue

Pond wallpaper. He christened the bug Cannon's Birdcage, and it landed him on the front page of a million Silicon Valley blogs. Last I'd heard, he was attending Stanford for computer science.

He jumped off the stairs and hugged me. He smelled like expensive wood flooring.

"How's college? How's your mom and dad? They still run that little ice cream parlor?"

"Yes."

He stared at me, his expression intense and unreadable. "I love that place."

"Hello, Bee," called a solemn voice.

Turning, I saw Martha. She was blinking at me from behind her thick, mad-scientist glasses, which gave her the all-seeing, telephoto-lens stare for which she was famous. She'd given up her khakis and boxy Oxford shirts for ripped black jeans and an oversized T-shirt proclaiming something in German: TORSCHLUSSPANIK. She'd also dyed her thin brown hair neon blue.

"Hi," I said.

"It's absurd how you haven't changed," drawled Kip, his smile like a tiny button on formal living room upholstery. "You freeze-dry yourself in some cryogenic experiment? 'Cause it isn't fair, child. I got crow's-feet and gout."

Whitley was back, avoiding eye contact, grabbing her flesh-colored Chanel purse.

"You're coming with us, right?"

She seemed less than thrilled by the idea, now shoving her manicured feet into Lanvin flats.

"Actually, I—"

"Of course you are," said Cannon, throwing his arm around my shoulder. "I'll scalp you a ticket. Or I'll scalp someone for a ticket. Either way, we'll figure it out."

"*Laissez les bon temps roulez,*" said Kip, raising his glass.

There was a Texas-sized stretch of silence as we filed outside, the only sounds our footsteps on the pavement and the wind ransacking the trees. My heart was pounding, my face red. I wanted nothing more than to sprint to my pickup and take off down the drive at a hundred miles an hour, pretend none of this had happened.

"We taking two cars?" asked Martha.

"We're five," said Whitley. "We'll squeeze into mine."

"Promise you'll glance in that rearview mirror at least once, child?" asked Kip.

"You're hilarious."

We piled into her hunter-green convertible Jaguar. Whitley, with a severe look—which I remembered meant she felt nervous—pressed a series of buttons on the console screen. The engine did an elegant throat clear, and the top half of the car began to peel away like a hatching egg. Then we were speeding down the drive, Whitley accelerating like a veteran NASCAR driver, swerving into the grass, mowing through rhododendrons. I was in the backseat between Kip and Martha, trying not to lean too hard on either of them.

Kip tossed his pink wig into the air.

"Ahhhhh!" he screamed, head back, as the wig landed in the driveway behind us. "After a long absence, the band is back together! Let's never break up again! Let's go on a world tour!"

What about the lead singer? I couldn't help wondering as I looked up at him.

Aren't you forgetting Jim?

——

The opening band had already started when we arrived. There wasn't time to talk. There was only this anxious pushing through the packed crowd outside while Whitley approached the bouncer. Martha went in to secure the table, and Cannon went around asking guys with buzz cuts and Budweiser breath if they had an extra ticket, all of which left me crammed pointlessly against the side railing.

"You guys go in without me!" I shouted at Kip, who'd materialized beside me.

"Hush." He linked his arm through mine. "Now that we found you again, we're never going to let you go. I'm your barnacle, child. Deal with it."

I laughed. It seemed like the start of the first true conversation that night.

Kipling and I had always been close. Tall and lanky, with rust-red hair and "an ancient gentleman face"—as he described himself—he was the most fun stuffed into a single person I'd ever met. He was eccentric and strange, like some half-broken talisman you'd find on a dusty shelf at the back of an antiques store, hinting at a harrowing history and good luck. He was gay, though claimed to be more interested in a story well told than in sex, and saw Darrow more as a country club than as any institution in which he was meant to learn something. A study date in the library with Kipling meant constant interruption for his anecdotes and observations about life, friends, and the host of colorful characters populating his tiny hometown of Moss Bluff, Louisiana— like we weren't holed up in muggy cubicles stressed about SATs, but relaxing on a porch shooing flies. While he was as rich as the others ("defunct department store money"), he had had what he called a "busted childhood," thanks to his scary mom, Momma Greer.

Little was *actually* known about Momma Greer, apart from the details Kipling let slip like a handful of confetti he loved to toss into the air without warning. When he was a toddler she locked him alone for days in Room 2 of the Royal Sonata Motel ("ground floor by the vendin' machines so she could sneak out without payin'"), nothing to eat but a stash of Moon Pies, no company but Delta Burke selling bangles on QVC. Her negligence had led to a pit bull, chained up in a backyard, attacking Kipling when he was five, biting off three fingers on his left hand, and leaving him with a "mini shark bite" on his chin—disfigurations he paraded like a Purple Heart.

"Just call me Phantom of the Opera," he'd say, gleefully fanning his severed hand in front of your face. When the court finally removed Kip from his mom's custody, sending him to live with an infirm aunt, he kept running away to try to get back to Momma Greer.

Last I'd heard she was in a mental institution in Baton Rouge.

I wanted to ask how his year had been, but at that moment, Whitley, in true Whitley fashion, came over and without a word grabbed my wrist, pulling me through the crowd. She'd come to some understanding with the doorman. He let me in without a ticket, stamping my hand, and then we were all at a reserved table in the front watching a girl with stringy hair pretend she was Kurt Cobain.

It was strange. The drummer looked like Jim. I wasn't sure anyone else noticed, but he looked like Jim's younger brother, all milk-chocolate eyes and bedhead, the rueful air of a banished prince. It was deafening inside, too loud to talk, so all of us just stared at the band, lost in the swamps of our thoughts.

Maybe I was the only one lost. Maybe they'd all had amazing experiences in college, which had shrunk what had happened to us in high school, turned even Jim's death into a faded T-shirt washed ten thousand times.

Once upon a time at Darrow, they'd been my family. They were the first real friends I'd ever had, a collection of people so vibrant and loyal that, like some child born into a grand dynasty, I couldn't help but be awed at my luck. We'd been a club, a secret society all the other students at Darrow eyed with envy—not that we even paid attention. Friendship, when it runs deep, blinds you to the outside world. It's your exclusive country with sealed borders, unfair distribution of green cards, rich culture no foreigner could understand. To be cut off from them, exiled by my own volition as I had been for the past year, felt cheap and unsettled, a temporary existence of suitcases, rented rooms, and roads I didn't know.

Jim's death had been the earthquake that swallowed cities.

Although I had spent the past year certain my friends knew much more about it than they'd let on, I also knew with every passing day the truth was drifting farther out of reach. I'd checked Whitley's Snapchat and every now and then I saw the four of them together. They looked so happy, so nonchalant.

Like nothing had happened.

Yet now, I could see that the dynamic between them had changed.

Kip kept drumming his disfigured hand on the table. Whitley kept checking her phone. Martha seemed to be in an unusually bad mood, throwing back shots the bartender kept sending to our table—something called the Sinking of the *General Grant*, which tasted like crude oil. I caught her staring at me once, her expression faintly accusatory. I smiled back, but she turned away like one of those jungle plants that shrivel at the faintest touch, refusing to look at me again. Once, as Cannon leaned forward to whisper something to Whitley, he tucked her hair behind her ear, which made me wonder if they were back together. Then it seemed more habit than anything else.

When the opening band finished, I wanted to disappear. I wanted to take a taxi back to Wincroft, climb into my dad's truck, drive off, and never look back. What had I expected—for the truth to be right there, obvious as a giant weed growing among tulips, waiting for me to yank it out?

But I stayed. I stayed for the next band, the band after that. I drank the Moscow Mules Whitley put in front of me. I let Kipling pull me to my feet, and I danced the Charleston with him, and the fox-trot, letting him spin me into the beach bums, and the prep-sters, and the Harley-heads under the shaking paper lanterns and posters of sunken ships.

Just a little while longer, I kept thinking, *and I'll bring up Jim.*

When the next band finished, Whitley wanted to go back to Wincroft, only no one could find Cannon. As it turned out, he was in the bar's back alley, helping a girl who'd had too much to drink and was passed out by the fire exit.

"Here comes Lancelot," said Whitley.

Perched along the railing, we watched while Cannon tracked down—with the efficiency of a lobbyist working Capitol Hill—the girl's missing friends, purse, sandals, and iPhone. He even located her hair clip, which he used to gently pin back her hair so she'd stop throwing up on it, which led the girl's newly located, equally drunk friends to stare up at him in wonder.

"Are you human, dude?"

"Do you have a girlfriend?"

"Who *are* you?"

Cannon ran a hand through his hair. "I'm Batman."

"Here we go again," sighed Whitley.

Cannon was not handsome. He was slight, with dirty blond hair and pale, out-of-focus features. But he had atomic intensity, which never failed to shock and awe when unleashed upon the world. Moving like a highly charged ion, capable as a machine gun, the first week of freshman year Cannon hacked Darrow's intranet to display its flaws (becoming the school's de facto tech guru). He revamped the decrepit sculpture garden and the wres-tling gym. He was class president, and organized marches, marathons, and fund-raisers for endangered species and girls' rights. Cannon was the first to admit that his outgoing, sociable nature and activism was compensation for being a tongue-tied computer geek as a child, worshipping Spielberg movies, eighties pop songs by the Cure, and Ray Kurzweil, no friends to speak of but an imaginary fly named Pete who lived inside his computer. He was adopted, raised by a single mother, a judge in the superior court of California. And while at first glance having Whitley Morrow as his girlfriend—besting Darrow's country club boys who were IIIs and had middle names like Chesterton—seemed like a mistaken case of the princess accidentally ending up with the sidekick, the more you knew Cannon, the more you realized the role of prince was far too trivial for him. He was the king—at least, that was what he was aiming for. He was the most silently ambitious person I'd ever met.

"Any more distressed damsels you need to save?" Whitley asked as Cannon strode back over, having helped the girl and her stumbling friends into an Uber.

He held out his arms in mock triumph. "The bartender looks like he's coming down with a head cold. But no. My work here is done."

"Thank the Lord, 'cause I need my beauty sleep," said Kip with a yawn.

We piled into the Jaguar.

The problem was, no matter how many times Whitley pressed the buttons on the console screen, the convertible top wouldn't go up. It wouldn't go up manually either.

Cannon volunteered to drive, but Whitley insisted. It began to pour, so hard there was more rain in the air than air. The thirty-five-minute ride home was this terrible ordeal, all of us in the backseat hunched together, drunk and freezing. At one point Martha threw up all over her feet, all of us shivering under E.S.S. Burt's creepy London Fog trench coat, which Whitley had found in the trunk. Whitley began to cry that she couldn't see the road. Tearing around a curve, we nearly collided with a tow truck.

The driver blared his horn. Whitley jerked the wheel, tires screeching. Everyone screamed as we barreled off the road, bouncing to a halt in a ditch, Kip hitting his head on the seat. Killing the engine, Whitley started to sob, screaming at Cannon that it was all his fault, that as always he'd needed to impress a bunch of girls just to massage his screaming insecurity for five minutes and now we'd almost died. She snatched his baseball cap off his head and threw it into the dark. Then she scrambled out, shouting that she was finding her own ride home, running into the woods. I sensed her tantrum had to do with the rain and almost ending up in a car accident—but also with me, how I'd shown up out of the blue.

Cannon went after her. A few minutes later, he brought her back. She was crying and wearing his hoodie. He tucked her carefully, like some wild bird with a broken wing, into the front seat, whispering, "It's gonna be all right, Shrieks."

It was Cannon who got us home.

——

As the five of us went clambering into Wincroft, dripping wet and drunk, it felt normal for the first time. It felt like the old days. Thank goodness for the defunct top on that convertible.

Our brush with death had thawed the ice. We were giddy, teeth chattering as we pulled off our wet clothes, leaving them in a soggy pile on the floor, which Gandalf kept circling while whining. Whitley disappeared upstairs. Martha was on her hands and knees in front of the fireplace, moaning, "I can't feel my legs." Cannon went down to the wine cellar, returning with four bottles of Chivas Regal Royal Salute, and poured shots in pink champagne glasses. Whitley dumped a giant mound of white terrycloth bathrobes on the couch like a pile of dead bodies.

"I've never been so scared in my whole life," she said, giggling.

That was when the doorbell rang.

We all sat up, staring at each other, bewildered. Mentally counting. We were all here.

"Someone call Ghostbusters?" slurred Martha.

"I'll go," volunteered Cannon. A sloppy salute, and he disappeared into the foyer. None of us said a word, listening, the only sound the rain drumming on the roof.

A minute later, he was back.

"It's some old geezer. He's two hundred years old."

"It's Alastair Totters," said Martha.

"Who?" Cannon snapped.

"Time-traveling villain in *The Bend*," mumbled Martha.

"No, no," whispered Kip, gleeful. "It's the proverbial kook with Alzheimer's who wandered away from his nursing home during Elvis Social Hour. *Without* his medication. They're always without their medications."

"I'll invite him in for a nightcap?" asked Cannon, sighing, a mischievous wink.

"No," hissed Whitley. "That's how horror movies start."

"Chapter three," Martha muttered.

"Hey," said Cannon, pointing at Wit. "That's not very nice. *I'm* inviting him in—"

"NO!"

Then we were all racing, giggling, tripping over each other as we bumbled to the foyer to see for ourselves, tying up our bathrobes, taking turns to check the peephole, bumping heads. I assumed Cannon was somehow playing a trick on us, that no one would actually be there.

But there he was. An old man.

He was tall, with thick silver hair. Though I couldn't make out his face in the shadows, I could see that he was dressed in a dark suit and tie. He leaned in, smiling, as if he could see me peering out.

Cannon opened the door with a bow.

"Good evening, sir. How may we help you?"

The man didn't immediately speak. Something about the way he surveyed us—methodically inspecting each of our faces—made me think he knew us from somewhere.

"Good evening," he said. His voice was surprisingly rich. "May I enter the premises?"

No one answered, the question being too presumptuous and strange. I gathered he was not senile. His eyes—deep green, gleaming in the porch light—were lucid.

"Oh, you live next door," said Whitley, stepping beside Cannon. "Because if this is about Burt's sailboat, the *Andiamo*, being marooned in front of your dock, he told me to tell you he had problems with the anchor and he's working on getting a tow next week."

"I do not live next door."

He stared at us another beat, his face expectant.

"It's really best if I come inside to explain."

"Tell us what you want right there," said Cannon.

The man nodded, unsurprised. It was then that I noticed two bizarre things.

One: he looked like Darrow's musical director, Mr. Joshua. For a moment my drunken mind believed that it *was* Mr. Joshua, that something terrible had happened to him in the year since I'd last seen him. He'd suffered some tragedy and aged twenty-five years, his hair going silver, his face growing tattered. But it wasn't Mr. Joshua. Mr. Joshua was slight and rosy, quick to laugh. This man was bony, with a hawkish face, one that would look at home on foreign currency or atop a monument in a town square. It was as if he were the identical twin brother of Mr. Joshua, as if they'd been separated at birth and had totally different life experiences, Mr. Joshua's nurturing and this man's harrowing, bringing him to look the way he did.

Two: there was no car in the driveway, so the question of how he'd come here without an umbrella yet remained perfectly dry hung in the air, vaguely alarming, like a faint odor of gas.

"You're all dead," he said.

CHAPTER 3

"Oh, dear. You'll have to excuse me. That's not accurate."

The old man placed a hand over his eyes, shaking his head. "I overshot it. Went for the dramatic, *Masterpiece Theater* effect. I apologize. Let's try that again, shall we?"

He cleared his throat, smiling.

"You're all nearly dead. Wedged between life and death. Time for you has become snagged on a splinter, forming a closed-circuited potentiality called a Neverworld Wake."

Quite pleased now, he nodded and took a deep breath.

"This phenomenon is not specific to you. There are such moments occurring simultaneously in the past, present, and future all around the world and across the universe, known and unknown, crumpled and unfolded. Time does not travel in a straight line. It bends and barrels across tunnels and bridges. It speeds up.

Slows down. It even derails. Well then. This hitch, as we might call it, is where each of you exists at the moment. And it is where, until further notice, you will remain."

He bowed like the longtime ringmaster of a down-at-heel traveling circus, with gracious ease and a hint of exhaustion.

"I am the Keeper," he said. "I have no other name. The way I look, act, the tone of my voice, my walk, face, everything I say and think is the sum total of your five lives as they were lived. Think of an equation. This moment equals your souls plus the circumstances of reality. Another example? Imagine if each of your minds was placed inside a blender. That blender is turned on high. The resulting smoothie is this moment. If there were someone else with you? It would be a slightly *different* moment. I'd be saying something else. I'd have different hair. Different hands. Different shoes. Docksiders rather than Steve Maddens.

"I digress. The circumstances of reality. You're doubtlessly wondering what I meant by that. *Well*."

He sniffed, smiling.

"Each of you is, at present, lying kinda sorta dead on the side of a coastal road. This is due to a recent head-on collision with one Mr. Howard Heyward, age fifty-eight, of two hundred eighty-one Admiral Road, South Kingstown, who was driving a Chevrolet Kodiak tow truck. Time is standing still. It has become trapped inside an eighth of a second like a luna moth inside a mason jar. There is a way out, of course. There is one means by which the moth can escape and time can fly irrevocably free. Each of you must vote during the last three minutes of every wake. You must choose the single person among you who will survive. This person will return to life. The remainder of you will move on to true death, a state permanent yet wholly unknown. The decision must be unanimous, save one dissenter. There can be only one who lives. There are no exceptions. Do you have questions?"

No one said a word.

All I could think was that he was senile after all. He also seemed to have once been an actor, because he had intoned his speech like the baritone narrator of some old 1950s TV Western starring John Wayne, his voice lilting, old-fashioned, and grand. There was an effortlessness to his every word, as if he'd given this memorized speech dozens of times before.

He was waiting for one of us to say something.

Kipling started to clap. "Bravo."

"Hold on," said Martha, scowling. "Is he selling Bibles?"

"What do you want?" demanded Cannon.

The man shrugged. "I am a simple resource. I desire no compensation, monetary or otherwise. Nonetheless, I wish for you to succeed."

"Succeed at what?" asked Whitley.

"The vote."

"Listen," said Cannon. "It's been a long night. Tell us what you want."

"It appears my delivery was a bit rushed for your comprehension. Would you like the news a different way? Dramatic reenactment? Flash cards? A second language? Italian tends to soften the blow of even the most ominous prognosis, which was why Dante used it for the *Inferno*." He cleared his throat. *"Buonasera. Tra la vita e la morte, il tempo è diventato congelato—"*

"That's enough," snapped Cannon. "Get the hell off this porch."

The man was unfazed. He smiled, revealing small gray teeth.

"Very well. Good luck to you all. Godspeed."

He hopped nimbly down the steps, striding out to the driveway. Within seconds he was drenched and vanishing into the yard beyond the lights. We listened to his footsteps sloshing through the grass.

"My brain just exploded," said Martha.

"Worst door-to-door salesman *ever*," said Kip, shaking his head. "I think he learned his sales techniques from Monty Python. What did he call us?"

"Dead," I whispered.

"Right. I've been called many things. Deadhead. Dead*beat*. Never just plain old dead. Has a sort of bleak ring to it."

"He's a Jesus freak," said Whitley, nibbling her fingernail. "Right? In some cult? Should I call the police? There may be others out there. They might be waiting to break in here and slaughter us or something."

"He's harmless," mumbled Cannon. Yet he seemed unnerved. Scowling out at the empty driveway, he suddenly seized an umbrella and barreled outside just as another monstrous clap of thunder exploded and the rain fell harder. He stomped into the yard, looking around, disappearing in the same spot as the old man.

We waited in silence, apprehensive.

A minute later, Cannon reappeared.

"Must have headed back to the road. No sign of him."

"Let's check the security cameras," said Whitley.

They headed downstairs to the surveillance room, and Kip and Martha—muttering about needing "a stiff drink before the ensuing elderly zombie apocalypse"—shuffled back into the living room.

I remained where I was, staring outside.

There had been something legitimately upsetting about the old man. All the eloquence, the formal speech, the accent—at once like a cable newscaster's and someone who'd spent a year abroad in England—seemed only to conceal a deep calculation. As if what he had told us were only one small piece of a grand plan.

I watched the woods, searching for movement, trying to steady my drunken head.

Suddenly, music erupted from inside, overlaying the storm with a soundtrack, softening the night's edge. With a deep breath, I shut the door and bolted it. Whitley was right. He was probably just looking to recruit people for his church.

Still, I walked past Kip and Martha, curled up stroking Gandalf on the couch, and took out my phone, stepping into the hall. My mom answered on the first ring.

"Bee? Is everything all right?"

I could tell from her anxious tone that she and my dad were both still awake, doubtlessly reading in bed: Dad, one of his thirty-pound presidential biographies, Mom *trying* to read a thriller by James Patterson, though she'd probably been skimming the same paragraph four, five times before blurting "I don't understand why she had to go see them. They still have some mysterious hold on her." Then Dad, with the patient, knowing stare over his glasses: "If she wants to see them she can, Victoria. She's an adult. She's stronger than you give her credit for."

I realized I had no idea why I was calling, except to hear her voice.

"It's too late to drive back, so I'm spending the night," I said.

"Well, your father needs you at the Crow for opening. Sleepy Sam called to say he's having a tooth pulled."

"I'll be there."

She lowered her voice: "How's it going with them? Can you talk? You sound upset."

"Everything's fine. I love you."

"We love you too, Bumble. We're here if you need us."

I hung up, just as Whitley and Cannon were returning from the surveillance room.

"No sign of him on the cameras," said Cannon.

"He's gone," she said.

"This night gets an A-plus in weird," slurred Martha.

"Wasn't it hilarious how he asked to be called the Keeper?" said Kip, shaking his head. "The man looked like more of an Eastern European Santa Claus."

Whitley wrinkled her nose. "That was my Internet password for everything for *years*. I'm not even kidding. The keeper one-two-three."

In the end, the consensus was he was Just One of Those Things, one of life's untied shoelaces. As the thunderstorm raged on, however, lightning cracking and thunder yowling, at one point a giant oak branch crashed onto the back deck, demolishing the entire railing.

We jumped, staring at each other, doubtlessly imagining the same thing: here it was, the beginning of the horror to which that funny old man had been the creepy prelude.

Only nothing happened.

Another hour passed. Whitley talked about being sexually harassed by her boss at the San Francisco law firm where she'd had an internship all summer. Cannon couldn't tell if he was in love with his girlfriend, an international fencing champion.

"Love is this elusive bird," he said. "You're the lifelong bird-watcher, looking for this rare red-plumed quail people spend entire lives trying to see for three seconds in a cherry tree on a mountaintop in Japan."

"You're mistaking love for perfection," I said. "Real love when it's there? It's just *there*. It's a metal folding chair."

When no one said anything, I realized, embarrassed, I'd blurted this as a clumsy way to bring up Jim. And I was about to. Then Whitley got up to get more Royal Salute, and Kipling muttered that he hadn't been this wasted since he was nine, and the moment was gone.

"I'll tell you what love is," said Martha, gazing at the ceiling. "It's the Heisenberg uncertainty principle. Once you think it's there and give voice to it? It's not there anymore. It's over here. Then way over *here*. Then here. You can't trap it or contain it no matter how hard you try."

It was the first time I'd ever heard Martha speak in such a way—the first time for the others too, if their surprised glances were any indication. Being allergic to romance was her shtick. If ever you asked her whom she had a crush on, she'd blink at you like you had three heads: "Why would I waste *time*—a highly precious, constantly diminishing resource—on transitory neurological fluctuations of adrenaline, dopamine, and serotonin?" When she saw couples holding hands in the halls, she gave them a cartoonishly wide berth.

"In case they're contagious," she said. And she wasn't joking.

The conversation meandered on as rain peppered the windows.

At one point Kip started calling me Sister Bee again, which made Cannon blurt that I was the one person at school no one, not a teacher or student, a parent, a maintenance worker, or even an *ant,* could ever say anything bad about.

"And your nice isn't even irritating," said Cannon.

"Remember how in biology," said Kip, smirking, "Bee didn't even tell Mr. Jetty that Chad Burman had just thrown up his entire lunch all over the back of her blouse? She just sat there heroically answering his question about osmosis and then excused herself."

"And the field trip to D.C. when Mr. Miller had to go home to his pregnant wife, and rather than summon another teacher from campus to chaperone, Ms. Guild just asked *Bee.*"

They cackled with laughter.

"It wasn't that big a deal," I said.

During this conversation, Whitley remained tellingly silent, a smug expression on her face as she stared at the floor, as if she begged to differ, as if she wanted to laugh.

When is it coming? I wondered with a shiver. *The conversation about Jim?*

The absent leader. The sixth member. The killed one.

Weren't they dying to talk about him? Jim, whose shadow stretched behind him long and dark, as captivating dead as he was when he was alive. Jim the poet. Jim the prince.

Of course they were thinking about him. How could they not?

Yet it seemed he was the locked shed on the forsaken property everyone was too scared to approach, much less peer inside all the filthy windows.

Not long after, I passed out. When I woke up, peeling my cheek from the couch cushions, Whitley and Cannon were asleep under a blanket in front of the fireplace. Kip was snoring on the love seat. Only Martha was awake. She appeared to have sobered up and was sitting across the room in a club chair, reading with her chin in her hand.

"Hey," I croaked, rubbing my eyes. "What time is it?"

"Four-fifteen."

It was still dark out, and still raining.

"Can't sleep," Martha said with a wan smile. "It's that old man. I feel like he's still out there."

Her remark made me glance out the windows, shivering.

Whitley had turned on every light, and I could see the giant fallen branch, the gardens and pool, the stone path leading down to the dock.

"I'm sure it's fine," I whispered.

We went on talking, though eventually the silences between our words stretched out farther and farther, like the distance between a final chain of tiny islands before the open sea.

Martha and I had never been close, though by rights we should have been. As the only scholarship kids at Darrow, we were two rescue mutts of humble bloodlines and skittish temperaments thrown into a kennel of world-class purebreds.

She'd attended Darrow on a physics scholarship established by a genius alumnus who'd worked on the God Particle. She'd been the first winner in twenty-eight years. Valedictorian of our class, she went to MIT on a full ride for mathematical engineering.

She'd been raised in South Philadelphia by a single dad, and her family was even poorer than mine. I never met her dad, though Cannon once said he owned a gas station and went by the nickname Mickey Peanuts. Jim told me Martha had had a considerably older sister who'd died of a drug overdose, and that death was the reason Martha's mother left. But Martha never mentioned a sister, and any talk of her mom was in connection with a single trip to Alaska she'd taken when she was ten.

I'd spent hours in her company, yet I couldn't tell you who or what Martha ever loved beyond this weird underground fantasy novel called *The Bend*. The book was why she wallpapered her dorm room with mysterious posters of steam trains and scoured Reddit forums for other megafans, known as Benders. She even dressed up—with a surprising lack of embarrassment—once in a top hat and spectacles, or a gray barrister's wig—to celebrate the apparent birthdays of the characters. She always kept a copy of the book at the bottom of her backpack, pulling out the doorstop of a thousand torn-up pages—crudely Xeroxed, bound with frayed twine—at the start of class, reading, it seemed, to avoid talking to anyone.

At heart she was Jim's friend. They'd met when they were kids at some invitation-only camp for the gifted, housed in a nineteenth-century mansion in upstate New York called Da Vinci's Daughters and Sons. Jim was there because he'd composed an entire musical about Napoleon, which had been staged at his Manhattan private school and gotten him profiled in *New York* magazine. Martha was there because she'd built a working airplane engine in her garage.

It was Jim who urged Martha to apply to Darrow, Jim who sought to have her around. Over the years she'd become an integral part of our group, giving every situation its deadpan punctuation or making some awkward reference to a chapter in *The Bend* that no one understood. And yet I always suspected Jim had been her only true champion, that Cannon, Wit, and Kip accepted her the way one accepts a lifelong inconvenience, like asthma or a spouse's beloved cat. He never stopped insisting she was amazing, that one day when we were sixty we'd look back and think with disbelief, *I was friends with Martha Ziegler.*

"Which will be like saying you were friends with Steve Hawking. That's how big she's gonna be."

The two of them had a shabby shorthand, laughing at things only they found funny, arms slung around each other's necks like old cardigans. While it didn't make me jealous per se, it could lead me to notice something Martha did—heavy glance, weird remark—that would set off alarm bells, and I'd entertain my long-standing suspicion that she was harboring a burning secret: she was in love with Jim. It was why she'd never liked me.

I could only assume she'd been heartbroken by his death. In the aftermath—the ten or so days before summer break—she was glum and taciturn, scuttling out of Final Chapel ahead of the entire school like some startled attic bat. She was agitated. Dimly I recalled how she'd left school suddenly the day before I did, vanishing without saying goodbye. Whitley, ever attentive to the embarrassing things people wished to hide, couldn't stop saying, "Something's up with Martha."

Now here she was, staring at me with that stark telephoto stare I'd always found nerve-wracking. Whatever she had felt about Jim's death, whatever had been uprooted, was hidden now, like a pod of blue whales thundering through the depths of an ocean with a still surface.

I realized that she'd just asked me a question.

"What?"

"I was wondering if you still made those dream soundtracks."

She was referring to my hobby of creating albums for movies I made up. It was just something I did. I didn't know why. As a child I'd always been painfully shy, so terrified of speaking in class, my teachers often thought I had a stutter or a hearing problem. I began crafting pocket-sized books with lyrics and hand-drawn art for movies I wished existed, like the soundtrack to a hit teen vampire movie called *Blood Academy*. Or *Dove Nova*, the biopic of a Swedish teen pop star who vanished into thin air, her disappearance forever unsolved. There was no point to these albums. I couldn't even explain why I made them, except that I liked to imagine they were artifacts of some other world that existed beyond the one we could see, a world where I wasn't timid, and unsaid words didn't collect in my mouth like marbles, and I was brave. They were my what-ifs, my *glass menagerie,* as Jim said.

One night freshman year during a snowstorm, the whole school was in the auditorium for Holiday Dance when the power went out. I had accidentally ripped the back of my dress, so I left Jim to run back to my dorm to change. To my surprise, I encountered Martha in the dark of the common room, reading *Pride and Prejudice* with a flashlight, so absorbed she hadn't realized one of the windows was wide open and snow was collecting in the corner three inches thick. We ended up hanging out for two hours, just the two of us. It was the only time we ever did. For some reason, probably in the hopes of making things less uncomfortable between us, I'd shown Martha my collection of dream albums. Ever since then, when we were alone, she tended to ask about them, like they were some one-size-fits-all subject she could rely on to get me to talk. It could be a little unnerving.

"No," I said, feigning a yawn. "Not really. I think I'll go find a bed upstairs."

She nodded, her face solemn. "Good night, Beatrice."

I slipped out—Martha returning to her book—and trudged upstairs, finding my favorite guest room at the end of the hall. I pulled back the comforter and slung myself into bed.

Any other night I would have been kept awake by the memories inside that room. I was curled up under the heavy covers, same as always. The only thing missing was Jim snuggled beside me, composing lyrics by the light of his cell phone.

I set my alarm for six and closed my eyes. I'd sneak out before any of them were awake.

And that, for better or worse, would close my final chapter on Wincroft.

CHAPTER 4

When I awoke it was light out.

I was freezing and covered in sweat. No, not sweat, I realized after a moment, blinking. It was rain. I was soaked because I was sitting in the backseat of the Jaguar convertible, the top still down. It had been parked, seemingly by someone very drunk, in a flower bed in the front yard of Wincroft.

It was still pouring rain. Kip and Martha were beside me, wearing confused expressions.

"What are you doing?" Kip asked me. He was soaking wet, his eyes bloodshot. A raindrop dangled off the end of his nose. "Where are you taking us?"

I had no clue what he was talking about. I scrambled out of the car, raced across the driveway to the mansion, and threw open the front door. I nearly collided with Whitley. She was frozen in the foyer, wearing the same outfit she'd had on last night. She surveyed me with a look so stunned, I understood immediately that something terrible had happened.

"What? What is it?"

She only stepped past me, staring out the door, speechless.

I hurried past her into kitchen. Shivering, I took inventory of my body. I felt fine. My head was clear. Yet somehow I'd overslept. I wasn't going to make it to the Crow by opening. My parents would be scrambling to keep up with the morning crowd, then lunch, and my dad would be so strapped he'd forget to tell people about the specials, and my mom would use this as an excuse to say they didn't need specials anymore, they were too expensive, which was sometimes enough of a spark to make them start arguing, which they rarely did.

Cannon was standing at the kitchen island typing on his open laptop.

"See, look!" he shouted over his shoulder, seemingly believing I was Whitley. "*New York Times*. It's the exact same thing."

I stepped beside him. He was amped, like he'd had about six cups of coffee.

"What is it?"

"What is it?" he mocked, turning to me. He grabbed my head, directing it at the screen.

" 'Senate Pushes for New Immigration Initiative,' " I read.

"The *date*," he snapped.

"Friday, August thirtieth. So?"

"So? *So?* It's yesterday."

Scowling, he was tapping the keyboard, loading CNN.

"CNN. *The Post. Time.* All of them say the same thing."

He shoved his iPhone into my hands. I blinked stupidly down at the date overlaying a photo of what had to be his fencing-champion girlfriend.

He was right. *August 30. 5:34 p.m.*

There had to be an error with the International Date Line. Terrorists had hacked the network. As if reading my mind, he held up his wristwatch, the hour and minute hands set to 5:35, the date turned to 30.

"How could hackers get into my TAG Heuer?"

I could only stare.

At that moment, his phone rang. Someone named Alexandra. He snatched the phone.

"Alex. Hold on. Now, wait a—wait a— Tell me what day and time it is. The date and time. I'll explain in a sec—would you tell me the goddamn *date*? I'm not asking you to recite the Declaration of— WOULD YOU PLEASE JUST SHUT UP AND TELL ME—"

Whatever Alex's confused response was, Cannon furiously hurled the phone at the sliding glass doors. He collapsed on the couch, staring wild-eyed at the floor. I hurried to my purse and dug out my phone, which was actually pretty strange because the last time I'd seen it, it'd been upstairs.

My phone read the same thing. *August 30.* With a shiver of panic, I dialed my mom.

"Hi, Bumble—"

"Mom. *Mom?* Where are you?"

"On our way to the Dreamland to see *His Girl Friday*. What's the matter?"

"You didn't see the movie yesterday?"

"Yesterday?"

"Mom, what day is it?"

"What? Why are you shouting?"

"What's the date?"

"It's—it's Friday, August thirtieth."

"Are you positive?"

"I'm looking at the dashboard right now."

"It's the thirtieth," I heard my dad chime in.

"Mom, I called you last night, remember?"

"Last night? What?"

"Last night I called, and said I was spending the night at Wincroft, and you asked me to be in for opening because Sleepy Sam was getting a tooth pulled."

"Sam is out tomorrow? He called *you*? Sam is out tomorrow," she told my dad.

"He called Bee, after we've made sure he has our number about nineteen times?"

"Bee, what's going on up there? Is it awful? Why don't we come get you?"

I hung up, blood rushing in my ears.

My mom called back, but I was too shaken to answer.

I sat on the couch, trying to calm down. This had to be some kind of lucid dream. I willed myself to wake up. *Wake up.* After a moment, I realized Kip and Martha had drifted inside. They were standing stiffly with stricken expressions, like they'd just woken up from sleepwalking. Whitley had stepped back into the kitchen, her every gesture slow, as if pretending to walk on the moon.

"Y'all?" whispered Kip, his voice scarcely audible. "Was there an earthquake? Or some end-of-days world event we're just finding out about?"

That was when the doorbell rang.

I didn't wait for the others. I jumped off the couch, sprinting past Kip and Martha, and yanked open the front door.

"Perhaps this time I'll be invited in for tea," said the old man.

CHAPTER 5

"The first thing you must do is stay calm," said the Keeper. "Panic will get you nowhere."

He was making tea.

He had asked for tea when he'd strolled inside, and as we were all too alarmed to react to what he was saying, he had, incredibly, started making it for himself. He filled the kettle, turned on the gas stove, and grabbed a mug from the cabinet, as if he had visited this house many times before.

"If it's any reassurance, remember one thing," he continued, his fingers nimbly straightening his dark blue silk tie. It caught the overhead light, and I saw it had a discernable pattern of stags identical to the stag presiding over the entrance to Darrow.

"Others have gone through the Neverworld before you. Many

more will after. Hundreds of millions of others will expire never having had the opportunity that each of you has. So you must look at this as a gift. A chance to change history, for your choice of who will live will affect billions of moments barreling into the future for infinity. In other words, there is a precedent, and you aren't alone. You must rely on each other. Each of you is a key, the others your locks. This isn't a nightmare, and it isn't a dream. It's a crack you will continue to fall through until you vote. The sooner you accept where you are, the sooner you will all escape."

The old man here, *again,* wearing the same dark suit, speaking in the same grand voice, was so incongruous and strange, none of us could really pay attention to anything he was saying. Whitley and Kip were standing by the kitchen island, staring openmouthed at him, as if he were a poltergeist. Martha was on the couch, stone-faced, her feet planted like she felt faint. I was doing my best to follow what he said, in case there was some clue that might reveal who he actually was. Yet all the while my mind was screaming, *It's a prank. It's a prank.* It had to be. Somebody— international terrorists, hackers from Anonymous or some other group—was playing a cruelly ingenious trick.

I noticed Cannon had disappeared upstairs. Now he reappeared, hauling his duffel.

"I'm out," he announced.

"What?" asked Whitley, alarmed. "Where are you going?"

"Airport."

"But it's yesterday," said Kip.

"No, it's not. Of course it's not. Yeah, we can't explain it, but there is an explanation. I'm sure the physics department at Harvard is working on this as we speak."

"I'm afraid the physics department at Harvard is ignorant of your plight," interjected the Keeper, wringing out the tea bag on a spoon. "They've got their hands quite full trying to solve quantum gravity. Specifically, the vacuum catastrophe."

Cannon surveyed him coldly. "I'm going home."

"To do what?" asked Kip. "Complain? 'Ma? Uh, today's kinda yesterday'?"

Cannon shrugged. "I'll be damned if I'm staying here with him."

He left. We listened to the front door slam. Then, suddenly, Whitley was scrambling after him. And Kipling. Martha too. They were all moving, running away as if they'd just learned the old man was wearing explosives. They grabbed car keys, handbags, sweatshirts, phones. I didn't want to be left alone with him, so I grabbed my bag and ran out into the downpour too. They were sprinting to their cars, engines roaring to life, windshield wipers flying. By the time I'd started the Dodge truck and reversed, all four cars were gone.

The Keeper had walked out onto the front steps. He took a sip of his tea.

The reality of the situation, that we were just leaving him there in the house, a complete stranger, was too wild to fathom.

"Don't worry!" he shouted cheerfully at me over the rain. "I promise not to steal the silver."

I floored the gas. As I roared down the driveway, I had the

acute feeling of being chased. Yet, rounding another bend, I saw no one behind me. When I took a final glance back at Wincroft, the red brick mansion sinking behind the hill, even the Keeper appeared to be gone.

———

It began to get dark. The rain was relentless, the sky black and blue. As soon as I'd gone a few miles, peering in at every driver to make sure they were alive and not ghosts, aliens, or zombies (most doing double takes, wondering what my problem was), I began to relax. All the drivers looked human, alive, and ordinary, chewing gum, fiddling with the radio, utterly at ease with what day it was, what time it was.

Everything was normal.

I called my mom again.

"Bee?"

"Where are you?"

"In the movie. What's going on? You scared us, the way you sounded before—"

I drove straight to the Dreamland in Westerly. My parents were waiting outside, ashen. I parked in the fire lane, leaving the engine running. I wrenched the door and ran, throwing my arms around them.

They were real. I wasn't dreaming. It was going to be all right.

My mom was distraught. "You're never speaking to any of those people again—"

"Victoria," admonished my dad.

"What? *Look* at her. She's completely undone. We're not going through this again. No. Those kids are rotten. Spoiled. They'll live their entire lives without ever turning around to see the mess they've made, Mommy and Daddy always running after them with a maid and a checkbook."

"They're just kids."

"*Just kids* left our daughter barely able to eat or sleep for two months, if you remember."

"That was shock. And grief."

I was crying, but of course they couldn't understand the real reason, that it was relief. The day that had already happened—whatever it was—hadn't been real.

This was real.

I managed to calm my parents down, and we went to dinner at the Shakedown. We talked with Artie, who gave us free apple pie. We strolled along the boardwalk and talked about the umpteenth offer from developers who told my dad he had to sell the Captain's Crow so they could build condos. Though my parents were alarmed, not just by my abrupt appearance, but by the uncharacteristic gusto with which I was approaching spending an evening with them—something I had done with relative apathy all summer—they said nothing. They pretended they believed my excuse for abruptly leaving Wincroft: "I had to get out of there. We've all outgrown each other, you know?"

They also humored my manic need to keep the night going, to walk a little farther down the boardwalk, to stare in at every sailboat painting in every window of every art gallery, to walk out to the old swings on the beach where someone had spray-painted on the wall LIFE IS BUT A DREAM, thereby postponing the inevitability of driving home and going to bed.

I was afraid to sleep, because the glaring fact that *I had already lived this day* nagged like a bad pop song that wouldn't leave my head.

We got home just after midnight. Dad drove the Dodge RAM as I said I was too tired, though the real reason was I was scared to be alone in the car. We filed into the house, my dad yawning. My mom loaded the dishwasher.

"Will you stay with me until I fall asleep?" I asked her.

"Of course." She smiled, though I could tell the question worried her. The last time I'd asked her to do that, it was just after Jim died.

She sat on my bed as we talked about changing the menu at the Crow, the community vote to tear down a drawbridge. I knew she wanted to ask me about them, my old friends, what had happened tonight, but thought better of it.

At one point she stood up to inspect the white daisy wallpaper of my room.

"I can't believe it. Your dad said he fixed this."

She scratched at a seam in the corner, tugging the edge. A large chunk immediately peeled from the wall.

"Are you *kidding* me? There's actually mold here."

"It's a sign you and Dad should sell the Crow and retire to Florida."

She crossed her arms. "Do I look like someone who wears a visor?"

I began to feel heavy sleep falling over me. She said something about my dad's bad back, how it was hurting him more than he let on. I held her hand as I passed out.

My mom's hand was real. What had come before was not. So a day had decided to repeat itself. *Is it really that big a deal?*

What lies the mind will tell to keep you safe.

The mind does its best to lessen the impact of any catastrophe. It really tries its best. But then the distance between reality and woven fantasy becomes too great for even the mind to bear. All those words of calm and relief, the hope that everything will be all right in the end, can't help stretching and tearing and fading to nothing.

Then you wake up screaming.

━━━

I woke up in the downpour in the backseat of the Jaguar, Martha and Kipling beside me again. When I sprinted away from them into the house, I was shaking so badly I had to sit on the couch, feet apart, hands on my knees, trying not to hyperventilate.

I was here again. I was back at Wincroft. At least I was alive. But was this life?

Gandalf was running in circles around the living room, barking.

"No. No. No!" shouted Cannon.

He was at the kitchen island typing on his laptop again, though—undoubtedly after seeing that the date was the same— he slammed it closed and threw it across the room.

I realized dazedly, glancing up, that Whitley was outside, in the throes of one of her rages. Completely soaked, she was pulling the white umbrellas out of the patio tables and launching them over the railing.

Her temper had been legendary at Darrow.

"Psychotic fits," the cattier girls used to hiss.

I'd always found it enviable—that Whitley could be so beautiful and smart, and on top of that so unconcerned about causing a scene or curbing her biblical emotions. It seemed unfairly glamorous, like she was the untamable heroine of a Victorian novel. (Even the oft-gossiped-about phrase around school—*Lansing's temper*—sounded gorgeously bygone, like the name of an exotic illness with no cure.) To be so wild—it was how I longed to be. Wit surged into battle. I froze. Whitley threw her head back and screamed. I was mute. Her rages were Olympian, five-star, multi-platinum. They came from some boiling place inside her not even she could explain. Face flushed, eyes flashing, she'd demolish her dorm room, rip pages from every textbook, punch walls, overturn tables, tell off a teacher with zero care for tact, mercy, or an aftermath. It always seemed to me in those moments that Whitley was witnessing some alternative world invisible to the rest of us, something ugly and so vast it couldn't be fit into the English language.

Her rages got her sent to the infirmary. They would have gotten her kicked out if it weren't for her mom, the Linda, CEO of the pharmaceutical group Lansing Drugs, flying in from St. Louis in her fat mink to smooth everything over, which meant funding another wing for the library. It was the reason Whitley got special permission to leave school to go see a psychologist up in Newport. Whenever a fit happened, I'd always run to her side and hold on to her, like some astronaut trying to make sure my colleague didn't float out into space.

Now, as I watched her seize a deck chair and throw it over the railing screaming, I could only observe her blankly, unable to move. I couldn't help her. I couldn't help myself.

Kipling and Martha had wandered in and were looking around the kitchen like people visiting their property after a tornado.

"We have to call someone," Kipling said, his voice shaking. "The FBI. The CIA?"

"And say what?" asked Martha, turning to him. "Time has become a broken record?"

"There've got to be others going through this. It's a national emergency."

"I'm sure Anderson Cooper's all over it," muttered Cannon. He was on the floor, hands linked around his neck like he was in a bomb shelter. " 'Today. A new kind of breaking news. Yesterday is today. *Again*. More on this story as it never develops. Tweet us your experiences with hashtag Groundhog Day is real.' "

Kipling grabbed the remote and turned on the TV, flipping through channels, every one yelping something normal. *Coming up, we'll show you how to make a three-minute omelet. Keeps whites white and colors brand-new.*

The doorbell rang.

No one moved.

Within seconds the Keeper had strolled inside, a sympathetic, even grandfatherly look on his face. There was something insidious about him now: same suit, same tie. I felt like I was going to be sick.

"This will be the worst of it," he said. "It's the second wake that feels the most catastrophic."

"Tell us what to do," said Martha.

"I did. Take the vote."

Take the vote. As if it were just a matter of making a left turn rather than a right.

Whitley must have spotted the old man from outside, because suddenly she heaved the sliding door open and stood in the doorway, panting and scowling at him, gusts of rain blasting around her like a storm scene in an old movie. Before anyone could stop her, she was sprinting inside. She grabbed a Chinese vase off a table and slung it at the old man's head.

He crumpled to the floor. Cannon ran to Whitley, but she brutally elbowed him off, grabbing the Keeper by his necktie and forcing him into a chair. Then she was barreling into the kitchen, pulling open drawers, tossing pots, ladles, cooking spoons to the floor.

"The cycle of violence is actually a pointless denial of reality," said the Keeper, holding his head.

Whitley was back in front of him with cooking twine, brutally tying up his wrists, brandishing a fourteen-inch carving knife inches from his jaw as she sliced the string. Crouching, teeth gritted, she moved to his ankles. The Keeper didn't protest, only watching her, bemused, like a father when his four-year-old decides to bury him alive at the beach.

She dragged a stool over and sat in front of him, brushing her hair out of her eyes.

"Start talking."

"About what?" asked the Keeper.

She smacked him hard across the cheek.

"Whitley," reproached Cannon.

"Tell us who did this and how we get out of here."

The Keeper closed his eyes. "I've already told you. The vote. As for *who*? There is an infinite number of possibilities. The universe, God, the Absolute, the Supreme Being, He Who Actually Is, Adonai, Ahura Mazda—"

She slapped him again.

"Wit," whispered Kipling. "You think it's wise to go all Tarantino on this poor man?"

"He's not poor. He's toying with us."

She slapped him again. The Keeper remained unperturbed, blood trickling from his nose. I started to cry. And yet I made no attempt to stop her. None of us did. We stood there, frozen, all doubtlessly wondering—terrible as it was to admit—if hurting the Keeper might reveal something, something that would end this. He'd confess it was an elaborate game; the curtain would fall, scenery crashing. We'd laugh. *How hilarious. You really had me going there.* I also couldn't help hoping that, as with so many nightmares I'd had as a child, if things became sufficiently strange, the dream would at last puncture and I'd wake up.

Whitley hit him again.

"The final three minutes of every wake you will each vote for the single person among you who will survive—"

"Why only one?" asked Martha sharply, stepping beside Whitley.

"I can't explain the whys and hows of the Neverworld. They were determined by you."

"But if time has stopped," asked Cannon, "why can we return to our normal lives?"

"Only for eleven point two hours. Six hundred and seventy-two minutes. The length of your wake. For Cannon and Whitley it's six hundred and seventy-five. At the end of that time, you will all wake up in the Neverworld again, as surely as Cinderella's stagecoach turns back into a pumpkin. Even though your accident produced a snag in the space-time fabric, a crinkle in the cloth, the present world hasn't disappeared. It remains alive all around you, a bullet left in the gun chamber."

"What is the significance of our arrival time in the wake?" asked Martha.

"The beginning and end of a wake are based on an infinite number of factors, including violent impact, strength of connection, and random chance."

Whitley, seemingly unable to hear another word, flung down the knife. She seized her phone off the kitchen island and had a curt, unintelligible conversation before hanging up, shoving her feet into her Converse sneakers.

"What are you doing now?" asked Cannon.

"Driving to T. F. Green."

It was the airport for private jets outside Providence.

"I booked the jet to Hawaii. We're leaving in an hour. Let's go."

"Won't change a thing, I'm afraid," said the Keeper.

She glared at him. "We will be in a plane thirty-six thousand feet over the Pacific Ocean at the end of the—what did you call it, the *wake*? What's going to happen? We just vanish out of our seats like some Willy Wonka magic trick?"

"You'll see," said the Keeper.

———

Everyone went with Whitley except me.

I couldn't. I was too devastated, too scared to move so far away from my parents, to be trapped in a box in the sky with them.

Them.

They were *them* to me too now. I wasn't one of them, not anymore. If this situation had made anything clear, it was that: that the very people I'd once loved and trusted most in the world had become total strangers.

What had I done to deserve this? To end up in hell with *them*?

I couldn't think about it. No, I couldn't let my mind move ahead. It had to stay on a tight leash tied to this moment. It was all I could handle.

I watched them pile with varying degrees of conviction into Cannon's Jeep. It was obvious that they suspected Whitley's plan, an impetuous flight westward to a tropical island, was futile. Yet they went ahead. For a show of solidarity? Some last, vain hope that it might actually work, that the Linda's Gulfstream V tearing through the pink cotton-candy clouds with its beige calfskin seats and trays of fanned-out mango slices would be the loophole, the wormhole, the Get Out of Jail Free card to puncture this nightmare?

I stumbled down the steps, barely aware of the rain drenching me as I climbed into the truck. As I backed out, I saw that the Keeper had managed to free himself from Whitley's knots. Once again he was at the entrance, his face bloody and red, Gandalf at his side, as if the dog had always belonged to him.

This time the old man didn't utter a word. He didn't have to. His smile at me as I drove past him said it all.

See you later.

CHAPTER 6

You can't stay awake.

We tried that. No matter how many cups of coffee or how many cans of Red Bull or Monster energy drinks you down, no matter how many caffeine pills or how much ginseng you take, your body gets pulled into the heaviest hollow of sleep you've ever felt in your life. The next thing you know, you're right back where you started.

Back at the wake.

You can't kill yourself either.

Kip tried that. He hanged himself with one of E.S.S. Burt's belts in an upstairs bedroom. I didn't see him. Martha told me. The next wake, as usual, he was right beside me in the backseat of the Jaguar, a healthy color, no black-and-blue marks around his neck, no swollen face.

Like nothing had happened.

"We're immortal," said Cannon. "We should take over the White House."

"In eleven point two hours?" said Martha. "That's not enough time to drive to Chicago, much less rule the free world."

Tell your parents. Call the police. Have the Keeper arrested. Call a shrink. Check into the psych ward of Butler Hospital and ask the attending physician to make tomorrow arrive, please. Confess to a priest. Tell a bus driver, a cabdriver, the tired waitress at the twenty-four-hour diner who's seen it all, the bent-over elderly woman in the frozen foods section of Price Rite buying a shocking number of pepperoni Hot Pockets, the man in the leather jacket browsing engagement rings at Kmart. Read the two hundred and fifty-two books in the science section of the Warwick public library, and a zillion textbooks on Google Books, trying to determine if ever in the history of the world some sage like Copernicus, Aristotle, Darwin, or Hawking has ever written or even hinted about such a thing as errors in time, cosmic waiting rooms, lethal lotteries in limbo, human terrariums in hell.

"What's the subject you're searching for again?" the librarian asked me.

"It's called a Neverworld."

She typed on the keyboard, shaking her head.

"Nothing comes up in the Library of Congress."

We tried every one of these things in the beginning.

Every time, we woke up in the exact same place, exact same time. We were songs on repeat, flies in a mason jar, echoing screams in a canyon that could not fade.

The ongoing experience of Recurring goes against the very heart of being human, and it is—I will tell you this without flinching—unbearable. The mind rages trying to disprove it. When it can't, the brain breaks down with shocking ease. The psyche is fragile. It is a child's sand castle in an incoming tide. Never before had I understood how little control we had over our world, or really anything except our own actions, and now my little life didn't even belong to me. We were helpless passengers strapped inside a spaceship circling Mars. The sun, the sky, the stars—how long did I stare at them, lying on the deck chair by the pool in the pouring rain, wishing I could just be them, a collection of gas and fire? I'd even take a beetle, a blade of grass, anything, so long as it was outside the Neverworld.

"Take the vote," urged the Keeper. "Just take the vote."

We took the vote. Of course we did.

We voted for the first time early in our arrival in the Neverworld. Twilight Zone. Purgatory. Doomed-Fate-*Survivor*-Homeroom-*Freaky-Friday* Bullshit. We called it all kinds of names, as if insulting the unknown forces keeping us here would make them change their minds.

We assembled in Wincroft's library like colorful characters in the final pages of a murder mystery waiting for the genius detective to unmask the killer. We sat in club chairs. Whitley served champagne. We wrote the name of our chosen survivor on a scrap piece of paper, the Keeper collecting them.

"There is no consensus," he announced.

The second time we voted, we each gave a speech beforehand in an attempt to persuade the others why we deserved life and not the others. We were defense attorneys in a courtroom speaking to a jury of the prosecutors, a circular setup of justice that would never work. The speeches ranged from altruistic (Cannon) to woodenly scientific (Martha) to childish and tone-deaf (Whitley, revealing a charitable streak she'd never had before, announcing she'd supply the entire continent of Africa with clean water). Kipling, when he stood up to speak, fell over, he was so drunk.

"You should vote for me because you *shouldn't* vote for me," he said. "I'm a mediocre, fucked-up shithead."

I spoke last.

All I said was that I was an ordinary girl destined for an ordinary life, but they could vote for me because I'd make it my aim to do small acts of kindness every day.

As I said it, I was acutely aware that I sounded as disingenuous and desperate as they all did. Even worse, none of them were listening. They watched me, sure, but their attention was buried under the weight of their fates, fastidiously, hungrily inspecting it like Gollum inspecting the Ring, wondering if the Neverworld was real.

I couldn't blame them. I was a blubbering mess too. Rarely had I passed the eleven point two hours without bawling as I drove to Westerly to see my parents at the Dreamland, usually just observing them without their knowledge, because to actually spend time with them made me sob uncontrollably the next wake. I'd tried explaining to them what was happening.

"I've been in a car accident, and I might die, and this limbo is called the Neverworld Wake according to this weird old man who won't leave us alone."

They always listened. Yet I could see that the only real feeling they had was devastation, believing that Jim's death had messed me up even more than they'd realized and I needed twenty-four-hour psychiatric care. So I'd gotten in the habit of sitting in the theater, unseen, a few rows behind them, beside this massively fat guy in a Brooklyn Book Drop T-shirt. I always smiled at him, thinking: *Do you realize how lucky you are? You have a tomorrow.* I ate popcorn, watched *His Girl Friday,* and snuck out before the lights came on.

The result of that vote was no different.

"There is no consensus," said the Keeper.

We all voted for ourselves. I couldn't foresee a time when we wouldn't. It was all we had to keep us going: the possibility, however remote, of getting out of here, of getting back to life.

And all the while the Keeper watched us.

He was still there, appearing when least expected. Sometimes he came inside and made tea. Sometimes he worked on the Wincroft grounds as a gardener, wearing a black hooded slicker. In spite of the rain—which would, during some wakes, turn impossibly to snow, temperature dropping, swirls of snowflakes spinning like miniature tornadoes through the air—the Keeper trimmed vines, rosebushes, ivy, and privet, the wisteria and lilac knotting the trellis. He swept the stone paths and hoed flower-beds. He stood atop a green ladder and cleared dead leaves from the gutters, wiped the glass panes clean on lanterns and lamps. He removed lichen from the wings of the crow gargoyles silently cawing.

Other times he could be spotted from a distance, a faceless

silhouetted trespasser hurrying across the lawn and into the woods, as if taking a shortcut through Wincroft on his way somewhere else, somewhere unknown.

—

I don't know how long we'd been in the Neverworld when we had the fight.

Time was vague here. It miraged and optical-illusioned the more you tried to look back on it, or fit it into a traditional monthly calendar. On close inspection, the hours were real. But if we tried to add them up into some larger understanding of the passage of time—how long we'd been here—they evaporated and grew unclear.

The passing of four wakes felt the same as four hundred.

The more wakes that passed, the more terrified I became. I could feel the others growing listless and distant, as if disinterested in ever actually leaving.

"I vote for Kanye!" shouted Cannon, raising his glass. "Kanye is my choice for who lives."

"There is no consensus," announced the Keeper.

Whitley began to drink all day. So did Cannon and Kipling. Then all three started helping themselves to the pills E.S.S. Burt kept in his master suite, hundreds of orange bottles of uppers and downers lining the medicine cabinets like candy in a sweet shop. It wasn't uncommon for them all to be either manically hyper or unresponsive and lethargic. Kipling paced outside, having conversations with the rain, wearing nothing but that pink wig and a green silk peacock-patterned bathrobe belonging to one of Burt's girlfriends.

Once, while gathering everyone for the vote, I couldn't find him. Searching the mansion, I finally spotted him floating in the pool on a swan raft in the torrential rain.

"Kipling!" I grabbed the leaf net and used it to haul him to the side.

He could barely open his eyes. "Hello? You there, God? It's me. Judy."

"Kipling. Can you hear me?"

"I'd like to order room service, please. I'd like the spaghetti Bolognese."

He rolled off the raft into the pool, sinking. I pulled off my shoes and raincoat and dove in after him, finding him drifting motionless along the bottom. Madly I kicked him back to the surface.

"Kipling! Can you hear me?"

" 'It's the final countdown,' " he sang, his eyes slits.

I was the lone nurse working in a madhouse.

While Martha had remained sane, she had also decided to remove herself, washing her hands of the situation, it seemed, ducking out without word at the beginning of every wake. She spent the day outside. A few times at dusk I caught sight of her wandering the woods fringing the far lawns, hauling her black bag, studying the treetops with a pair of binoculars like some professional bird-watcher, or an environmentalist recording evidence of acid rain. She'd fumble in her bag, which looked so heavy I wondered if inside was a copy of the same underground book, *The Bend,* she'd lugged around Darrow. Instead, she'd remove a thin black notebook and scribble in it for a minute before trudging on. Once, I ran after her.

"Martha!"

She kept walking, pretending she hadn't heard me.

"Martha! Wait!"

She stopped and turned. I could see she didn't want to be bothered—certainly not by me.

"I'm worried about them," I said.

She nodded. "So?"

So? I could only stare at her, rain coursing down my head and arms. Hadn't she witnessed what was going on? Didn't she care?

"They're going crazy. They're not taking it seriously anymore. I don't know what to do."

She shrugged. "It's all part of the acceptance."

"What are you talking about?"

"When criminals are sentenced to life in prison, there's a ninety-four-percent chance of mental collapse within the first year." She shrugged. "Just leave them alone."

"No way. We have to stick together."

To my shock, with another awkward shrug, she began to walk away.

"Where are you going?" I shouted.

She didn't answer.

"I need your help! *Please!* Don't you want to get out of here?"

She held up a hand—a mild gesture of acknowledgment to a child having a tantrum—and kept walking.

We were shipwreck survivors in a raging sea. Now they were forcing me to let go of their hands so they could sink into the waves and drown.

I was going to be stuck here forever.

Here, in the Neverworld, where I'd never grow old.

Never have a family.

Never fall in love.

I was an immortal vampire without any perks. No bewitching beauty, no golden eyes or shimmering skin, no ability to run three hundred miles an hour and flip cars over.

I was a ghost with no haunt. I couldn't turn TVs to static or swivel porcelain doll heads 360 degrees, causing normal humans to have nervous breakdowns. I couldn't make toddlers stand in zombie trances in living rooms, captured in shaky found footage in the dead of night.

I was a ticking clock in a timeless world.

Without time, nothing had meaning. Never before had I understood how crucial the passage of time was to caring about something. It gave it an expiry date, a wick, a rush, a burn. Without it, everything sat in place, dumbly waiting.

In my darkest moments I thought of Jim.

I'd come to Wincroft to find out what happened to him. Now even that question, the one I'd spent the past year turning over and over in my mind, shriveled and flattened in the face of the Neverworld, like a little worm on the driveway in the beating sun.

The night of the fight, I'd just returned from the Dreamland. Letting myself into Wincroft, I heard screaming coming from upstairs. I sprinted up the staircase, realizing they'd locked themselves in E.S.S. Burt's bathroom in the master suite.

I knocked. "Is everything okay?"

There was no answer but snickering.

"It's almost time for the vote."

This was met with more laughter.

"Hello?"

The door was flung open. Whitley stood there wearing an oversized red-sequined evening gown. Her eyes were bloodshot and smudged with eyeliner. Kipling was draped like an exhausted panther over the edge of the tub. Cannon was sitting on the counter, bandana tied marine-style around his forehead. It was obvious from their flushed faces—and the array of empty Dom Pérignon bottles scattered across the tiles—that they were wasted.

"Sister Bee, charmed to see you," Whitley said primly. "We won't be joining you. *Ever.*"

"What?"

"We aren't voting. We're staying at Wincroft until the end of time. So there."

She rolled her eyes at the look on my face.

"Oh, God, Bee. Stop mothering everyone. Your good-girl nun act is never getting you chosen. In fact, it'll be over my maggot-infested body that I ever allow some Mother Teresa type to triumph on to life. No way. It goes against my very life philosophy that one must get filthy to live. You must get down in the dirt or you've done nothing."

"I'm not Mother Teresa. I'm not a nun. I'm not even that good."

She waved her hand as if shooing a fly and turned, idly surveying her reflection in the mirror.

"It's not about the vote," I went on. "It's about staying together. We could lose ourselves forever in this place. Remember what Jim used to say about friendship? About *us*? What we have is a loyalty that can see us through anything."

Whitley bit her bottom lip, trying not to laugh.

"You still love him. *Wow*. He was the only person you ever saw in a room. And it's still true, even though he's dead. By the way. Did you ever wonder why he chose you? Out of all the girls at school?"

She rubbed some lipstick off her chin. I braced myself, because I knew what was coming. Her tantrums always began this way: she made some grand opening statement like a veteran prosecutor holding a jury rapt, the perfect set of words to slice her target in two.

"He chose you because a plain setting makes the diamond sparkle brighter."

I said nothing, willfully reminding myself to ignore whatever Wit said when she was angry. Yet I felt my face flush, a nervous voice in my head chattering *It's not true*.

"I disagree," said Cannon, frowning. "The problem always was that *you* loved Jim."

"He's right," muttered Kipling. "It was obvious, child. Like a wart on a lifeguard's big toe at a public pool."

"Oh, please." Whitley glared at him. "You were obsessed with him. Admit it. Don't think we didn't see you ogling him, your Southern accent going all syrupy around him, like you thought you could seduce him with some third-rate community-theater impression of Truman Capote. And *you*." She turned to Cannon. "You were happy when he died."

"I was gutted," he answered in a clipped tone.

"Gutted with *glee,* maybe."

Cannon glared at her, his face implacable. "You hate the Linda? Well, too bad. You're her to a tee. All that's missing are the face-lifts, the cankles, and the army of men who have fled you like a storm warning for a Category Five hurricane. But don't worry, angel. That will come in time."

"There is no time," noted Kipling, holding up a finger, half asleep. "Not anymore."

Whitley stared at Cannon, mouth open, shoulders trembling.

"Cannon didn't mean that," I whispered, touching her arm.

She threw off my hand, seizing a bottle from the floor. Cannon ducked as it exploded against the mirror behind his head.

"You're all monsters! *Get out of my house!*"

She elbowed me out of the way as she fled. Seconds later, she reappeared at the end of the hall brandishing a shotgun, aiming for my head. I took off down the staircase as a shot blasted the ceiling, chandelier swinging, bits of plaster and molding crashing to the ground.

"Get out! Termites! Leeches! Rats!"

More shots rang out as I reached the front door and pulled it open, colliding with Martha.

She was wearing a green poncho, soaking wet from the rain.

"Beatrice? What's the matter?"

"Worms! Maggots! Those disgusting fish at the bottom of the ocean with switchblade teeth! GET OUT! ALL OF YOU!"

I didn't answer. I sprinted outside to my truck and took off, blasting across flowerbeds, mud puddles, broken branches, swerving back onto the driveway as I tried to catch my breath.

———

I had to get away from them. I had to clear my head.

Everything they said, I kept reminding myself, was just the Neverworld talking. Being stuck here, day after day, made you think and feel the darkest things, as if daring the universe, God, whatever was out there, to prove that they weren't true.

A plain setting makes the diamond sparkle brighter. You loved Jim. You were happy when he died.

I didn't want to think about it. I drove straight to the Captain's Crow, letting myself in with the spare key my dad kept stashed behind the outside wall thermometer. I'd make a grilled cheese, eat some Wreck Rummage, and fall asleep. I'd figure out what to do tomorrow, yesterday, today, whatever it was.

The moment I entered the restaurant, however, slipping through the tiger-stripe shadows, I realized something was very wrong.

The café chairs, normally overturned on the tables, had been tossed all over the floor. The glass on the display of ice cream was cracked. Within the smells of toast and sunscreen was something else—something rancid. I'd just slipped into the kitchen, wondering if Sleepy Sam had forgotten to take out the trash, when my sneaker kicked shards of glass. Bending down, I saw I'd stepped on my great-grandfather Burn's pencil portrait. It had moved from its usual place over the door. Somehow it had ended up by the stove, facedown, the frame broken.

There was a robbery. That was my first thought.

Then I felt the wake descending, the blackest of sleeps pulling over me like a coffin lid, and I realized something else was going on, something strange.

I heard a faint tapping. Looking up, I screamed. In the window overlooking the alley by the sink, a face stared in at me.

The Keeper.

His gaze was neither hostile nor friendly, only stark, his jaw slashed by shadow. I realized that he was cutting away the ivy and vines of honeysuckle that had overtaken the wall, which my mom had never gotten around to pruning.

When I stumbled outside to confront him, he was striding down the alleyway.

"Hey!" I shouted after him. "What do you want?"

He ignored me, splashing through puddles, the clippings in a bag tossed over his shoulder, rounding the corner.

"Leave me alone!"

It was then that it occurred to me what he was.

The Keeper was a reminder.

The vote. The vote. *The vote.*

CHAPTER 7

After the fight, they went their separate ways. The moment they sprang back to the wake, Kip, Martha, Cannon, and Wit dispersed like seeds off a dead dandelion. They left without a word, sometimes without even looking at each other.

I let them go. I had no choice.

Was it depression? Probably. Fury over their fate? That too. Or maybe they just wanted to see what it felt like to climb beyond the Danger signs and Keep Out barricades, the barbed wire protecting the edges of the lookout atop the skyscraper, and jump.

What happened to us didn't matter. Peril didn't exist. If the Neverworld Wake had one asset, it was that we could remain forever young, like the Alphaville song. We could live and die and live again, without consequence.

Kipling began hitchhiking.

The moment he appeared in the back of the Jaguar, he took off down the drive. After he did this countless times, his expression an enigmatic mixture of resolve and expectation—as if he were actually looking forward to something—I followed him. I tailed him out to the main road, where, just before the stone bridge, he began walking backward, sticking out his thumb.

It was always the sixth car that stopped for him. A brown Pontiac with a dented fender.

I watched him disappear into that Pontiac so many times, I just had to know what was so captivating that he couldn't miss out on it, not even for one wake. So I caught up to him.

"Where are you going?" I asked him.

He turned, startled to see me, then annoyed. *"What?"*

"Who picks you up in the Pontiac?"

He kept walking. "It doesn't matter."

"Where do you go?"

"Leave me alone, Bee."

"Just tell me."

"No."

"Why not?"

"None a your goddamn business."

"Then I'm coming with you."

"No."

He was furious. He actually looked like he was considering hitting me, or tying me to a tree so he could get away.

"Tell me and I'll go back," I said.

He scowled, wiping the streaming rain off his face. "Her name's Shirley."

"And?"

"And she takes me with her to her chemotherapy treatment in Providence. Then we go back to her crappy apartment by a Stop and Shop and watch *Night of the Living Dead*. I cook her shrimp jambalaya and make a tuna salad for her cat named Canary. She thinks I'm a runaway from Mississippi. Sometimes my name is James. Sometimes it's Jesus. She undresses in front of me and asks me to touch her. She's religious. Thinks I'm some kind of savior from a different planet because I know so much about her. We talk all night. Now would you please go find your own disturbin' experience to get lost in? This one is mine."

At that moment, the brown Pontiac rounded the bend. Probably because I was there, or because Kip had a fake smile on his face, quite different from his usual laid-back, lounging-porch-cat demeanor, the car slowed for a second—revealing a plain-faced woman, brown hair, white T-shirt, radio blaring the Cure's "Close to Me"—then accelerated away.

Kip ran after her, waving. "Hold on! Wait for me! *Shirley!*"

The car tore around the bend, vanishing.

"Look what you did!" he wailed.

"I'm sorry."

Shaking his head, he took off over the bridge. He tried flagging down the next car, a red pickup truck, then a van, but no one stopped.

"Leave me alone!" he shouted as he took off jogging down the road.

I let him go. I understood. He looked forward to Shirley because for some reason she made him forget he was in the

Neverworld. It was probably only for a minute. But that was a priceless minute in a century of worthless ones.

———

After I'd learned where Kip went, I followed the others.

I had to. If I had any hope of ever making it out of here alive, I had to make sure I didn't lose them completely, that they didn't fall into some psychological rabbit hole from which they'd never be able to emerge.

I also needed a mission. I couldn't sit through *His Girl Friday* one more time. I couldn't watch my mom tell my dad with only a look that she didn't like the seats he'd chosen because they were too near the screen. Then, two seconds later: the bearded homeless man dropped the can of Old Milwaukee on the floor, muttering, "Shit, man," and the old woman behind him left to go report him as the man in the Brooklyn Book Drop T-shirt stuffed a handful of popcorn into his mouth (dropping three kernels in his lap). This symphony of normality played the same way every time. I knew every word, stutter, quip, throat clear, sniff, cough, scratch, and burp, like the stage manager who'd watched the same performance a million times from the wings.

Then there was the fact that my parents seemed so happy together it made me feel even more alone.

I followed Whitley and Cannon next.

They snapped back to the wake three minutes before the rest of us.

When I sprinted into Wincroft, they were already gone. They

left no note. The only evidence was red brake lights retreating down the drive. Yet their cars remained in front of the house. This meant that they left in some other car, and together, which suggested that whatever wounds their words had left from the fight, they'd already healed, like the skin of superheroes.

That didn't surprise me. They never stayed angry at each other for long.

Checking E.S.S. Burt's classic car garage, I noticed wet tire marks on the floor. I went into his office, read through his insurance forms, and was able to figure out that the missing vehicle was a maroon 1982 Rolls-Royce Silver Spur.

For the next few wakes, I tried to catch up to them.

It seemed impossible. They hadn't driven to the highway or any of the obvious coastal roads, so where did they disappear to, and so swiftly? Only countless wakes later, when I turned down an unmarked, narrow dirt drive, did I see the black wood sign painted in elegant Victorian script.

DAVY JONES'S LOCKER. Another mile and there was a second sign: MEMBERS ONLY.

I pulled into the parking lot. Davy Jones's appeared to be some kind of exclusive marina crowded with yachts. There was a white clubhouse and an outdoor tiki bar. Tanned crewmen in blue polo shirts strode purposefully along the docks, wielding umbrellas and iPads.

Parked directly in front of me was one maroon 1982 Rolls-Royce Silver Spur.

Almost immediately I spotted Whitley and Cannon.

They were speaking to a group of retirees, three couples in

their sixties or seventies, the women with short dyed hair and lean bodies like little bits of punctuation. The men were fat and bald. They were laughing. In fact, Wit and Cannon were laughing *so much* as I slipped out of my truck, keeping the umbrella low so they wouldn't spot me, I couldn't help gaping, incredulous at their all-too-convincing impression of being totally normal—like two people with tomorrows.

They seemed to be waiting for something.

Apparently it was an invitation to board the super-yacht the *Last Hurrah,* docked beside them. Because not a minute later, they were stepping with phony wonder up the teak steps, past the helicopter landing pad, and vanishing inside.

Bewildered, I strolled up to the boat. The uniformed crew were preparing for departure.

"Where you headed?"

"Bermuda."

Minutes later, the yacht cast off. That night, like all other recent nights, Wit and Cannon never returned to Wincroft to vote. By the next wake they were already gone.

So what were they up to? And why did the question fill me with such dread?

———

I had thirty-three minutes.

There were forty-seven minutes between the time I woke up in the Jaguar and the time the *Last Hurrah* cast off for Bermuda.

By minute thirty-three it was too late. There were too many crew members buzzing around not to be spotted. I was caught a million times.

"Excuse me? *Who* are you?"

"Hey!"

"You're not authorized to be here."

"Is this the *Dream Weaver*?"

"Is this *Cleopatra III*?"

"I'm looking for Captain Martin. I'm his niece."

I'd leave, stuttering apologies, ignoring the looks of suspicion as I snuck back to my truck. I'd watch as Wit and Cannon boarded that same yacht and took off into the open sea.

My only hope lay in immediately, the instant I woke, grabbing Cannon's car keys and sprinting to his Mercedes—twice as fast as my truck—taking a shortcut along a dirt service road, and barreling ninety miles an hour through marshes and sand into the Davy Jones's Locker marina.

I'd park behind a tree and speed-walk to the small cruiser beside *Last Hurrah,* where, pretending to be boarding that boat, I'd wait for the teenage deckhand to check his cell phone, at which point I had twenty seconds to dash up the steps and duck into the first door I came to. It led into an ornate game room with a jukebox and pinball machines. I then had fifteen seconds to slip up three flights to the staterooms and vanish into the bedroom at the end of the hall.

It overlooked the marina. It was there that, by cracking the window, I was able to eavesdrop on the outrageous scene—or, rather, con job. Whitley and Cannon, posing as newly married college sweethearts from Columbus, Ohio, had just been informed of a critical problem with their rented yacht, thereby leaving their honeymoon in tatters. Loudly they lamented their plight, which happened to be overheard by the owner of *Last Hurrah,* Ted Daisy of Cincinnati, who invited the poor young couple aboard.

"Why don't you spend the week with us? Plenty of room here for everybody."

"That's very kind, sir," said Cannon. "But we couldn't."

"Nonsense. The downside is you'll spend your honeymoon with a bunch of old geezers. But we promise to stay out of your way. You'll have a chef, an activities director, and a range of toys at your disposal."

"What do you say, sugar?" Cannon asked Whitley.

She nibbled a fingernail. "I'm not sure, honeybun."

I marveled at the way they had their act down, like a couple of seasoned Broadway tap dancers. How many wakes had it taken them to figure out the perfect formula for eliciting the invitation to board the yacht? Ten? Ten thousand?

"You kids are coming with us. I insist on it. Ted Daisy. This is my wife, Patty."

"Artwell Calvin the third," said Cannon.

"Anastasia Calvin," said Whitley, shaking her head. "I really don't know what I did in a previous life to deserve such kindness. I think I'm going to cry."

———

What had I expected aboard the *Last Hurrah*? A relaxed vacation cruise? A beautiful, distracting dream where Whitley and Cannon could forget the Neverworld?

That wasn't it. Not at all.

I should have known. Their relationship at Darrow had always been incendiary. They had sex in closets and classrooms, on rooftops, in the woods, on the balcony of the chapel, never once getting caught. They stalked hallways with their arms around each other like boa constrictors, students and teachers alike eyeing them nervously, though no one complained. They were in the top five of our class, after all. Whitley talked about their love as an insatiable need. I saw it as a lethal bullet speeding toward a target. Whether that target was one of them or some unsuspecting third party, I had no idea. They fought, made up, hated each other, couldn't live without the other for even one second.

They called each other Sid and Nancy. They stole things for fun. Anything on campus, no matter how big or small, could be targeted, like Mrs. Ferguson's AP Physics exams; a $12,000 seascape from an art gallery; Rector Trask's XXL tartan vest, which he notoriously donned for Darrow's Holiday Feast; even a John Deere excavator from the library construction site. They'd help themselves to whatever it was, resulting in a weeklong uproar of faculty announcements and threats of expulsion, a few unsuspecting students being summoned into a dean's office to detail what they knew—until, with equal quiet and swiftness, the object reappeared. Their knack for burglary was not due to the usual reasons for acting out, like anger or some perverse craving for attention. It was a simple love for the art of deceit—being a step ahead of everyone—not to mention their ongoing need to outdo each other.

Everyone whispered they'd be legendary if they stayed together. I secretly thought their connection was *too* close, like twins. Cannon didn't have Whitley's temper, but he had her intensity and knack for manipulation, dropping a word here, an inference there, that would be the gram of uranium to turn a benign situation nuclear. They broke up couples, made teachers cry. When they finally called it quits senior year, their breakup was eerily silent, a biological weapon that had abruptly dispelled with hardly any smoke, defying all scientific explanation.

"Everyone knows adolescent love has a short shelf life," Whitley explained with shrug.

Now it was clear that Whitley and Cannon boarded the *Last Hurrah* for no reason other than that they'd decided that boat was their mad, twisted playground to tear into, as if they were two wild monkeys locked in a cage.

It was their padded cell. The soundproof room where they could scream their heads off.

The first night, I watched Wit get so drunk she vomited all over the dinner table on the platters of lobster and sirloin steak.

"Whoops," she said, wiping her mouth.

The second night, she danced provocatively with Ted Daisy. When his wife, Patty, saw what was happening, she called out in a drunken voice, "Ted! Ted?" like their fifty-year marriage had suddenly turned into a phone call with poor reception.

On another occasion, Cannon and Wit stripped down to their

underwear and, climbing up onto the ship's railing, screamed, *"Carpe noctem!"* Holding hands, they jumped, falling the fifty feet into the sea. Alarms sounded. Women screamed. Engines gasped to a halt. The crew members swarmed, shouting orders, two diving in with life vests.

"Find them!" shouted Ted Daisy, desperately peering over the railing. He looked like he was having a heart attack. "I'll be damned if I'm going to jail because of those wackos!"

"We're going to lose everything," wailed Patty.

"We should have tied them up the moment we realized something was mentally off with them. We should have called the coast guard."

"It's *your* fault!" screamed Patty, her stiff blond hair standing up like pieces of potato chips. "You invited them aboard because you wanted to impress that little blond piece of ass. You thought you had a chance with her. Ha! Hope you're happy now!"

Hysteria. Panic. Fury. Despair. Fear. Alarm.

It all happened aboard the *Last Hurrah* on a day that would not stop happening.

I watched from back rooms, spare bedrooms, an electrical supply closet. I put on the extra crew uniform I'd found, and no one looked at me twice. I kept waiting for the right moment to appear, to try to talk down Cannon and Wit, bring them back from the razor's edge. I couldn't find it. I knew them too well. When they were like this, there was no stopping them.

I remained where I was, peering out at the nightmarish scene through a crack in the door, terrified, sick, sometimes crying, wondering when it would stop.

Then one night Cannon smashed a decanter over Ted Daisy's head. Ted shoved him into a display case stacked with crystal goblets. They began wrestling, overturning coffee tables and the dining room table. Then Cannon was sitting on the man's chest, strangling him.

I'd had enough. I ran out of the closet and knelt beside Cannon, trying to pry off his hands. The old man was spitting and blubbering.

"Stop it!" I cried.

It took Cannon another minute to let go. I tried CPR, compressing the man's chest, counting the way my dad had taught me. I checked his pulse. He was alive, but barely.

"You have to stop," I whispered.

Cannon surveyed me like I was a distant relative whose name he couldn't recall.

"You're making it worse. Because *we* remember. These people don't. But you do. And the destruction will eat away at you."

"Oh, shut up, Bee," said Wit.

She'd risen from the sofa, where she'd been passed out cold.

"What are you even doing here? Spying? When will you realize we want nothing to do with you? We're not your friends anymore. You blew that when you went MIA after Jim. You think you can just ditch your friends like that and get away with it?"

She shuffled toward me, her eyes red and threatening. I turned and ran, barging past the other guests, who'd been woken by the noise and were now, in their white terry-cloth robes and matching slippers, gaping in shock at the scene. I ran to the third-floor deck and spent the rest of the wake in one of the rescue boats, sobbing, hoping no one would find me.

I never returned to the *Last Hurrah*.

Cannon and Wit went the very next wake. Wit left me a message scrawled in high-drama red lipstick across the kitchen counter.

STAY AWAY.

The threat was unnecessary. I could never go back there.

Would repetition eventually render even the *Last Hurrah* boring, whereupon they'd return to Wincroft? Would one of them decide they wanted to live, to escape the Neverworld, to vote? Or would they simply move on to devouring something or someone else? The Neverworld held an infinite number of playgrounds, so it was possible, horrifying as it was to consider, that I'd never see them again.

I couldn't think about that. Not yet.

Instead, I turned my attention to Martha.

It was funny how I'd almost forgotten her. And I suspected it was just what she wanted.

CHAPTER 8

Martha no longer spent the day hiking Wincroft. Now she would hurriedly enter the mansion, retrieve a raincoat, and drive off, never returning.

"Where do you go?" I asked her.

She whipped around in surprise. She hadn't seen me sitting in the rocking chair on the porch. Recovering, she pulled out her car keys, then opened an umbrella.

"I visit this silly Baptist church buffet up in Newport." She shrugged, her face turning red. "I've turned it into my personal biosphere. Like I find a guy and see if I can get him to say 'I love you' by the end of the night. Or I approach a woman and see if I can get her to leave her husband. I'm trying to prove a theory about human nature. That anyone is capable of anything at any time, given a certain set of conditions."

She was lying. I could tell.

"Can I come with you?" I asked.

"I prefer to be alone, actually."

"What about when you were hiking around with binoculars? What were you doing?"

"Bird-watching."

She was lying about that too. She seemed fully aware I didn't believe her, yet she stared back at me, undaunted.

"Aren't you worried?" I asked, trying to ignore the anger in the pit of my stomach. "Upset? Scared? We've lost them all now."

She smiled thinly. "I suggest you resolve yourself to your fate, Bee."

And with that she turned and hurried down the steps to her car.

——

The next wake, I headed straight to my truck. While Martha was inside getting the raincoat, I hid in a driveway down the street, and when she pulled out, I followed her.

Unfortunately, my confrontation appeared to have tipped her off, because as soon as I pulled up behind her on the interstate, though I was three cars back, she took the first exit and drove in meandering circles around deserted office parks before pulling into Birchwood Plaza. She spent the next four hours wandering Urban Outfitters and Barnes & Noble and eating a calzone in the food court.

She knew I was there, watching her. Yet she was unconcerned.

The next wake, she did the same thing at a different mall. The third time, another.

There was no way Martha spent her Neverworld wandering malls. She was doing that because she knew I was following her. She seemed to be banking on my eventually growing bored and moving on.

So I did. I stopped. Instead, I devoted the next few wakes—or was it a few thousand?—to figuring out how to follow her unseen.

And so began my illustrious career in grand theft auto.

——

I was a panicky and apologetic thief.

Hundreds of times I was caught red-handed.

"Who the hell are you and what are you doing in my garage?"

"*Hi*. Sorry."

Thankfully—probably because there was something intrinsically sad about me, which could only be blamed on the Neverworld—everyone let me off the hook.

The only car I could steal without getting caught was a rusted white van emblazoned with the words MCKENDRICK PEST CONTROL.

It belonged to the McKendricks, a hyper militia-family of seven living in a modest ranch house four doors down from Wincroft. All seven McKendricks were always home, so to get my hands on the keys was the closing act of Cirque du Soleil.

It took me forever to get it right.

One: hide in rhododendrons outside the kitchen, waiting for

Bud McKendrick to wander into the living room for his Camel Lights. Two: dart into the kitchen pantry, trying not to trip on the bags of Healthy Weight cat food or the Macaroni and Cheese Storage Bucket with Gamma Lid from Target. Three: wait for Pete McKendrick to grab a Kit-Kat and head to the basement to watch *The Adventures of Jimmy Neutron,* Bud to go upstairs for a nap, and Gerry and Paul, the twins, to go play soccer in the front yard in the rain. Four: slip into the den, scaring Tupac, the cat, who jumps six feet into the air and climbs the curtains. Five: snatch the car keys off the table and duck behind the sofa as Laurel McKendrick takes forty dollars from her husband's wallet. "Heading to the store!" Six: run back into kitchen and try to avoid four-year-old Kendall McKendrick.

"Who are you?" she asked me, eyes wide in surprise.

There was no avoiding Kendall. No matter what, she always caught me.

It was the most incendiary moment of all: finding the perfect recipe of words that would stop her from wailing like a smoke alarm. I had tried everything. Nothing worked.

"I'm an angel."

"I work for the tooth fairy."

"I'm the Elf on the Shelf, and I need to borrow your daddy's truck."

How many times had I expertly trapezed my way through the McKendricks', only to crash to the ground, thanks to Kendall yelling her head off, prompting every McKendrick to descend on me.

"Dad! *Dad!*"

I'd run for my life as the McKendricks—all with variations on the same bulldog marine face—swarmed their front yard.

"Stop! Burglar!" they shouted through the rain.

"Dad, you're letting her get away!"

Good old Bud McKendrick never called the police. Probably because after five kids, it took more than some teenage housebreaker to rattle him. Frowning quizzically after me from the porch, more than a little blasé, he always let me go.

Finally there came the wake when I told Kendall the truth.

"My name is Beatrice Hartley. I'm trapped between life and death in a place called a Neverworld. I'm trying to make it out of here, and to make a long story short, I need you to be quiet and go watch cartoons with your brothers. *Now*."

She nodded mutely and padded downstairs.

Light-headed with amazement, I snatched Bud's Rams baseball cap off a chair, grabbed his Oakley sunglasses, unlatched the door to the detached garage, and ran out. I pulled on Bud's coveralls, hat, sunglasses, climbed behind the wheel of the van. Starting the engine, I was just wondering how in the world I was going to drive past the twins playing soccer, when Paul punted the ball into a neighbor's yard. I inched down the drive, turned right, pulled into another drive a few houses down, my heart hammering.

A minute later Martha drove past me.

I followed her Honda Accord all the way to Providence, to Brown University, to the third floor of a redbrick building on Thayer Street, to a corner office.

ARNOLD BELORODA, PH.D. read the brass plaque on the door.

I watched Martha knock. A male voice answered "Yes?" and she entered. I heard her say hi as the door closed, and though I slipped closer in the crowded hallway, straining to hear the muffled voices inside, I couldn't make out any more.

I Googled the name. Arnold Winwood Beloroda. He was an award-winning psychiatrist and professor emeritus specializing in group dynamic theory. He taught a host of classes at Brown. Making Ethical Decisions: The Good, Bad, and the Ugly. The Psychology of Manipulation and Consent. The Fantasy of Free Will. A senior seminar, Laboratory for Experiments in Social Persuasion. He had published thirteen nonfiction books, winning a slew of awards for one from the nineties, *Heroes and Villains*. According to the *Wall Street Journal*, it was about "the master-slave dynamics of concentration camps" and other situations in which "a large populace allows themselves to be controlled by a select few."

I scanned Beloroda's articles in the *Harvard Review*, the *Economist*, and *Scientific American*. What was so compelling about him? What was so critical that Martha had gone to such lengths to hide him?

Then it hit me. It felt like a pair of hands had begun to squeeze my neck.

While the rest of us had been wasting time warring against the reality of our circumstances, Martha had been using the Neverworld's infinity to study.

Beloroda had been teaching her how to manipulate the group so we would choose her.

She was figuring out how to win.

I tailed Martha over and over again. Every time, she drove to Brown's Cognitive, Linguistic, and Psychological Sciences building. Every time, she visited Beloroda. They remained holed up in his office for three, four hours. Clearly she'd figured out a way to hook him, captivate him with some high-level question about group dynamics or a detail mined from his own papers that served as the magic key to Open Sesame the close connection, the meeting of like minds. When they finally emerged, Beloroda—an elfin man with a turned-up nose and an overmanicured inky beard like a Rorschach test—was beaming at Martha (now hauling a pile of textbooks he'd given her, as well as a legal pad covered with notes), bewitched by the sudden appearance of such an engaging new student.

Sharing an umbrella, they always strolled outside, deep in conversation, and chatted for another twenty minutes on the sidewalk. Once I crept behind them, hiding in an alcove where a few students were smoking under the awning.

"You're absolutely correct," said Beloroda. "But here I would cite the philosophy of M. Scott Peck. In all groups there are four stages. Pseudocommunity. Chaos. Emptiness. And true community."

"Could you tell me more about the Milgram experiment?"

"Ah. The blind obedience to authority figures." Beloroda chuckled. "There's nothing I'd like more, but I'm afraid I'm due to join my wife at a party. How about we resume this conversation tomorrow after my Group Cohesion lecture?"

He was unlocking his car, climbing in.

"It was a delight to meet you, Miss Peters. Until tomorrow?"

He drove off. Martha stared after him, her affable smile abruptly falling from her face as she pulled up her hood and took off. She sat for the next few hours in a window booth at Greek Taverna, poring over the books, taking notes. When the diner closed, she moved to her Honda and read in there, seat reclined, overhead light on.

The longer I watched from the darkness of the park across the street, the more I felt a choking anxiousness and fear, as if the Neverworld were closing in on me.

Martha was brilliant. Martha understood. She was light-years ahead of the rest of us. She had summarily accepted the crushing reality of the Neverworld, and rather than fighting it, she had dedicated her time to figuring out how to master it.

I wanted to live, didn't I? I wanted to be chosen. Yet, staring at the pale light inside Martha's car, fighting back tears, I sensed I was too late, that I'd already lost.

My gaze suddenly fell on a dark figure pushing a wheelbarrow toward me down the path through the park. It was heaped with black compost.

I should have been used to the Keeper's presence by now. I should have ignored how no matter where I went, however near or far, when I least expected it, he would come to me like a terrifying thought, the Neverworld's omnipresent alarm, its memento, its tolling bell.

The vote. The vote. *The vote.*

The temperature had dropped. The rain was turning to snow again.

I sprinted to the McKendrick van, climbed in, and took off,

swerving into the road so wildly I almost hit a streetlamp. The Keeper paused to watch me go, a shovel balanced on his shoulder.

I caught a glimpse of his face through the swirling snowflakes, the chilling smile.

I couldn't imagine what Martha was planning. Whatever it was, I suspected it'd be so well considered and masterful, none of us would ever see her coming.

How right I was.

CHAPTER 9

How did I pass the next few wakes?

Was it months? Or was it years?

I was the only one left. Wincroft was my castle to rule, my tiny home planet. The solitude was infinite. Gandalf was there, but he backed away and barked whenever I tried to pet him, as if aware I wasn't quite real. I wandered the creaking hallways and musty rooms, had conversations with stuffed deer and grizzly bears. I read every book in E.S.S. Burt's library, sprawled across daybeds, love seats, and carpets; dining room tables, window seats, and grand pianos. I watched every show on every cable channel at every time. I ate chocolate. I played Scrabble by myself, and chess by myself, and sang pop songs. I drew everything I could think of—eyes, faces, landscapes, shadows. I made a dream soundtrack, song lyrics to a fake four-hour movie about the end of the world called *Ned Gromby's Last Day Alive Ever*, scribbling the mad rhymes about life and death, war and peace, all over the wallpaper and floors and ceilings of Wincroft. Wincroft was my bridge underpass spangled with my graffiti. I squeezed my eyes closed to beat back the silence, and sifted through memories of my old life as if inside them I'd find a key to a door that would lead me somewhere.

I visited the elderly. They were my favorite. Because they were locked inside their own Neverworlds too, impenetrable rooms of repetition and loneliness. I made a habit of ringing their doorbells with an excuse about selling early Christmas calendars for my church. I ate their fruitcake and petted their old dogs with bad breath before they scampered away with twitching backs. I sipped the weird tea and watched TV, inhaled the curdled house odors the owner was oblivious to. Most of all, I listened to the stories. I untangled the gnarled pileups of anecdotes and convoluted tales of dead husbands, failing health, childhoods of taffeta and milk that cost ten cents.

I figured if I remained in the Neverworld, alone, until the end of time, I would be like an ancient traveler wandering the side of the road with a calloused heart and hands, weighted with the world's tales and secrets.

At least then, if nothing else, I would be wise.

It was inevitable that I'd be sitting there, listening to the story about the broken engagement, the dead child, the cat, when suddenly I'd see the decay. It always came out of nowhere and made me jump. Every windowpane in every single window around me would be silently cracking. Or a family photo would suddenly drop down the wall with a thump, revealing a garish rectangle of wallpaper that hadn't seen daylight in forty years.

"*What* in the name of Jesus is going on . . . ?"

In Mrs. Kahn's case, it began with a faint popping noise.

"Damn raccoon's got in again," she muttered, tightening her robe. When she started shrieking in the den, I ran to her, astonished, to find her prized collection of snow globes—gifts from Paul, a lost suitor—detonating like grenades, water and snow and glass, plastic Santas, Eiffel Towers, St. Peter's Basilicas, exploding around the room.

Mrs. Kahn shielded her face. "It's the Day of Judgment!"

Of course, I'd noticed the deterioration before, back at my house with my mom. Again that night at the Crow. I didn't know why, or what it meant, but whenever I was away from Wincroft, the world began to decay and disintegrate around me.

It always made me scared. I ran away, muttering some excuse and that I'd be back tomorrow, leaving Mrs. Kahn, Mr. Appleton, Mrs. Janowitz, Miss Bellossi, bent over, disconcerted, as they inspected the rot, the mold, the cracks traveling like lengthening skeletal fingers along the windows. I'd sprint back to Wincroft to search the gardens and grounds for the Keeper. I wanted to confront him, demand to know what was happening.

Yet, bafflingly, whenever I willed him to appear, he stayed away.

The corrosion appeared to be getting stronger. What did it mean? Was the Neverworld going to swallow itself like a black hole? Were we running out of time to vote? Was it all because of what happened to Jim?

The answer jolted me like an electric shock.

Jim. It had to be because of Jim.

———

Then came the day Wit didn't leave.

I discovered her upstairs, buried under an avalanche of duvet, her face swollen with tears as she watched *Heathers* on her laptop. I stared at her, dumbfounded. I felt like some shipwreck survivor finding another person who'd washed up alive on my island.

She glared at me. "Leave me alone, Bee."

I was worried I'd frighten her away, so I did just what she said. I made her tea, left the mug on her bedside table, and ducked out.

The next wake, to my relief, she was there again, watching *The Breakfast Club;* the wake after that, *Goonies.* I always left her tea. Then, one wake, as I did, she threw off the comforter and surveyed me with a sad smile.

"Want to watch *Ferris Bueller* with me?"

Cannon reappeared a few wakes later. Mayhem, as it turned out, wasn't as much fun without an accomplice. He was as exhausted as Whitley, holed up in the library with his laptop in DOS mode, typing some mysterious hacker's command as the screen belched code. I printed out an obscure article written by a Stanford doctorate student about the future of Internet security and left it next to his laptop for him. The next wake, it was an essay about Steven Spielberg and brain cloning written by a freshman scientist at Harvard, then a blog posting by some genius sixteen-year-old Cambridge student about the future of robotics.

"How are you finding these articles?" Cannon asked once before I darted out. "I mean, they're so obscure."

With all my free time in the Neverworld, I've read the entire Internet. Twice.

"I just stumbled upon them."

He smiled. "They're really cool. Thanks, Bee."

Shortly after that, Kip stopped going hitchhiking. The moment he strolled into Wincroft, I couldn't help it. I threw my arms around him, hugging him.

"Sister Bee, you're breakin' my neck. I'm not Elvis back from the dead, child."

He pulled away, said nothing more, headed upstairs. Yet I could tell from his faint smile that he was happy to see me. That night I made him Boudreaux's Stomp Shrimp Gumbo, the recipe served in his favorite hole-in-the-wall café in Moss Bluff. I left him a bowl in the bedroom where he was holed up watching *Hoarding: Buried Alive* on TLC.

"How'd you get Auntie Mo's secret recipe?" he blurted, incredulous.

I had a million wakes to make her believe I was her long-lost niece.

"Just whipped it up," I said with a shrug.

So there they were, three wild animals I was doing my best to cajole into remaining at the zoo in captivity, rather than roaming the wild.

Then, one night, as the four of us sat reading in the library, I realized from the way Kip kept glancing curiously at the clock on the mantel that he was waiting for something. Martha must have said something to him about a group meeting, because when she appeared a few minutes after midnight, entering without a word, hauling her heavy black bag and taking a seat on the couch, he didn't look the least bit surprised.

"It's time," Martha announced.

Whitley and Cannon surveyed her in shock.

"Nice to see you too," said Cannon.

Martha gave him an official smile, clasping her hands like a judge.

"We've come back to where we started," she said. "It's as if the Neverworld's walls are slippery and slanted, always sending us back to where we began. I suspect, like me, you were each pursued by the Keeper, often when you least expected it?"

I nodded. So did the others.

"He's our caretaker. He tends us, keeping us alive and thriving, making sure we have the sustenance we need but also keeping us in check. This means he's capable of anything, being at once a guide and a taskmaster, a custodian and a thorn. Maybe he leaves you alone, or offers you a sprinkling of advice. Or else he hounds you, reminding you of the one thing you wish to forget. He will become anything to make you grow in a certain direction. Most of all, he is the chairman of a grand design we can't see."

No one said a word, all of us listening in wonder, in shock. The way Martha sat there—squared shoulders, steady stare. She was no longer the mute nerd who blurted unfunny comments at weird moments, the girl more comfortable buried in the pages of an underground fantasy novel than living in the real world. This was a new Martha, one who had studied with Beloroda. She was a confident presence now. I had no idea where she was going with this speech, but she'd given it considerable thought, her every word as carefully selected as stones in an ornate necklace, each one meticulously polished and gleaming.

"The Neverworld is real," she said. "To understand and conquer it, we must first understand and conquer each other. I've thought it over. We must set aside the question of who should live. We're not prepared for that. Not yet. Because there's another mystery we have to solve. It's dogged each of us in different ways since it happened."

"What are you talking about?" asked Cannon, frowning.

"Jim."

His name was like a gleaming sword pitching through the air, landing hard at our feet.

"It was suicide," whispered Whitley.

Martha stared at her, stony. "You don't *actually* believe that."

Wit seemed too uncomfortable to answer.

"I've been studying the Neverworld," Martha went on. "This place, among many things, makes us the most powerful detectives in the world. We can go back to the scene of the crime an infinite number of times. We can interview bystanders. Witnesses. The police. Every teacher, janitor, and student. We can polish our questions, manipulate, intimidate, blackmail. There are no penalties and no rules. We can find out what happened to Jim once and for all."

Martha's dark eyes found mine as she said this, sending a shiver through me.

"But the case was unsolvable," said Cannon.

"Yeah," said Kipling in a low voice. "The cops didn't get very far."

"They were pressured by the school board to wrap it up quickly. The sooner everyone believed suicide, the sooner Darrow could repaint the bloody walls. That's what our parents wanted. They wanted to sweep the scandal under the rug, for everyone to chalk the whole thing up to another doomed dream boy. The Legend of Jim Mason would be just another ghost story echoing through the halls."

"So we're Sherlocks for the foreseeable future," said Whitley.

Kipling raised an eyebrow. "I've always had a thing for herringbone and bloodhounds."

"I'm in," said Cannon.

"Me too," whispered Whitley.

"Beatrice?" asked Martha.

They all looked at me. I stared back, my heart pounding.

It was happening, after all this time: We were freeing the lion. Dredging the *Titanic* up from the bottom of the sea. We were unburying the man who'd been sealed inside the walls that night we went searching for the cask of the Amontillado.

We were going to find out what happened to Jim.

My Jim.

The cat-and-mouse game had begun.

PART 2

CHAPTER 10

The strange circumstances of Jim Livingston Mason's death had always seemed unreal to me, even though I experienced them firsthand.

As I thought back on it now, holed up in that library with my four former best friends, returning to each detail felt like trying to recall the rules of an imaginary game I'd played as a child.

Senior year, spring semester before finals week, my boyfriend, Jim, went missing.

Two days later, he was found dead, floating in the lake at Vulcan Quarry.

He was my first love, though those words don't begin to describe what he actually was. Moon. Voice in my head. Blood. Even though everyone and their grandmother will tell you young love never lasts, that its burn is much more fragile than it ever appears to the naked eye, I swore what Jim and I had was different.

He was beautiful in the unlikely way of some eighteenth-century hero galloping across moors on horseback: six foot three, honey-brown stare, uncombed black hair, cockeyed smile. But there was something else too. He was alive. If life force is a river's current, Jim's was so strong it could take off your fingers. He charged through an ordinary Monday as if he had been tasked with imparting a crucial secret about existence before Tuesday. He was a goofball, grandmaster of the Catchy Tune, the Double Entendre, the Shock Romantic Gesture, like giving me a vintage diamond Cartier pin in the shape of a bumblebee after he'd known me just a week. He wrote me a theme song called "The Queen's Neck." The worst thing about Jim was that his intensity attracted everyone. He was the light on a porch at night. Men and women, young and old, swirled around him, as if mistaking the attention of Jim Mason for a miracle dip in Lourdes. I couldn't fault them. He made them feel important and less alone.

He called me Amish, and Cahoots, and Hedy Lamarr. He said I had some quality of the past that he could never put his finger on, that I was meant for some long-forgotten, more innocent time.

"You're a Dusky Flying Fox," he told me.

"A *what*?"

"An extinct species of mammal known only by a single specimen. You were spotted once in 1874 on Percy Island off the coast of Queensland, Australia. No other examples of you were ever found. Yet here you are again, tucked away in an antiquated, not especially impressive boarding school in the wilds of Rhode Island. And no one knows about you but me."

He was analytical, agonizing, easily wounded, unable to let much go. The summer before senior year, he and a childhood friend were drinking and driving a speedboat off Long Island when they collided with a sandbar, hitting a fisherman's skiff. The fisherman and Jim's friend were fine, thank goodness, but Jim suffered a skull fracture and ended up unconscious for two days. As a result of his injury, he wrote six songs, four poems, and a rap song called "Bang-Up" about the incident. He vowed to give up alcohol. Once a month after the accident, he wrote letters to the fisherman, as if confessing to a priest.

That was just how Jim was. He saturated. He overflowed. He drowned.

"You have to design your life like it's a fresh America," he used to say, pulling his guitar onto his lap, his calloused fingertips dancing along the strings. "An unseen brave new world sits before you. Every. Single. Day. What are you going to do about it?"

Now Whitley, Cannon, Kipling, and Martha were watching me, uneasy. We'd never done this before. We'd never talked together about Jim's death. This had had to do with timing as much as the devastation of it. When every fact had been released by police and the administration had made their statement, finals week was finished. In a state of shock, unable to leave my bed, barely able to speak, I allowed my stricken parents to whisk me away from the treacherous kingdom of Darrow, back to the calming shelter of Watch Hill. It was days before I could stop sobbing, months before I felt anything remotely resembling fine.

"The body shuts down when it's too sad," said my dad.

——

"Where do we begin?" I asked now.

"Excellent question," said Martha. She looked at me, her dark eyes glinting behind her glasses. "What do *you* think happened to Jim? I always wanted to ask you."

There it was, the question I asked myself every day. So much so, it had turned me into a secret freak of nature, like a man who wanders around for years with a bullet lodged in his brain, normal on the outside, a gruesome marvel on the inside.

I was dying to spill my theories, what I knew but they didn't know I knew. It had been my whole reason for coming to Wincroft. But in this dizzying life-and-death dynamic in which we found ourselves, sharing them wouldn't necessarily be a wise idea. Not if I wanted to live. Martha asking this so pointedly sent a fresh wave of chills up my spine.

"I don't know," I said.

"It was an accident," interjected Kipling. "Had to have been, right? Say Jim was out at the quarry. Maybe he decided to get wasted. Sure, he'd sworn off booze after that boat crash, but maybe he was depressed. He was stressed about his musical. Didn't think he could pull it off. Maybe he slipped. The swim team kept those Pabst Blue Ribbons stashed all over. So maybe he was wanderin' the tall grass, which on a windy night could

112

be like gettin' caught in a car wash's Deluxe Wax Special, and, I don't know, he stepped too close to the edge and tripped?"

"When did Jim Mason ever trip?" asked Cannon.

Kipling shrugged, tipping back his head to squint at the ceiling.

"Freak possible," he said in a low voice. "That's what Momma Greer calls it when worst-case scenarios on steroids actually happen. She says all the big mysteries of history, like Marilyn's death, JFK, the Black Dahlia, the Lost Colony? They all came down to the freak possible." He nodded as if trying to convince himself, giving a lazy wave of his hand. "It's wild flukes. One-in-a-billion chances. Wrong places at the wrong time with a serious helping of bad luck. It's some crazy, gnarled tangle of destiny that can never be undone by any outside detective 'cause it'd sound too damn absurd." He looked at me, his face solemn. "The freak possible's what happened to Jim. I'd bet my life on it."

"Yeah," said Whitley, shrugging. "I mean, none of us knew he was heading to the quarry that night."

Everyone nodded, glancing tentatively at the others.

I suspected at least one of them was lying. I certainly was.

After all, on the night of Jim's death, none of them had been where they'd claimed.

I knew this because I'd gone looking for each of them, one by one.

I'd found nothing and no one.

—

Vulcan Quarry—or Vulcanation, as Darrow's students called it—was the abandoned quarry a mile from the center of campus.

If Darrow had one enduring legend, it was that quarry. Given its tantalizing proximity to school—the seventeen-acre property bordered Darrow's southeast woods—it was the off-limits no-man's-land kids whispered about and obsessed over, a far-off world to visit for pranks, hazing, hookups, and all other adolescent rites of passage, you name it.

Rumors about the quarry—how to find it, what happened to students who went there (most of whom were long gone from Darrow, so events could never be verified)—were part of the weekly goings-on at Darrow and served as a foundation to its lore. The quarry was as tightly woven into the fabric of the school as its official song, "Oh, Lord, Unbind My Heart"; its motto, "Truth, Compassion, Enterprise"; and even Marksman Library, the Gothic fortress of weather-beaten gray stones that stared out like a menacing stepfather from every brochure.

After World War I, Vulcan Sandberg Corporation created the quarry for mining granite. By the 1950s, they were bankrupt, the quarry forsaken. In the ensuing years, the crater filled with water, creating a lake two hundred feet deep. The grounds overgrew, with grass that reached your neck. The Foreman's Lookout—a wooden box like a pioneer-era saloon hoisted fifty feet into the sky, accessible only by scaling a narrow ladder—began to lean northward. Then there was the quarry itself, a hole in the earth the size of a small town. It sat there, gaping and ominous, impossible to look away from. It seemed to reveal some terrifying truth about the world the grown-ups wanted to keep hidden from us.

Darrow's football team used the quarry for Streak Night, the annual tradition of new recruits racing naked to the quarry and back. The crew team went swimming in the lake before state championships for good luck. Couples went there to lose their virginity, daredevils to brood. It was whispered that Vulcan Sandberg was actually a government cover-up, that the quarry had actually been the landing spot for an alien spaceship.

For Darrow's administration, Vulcan Quarry was a lawsuit waiting to happen, the enchanted wood they wanted to clear-cut to put an end to the dark fairy tales wafting off it like some toxic mist. There was always some board member protesting, collecting signatures to declare it a safety hazard, lobbying state representatives for it to be turned into a cultural center, a YMCA, a housing complex. In the meantime, it required new fencing and a twenty-four-hour police patrol. The town of Warwick—partly out of resentment over being told what to do by uppity out-of-towners, partly out of ineptitude—dragged their feet doing anything about it, though, and as long as I attended Darrow, the fencing around the quarry—rusted, riddled with holes, its faded signs halfheartedly declaring KEEP OUT—remained little more than a suggestion at best.

After Jim was found dead, however, he became the poster boy for the board's cause. Last I'd heard, the quarry was going to be turned into a reservoir and there was brand-new, state-of-the-art fencing around it.

Not that that would keep Darrow's students out.

If the administration knew the lengths to which the student body went to sneak out at night, to the quarry and everywhere else—dorm rooms, basement gymnasiums, boiler rooms—they wouldn't have believed it. There was a secret forum—AlbanzHax .biz—where students past and present anonymously revealed how to get in and out of every dorm without being caught.

All dark clothing. Porch ledge. Sneak past the window where Mr. Robertson is zonked out with an issue of Poets & Writers *over his chest. Get past him ur golden.*

The six of us snuck out to Vulcan Quarry all the time. We were already in the habit of stealing away to each other's rooms after curfew, clambering across ledges and landings to hash over boys, teachers, sharing a cigarette in the dark before hightailing it home, stealing back into bed. Sophomore year, Cannon found the crude map and pointers for the quarry etched into the tiles of the forsaken gym in the old athletic center. At midnight we escaped our dorms, meeting at the entry to the Philosopher's Walk. Barely able to suppress our laughter, we took off running down the tangle of dirt paths to get there.

Those were the best nights of my life.

I couldn't say why, exactly, this was so—only that I knew that as an old woman, when I thought back to my youth, I'd remember these nights, sitting with these five people along the harrowing window ledge of the Foreman's Lookout, gazing into that clear blue lake hundreds of feet below.

Our friendship was born there. There we were bound together. Something about seeing each other against that spare, alien backdrop of rock, water, and sky—not to mention the prohibited, dangerous thing we were doing—it X-rayed us, revealed the unspoken questions we each were asking. You could feel life burning us, our scars as real as the wind whipping our faces. We knew that nothing would ever be the same, that youth was here and nearly gone already, that love was fragile and death was real.

——

"What about the White Rabbit?" asked Martha now. "It never sat right with me. It was just too easy. The White Rabbit suddenly revealed to be Jim the *exact* moment he turns up dead?" She shook her head. "It went against everything I knew about him."

"You think it was a cover-up?" asked Whitley. "Some grand conspiracy concocted by the administration and Jim was the fall guy?"

"I don't know."

"You're right," I said to Martha. "There's no way he was the White Rabbit."

"How do you know?" Cannon asked me.

I just know.

——

The White Rabbit.

It was what everyone called the drug dealer at Darrow, someone who circulated the student body, invisible and invasive as a virus.

For most of my time at the school he was a bogeyman. No one had actually ever seen him—no one who would admit to it, at least. He did his deals in creative scavenger-hunt dead drops all around Darrow, like behind the frame of *Landscape #14* in the art gallery, or inside the ripped seat cushion of seat 104, row E, Orchestra Hall.

By the time I was a senior, the name had garnered such cult status, whenever anything weird happened, it was said to be the work of the White Rabbit. Even teachers knew the name. They'd doubtlessly held emergency meetings about him, trying to determine whether he was real or it was just kids dreaming up some Keyser Söze.

The biggest scandal concerned a freshman named Veronica Beers. She took some pills and went out of her mind during Winter Dance, fell down a flight of stairs, and got taken to the ER. She admitted the White Rabbit had sold her the pills. Tracing the phone number led to only a defunct prepaid phone.

Was he a lone wolf or a gang of hoodlums? A student or someone from the outside?

When the police found Jim, he'd been dead for two days. The cause of death was asphyxiation due to drowning, but he also had signs of a concussion and leg and spinal fractures, which the coroner believed were sustained when he hit the water.

Police searched Jim's room at Packer Hall, and they found hidden inside his Gibson guitar stashes of pot, Adderall, Ritalin, and cocaine. They concluded that Jim had been the infamous supplier, his death most likely suicide, though foul play in conjunction with some local criminal couldn't be ruled out.

The revelation spread like wildfire.

First Jim Mason's disappearance and death, then the shocking reveal of his secret life. It was the perfect one-two punch to leave us all breathless at the end of a teen slasher flick.

Of course the White Rabbit was Jim, everyone whispered. *Totally.*

It's always the one we worship the most we know the least.

He was, after all, Darrow's rock star, its heartthrob-musical-genius-Shakespeare, the boy who made spontaneous rapping, poetry, and wearing tweed caps cool (all small miracles unto themselves)—the kid everyone loved, longed for, yet simultaneously wished dead.

He had *it*. An energy force field.

He was the giant lit-up window with no curtains at night. You couldn't help stopping to look closer on your silent walk past him.

I never believed it.

There was no way Jim was the White Rabbit. Someone had set him up, I was sure. He never touched drugs or alcohol after his speedboat accident. And he wouldn't have sold it. He was a rescuer of broken-winged birds and lunchtime social outcasts. Nor did he need the money. His dad, Edgar Mason, was the inventor of the Van Gogh sneaker and the Poe hoodie, the man behind Starving Artist, a global leisurewear company he'd started in the back of his Jeep at nineteen. Jim's family was worth five billion, according to *Forbes*.

I'd spent the past year doubting my belief in Jim's innocence. I road-tested my theory obsessively, kicking the tires, trying to make the doors fall off. I wondered about all the occasions when

Jim said he couldn't meet me in the canteen during Evening Spells, how he was on a tear and had to stay sequestered in his dorm room writing. I wondered if he'd been lying to me every time he said he was at work on *Nowhere Man,* his musical about John Lennon.

My heart insisted no. He couldn't have been. He'd lied to me about other things.

Not about that.

———

"I know where to start," I announced.

The others had lapsed into thoughtful silence. Now they looked up at me, apprehensive.

"Vida Joshua."

"Kitten?" yelped Kipling in surprise.

"She knows something about Jim's death. I'm positive."

"How do you know?" asked Whitley sharply.

"Remember how Jim was acting that final week?"

Kipling arched an eyebrow. "Like I remember a hot summer with a water shortage, backed-up sewage, and zero air-conditionin'."

"He wasn't himself," I went on. "He was moody. A short fuse."

"All because of his musical," said Whitley.

"Oh, *Lord Almighty,* his musical," drawled Kipling, grimacing. "It was eatin' him alive."

"He was stressed about his musical, definitely," I said. "But there was something else going on too. Something I found out about."

They were watching me, rapt, waiting for me to go on.

"I'm pretty sure he was hooking up with Vida Joshua."

No one said a word. They just stared at me in shock.

"The day before he disappeared was the first night of Spring Vespers, remember?"

They nodded.

Spring Vespers—it was a two-night performance of skits, speeches, and original songs commemorating the end of the year and preceding finals week.

Around five, Jim texted me. He said he had a fever and chills, and was heading to the infirmary. I was shocked. After all, a medley of original songs from *Nowhere Man* was being performed that night. It was the cornerstone of Spring Vespers, the first time anyone had heard it, so for Jim to abandon his own production on the eve of its debut was very strange. Even if he was nervous about it, he'd never quit. Later that night, after eight, I was running late for Vespers, having stayed longer than I realized in the library. I veered behind the cafeteria on my way to the auditorium. It was the shortcut Jim and I sometimes took. That was when I saw him. Sitting by the loading dock. *Not* sick. At all. He was fine. Just sitting there in a black T-shirt and jeans, as if waiting for someone. Alone. I stood behind a tree and texted him.

How's the infirmary?

One hundred and two fever, he wrote back, plus a sick emoji. I *watched* him write this, completely nonchalant.

I'll come visit you, I wrote.

No. No. Don't. I'm going to sleep.

I couldn't believe it. I was about to confront him right then and there. Only that was when a car slinked up. Slow. No headlights. Taking care not to be noticed. Jim hopped off the ledge and climbed right in. Vida Joshua was driving.

"You saw her?" asked Cannon.

I nodded. "It was Mr. Joshua's beat-up red Nissan. The one he kept behind the music school with the keys in the ignition and the For Sale sign in the back window. The one the administration was always asking him to get towed."

"Poor Mr. Joshua," said Whitley. "If his head wasn't attached, he'd lose it."

"Did you ever confront Jim, child?" Kipling asked.

I nodded. "The next day. He didn't admit anything. But he was furious."

"Furious at you?" asked Martha, squinting skeptically.

I nodded.

Leave me alone, Beatrice. Stop spying on me. What are you, my father?

Jim's reaction had scared me. I'd never seen him like that before: trembling hands, tears in his eyes, anger like a sudden venom in his veins, making him scowl and spit and contort his face so he was unrecognizable. He'd been on edge for weeks, a mood I'd attributed to the pressure of getting his musical ready for Spring Vespers and recording the producer's demo Mr. Joshua had set up. *I want it to be glorious, Bee. I'm going for glory*. He had turned inside out with anxiety, self-doubt, despair. *The notes have lost their velvet,* he whined. What had once sounded like a haunting theme song had suddenly become shrill to him. His lyrics were clichéd. No amount of insistence on my part that they were good could convince him otherwise. Our relationship had become brittle, a series of botched conversations about stanzas and syncopated rhythms, finding a better rhyme for *dissipate.*

Figure eight? Exonerate? I'd try.

Just forget it, Jim would snap.

That afternoon, I'd given Jim every chance to explain what I'd seen, tell me the innocent reason he'd climbed into Very Flexible Vida's Nissan that night and lied to me about it.

But he didn't.

You want to break up with me over this? he screamed. *Good. I've had enough of your insecurities and childishness and your totally annoying inability to see the bad in people. Sometimes there's evil in the world, okay? Sometimes the sickness is right in front of you.*

His words had made me turn and sprint down the hill, hot tears blinding me. When I stopped and looked back, I saw in surprise that Jim wasn't following me as I'd expected. Instead, he was striding across the hill, a dark and consumed expression on his face, out of sight.

Like he was over me. Like we really were done.

That was the last time I ever spoke to Jim.

Two days later he was dead.

"The day after Rector Trask announced that Jim had been found dead," I went on, "it was all over the newspapers. That same day, Vida disappeared."

"What do you mean?" asked Cannon.

"She immediately left town, remember? They made the announcement."

"That's *right*," said Whitley slowly, wrinkling her nose. "At Final Assembly. 'And in further news, Miss Joshua is taking a job in stem cell research at the University of Chicago.' "

Kipling nodded, dubious. "It was like hearin' a chimpanzee got employed at the State Department."

"You thought she was fleeing the scene of the crime?" Martha asked me.

"The timing was strange," I said with a nod. "Like she was afraid of something. Anyway, I checked Facebook, and she's working as an assistant chef at Angelo's Italian Palace, living at home again. I always wished I'd had the guts to confront her. Now I do."

I took a deep breath and stood up.

"Who's coming with me?"

One by one, with uneasy expressions, they raised their hands.

CHAPTER 11

Vida Loretta Joshua was seven years older than all of us.

She was Mr. Joshua's only child. She'd graduated from Darrow and gone off to college in North Carolina, only she'd had some kind of mental breakdown—the exact nature of which remained vague—dropped out, and moved home.

When you visited the Joshuas' modest Tudor cottage on Darrow's campus, it was like visiting two ordinary people housing a pet leopard. This was because: (1) Vida Joshua was stunningly beautiful, with black hair, far-apart blue eyes, alien cheekbones, a face so symmetrical and arresting when she finally looked at you (which she only did after a prolonged delay) that it was like finding a wildcat lazily regarding you from a mountaintop as you squinted through binoculars; and (2) Mr. and Mrs. Joshua seemed to be afraid of their daughter. They addressed her in soft tones.

They tiptoed around (with no sudden movements) the spot where she could be found sunning herself on the living room couch with unwashed hair and baggy sweats, eating a bag of kale chips, watching *Real Housewives of Atlanta*. They seemed too scared to arrange her reentry to the wild (college) or get her into a rehabilitation sanctuary (therapy). So they just left her alone, bored and depressed, or whatever Vida was.

No one was really sure.

Sophomore year, Mr. Joshua twisted someone's arm to get her a job at Darrow. Vida started appearing in admissions, yawning as she shuffled unconvincingly between the copy machine and a computer; later she turned up in the Spanish department; then as assistant coach for JV field hockey, though when that didn't work out (apparently few were comfortable working alongside a big cat), they stuck her in the remote outpost of the art gallery. Most of the time she left the front desk unattended, and could be found outside in the back by the dumpsters, chatting with a random student, always a boy. Rumors swirled that her nickname at Darrow had been Very Flexible Vida, that she'd had sex with the entire wrestling team, that she'd fallen in love with a professor in college and stalked his wife, which had resulted in a restraining order that led to Vida's mysterious breakdown.

That was all I knew about her before I saw her with Jim. Once I saw them leave campus together, though, Mr. Joshua's nickname for his daughter, Kitten, seemed so fitting, because what had once been a cute little fluffball had suddenly morphed into a dangerous predator with a diet of horse carcasses and the capacity to kill without warning.

I hadn't even known she and Jim were friends. He'd never mentioned her. She had surveyed Jim from her spot on the living room couch with only marginally less indifference than she'd regarded me and everyone else. After he was found dead, though, she suddenly vanished from her job at the art gallery. Her ergonomic swivel chair, her mug of pens, the gallery printouts of price sheets and artists' statements of purpose mixed in with a welcome pack for a gym membership at the Jam, and Thai takeout menus—all sat there like nagging questions in the days following his death.

I found myself calling into question my every private moment with Jim, as if I were a miser locking myself in my room to stare down at the stacks of cash I'd stashed under my mattress, counting the money for the millionth time to make sure it was all there, checking that it wasn't counterfeit. In the intervening year, I kept tabs on Vida. I stared at her Instagram photos of camping trips in Wisconsin with some friend named Jenni who wore Bermudas; her loud move into a new apartment in Wicker Park (*Anyone know a good mover in the Chicago area????*), followed by a mute return home not three months later; her registration in a fashion design course; her interest in reflexology and a heavy-metal band called Eisenhower. I pored over these artifacts, looking for clues to her relationship with Jim. Occasionally I found them. She posted lyrics to a song Jim wrote—"Carpe"—to accompany a blurry photo she'd taken of a frog. *Once we had days when we ripped up the skies. Swore it was real, no deception, no lies.* On the one-year anniversary of his death, she posted a message on his Facebook page, which had become a living memorial. *Miss you Mason.*

In some of my darker moments, I considered sending her a series of anonymous messages, a sort of *I Know What You Did Last Year*, to see if I could smoke her out, get her to reveal what she knew, what she'd done.

I never did.

Never would I have believed Jim capable of betraying me by fooling around with Vida. Then again, we'd never had sex. We came close. At the last minute I always said no. Jim would roll onto his back, prop up his head, stare at the ceiling.

"What are you afraid of?" he'd ask with genuine curiosity.

I deferred with various versions of "I'm not ready," never having the guts to tell him the truth: that I was scared of losing the last piece of dry land I was standing on. I loved Jim, but our relationship could feel like a blackout sometimes. I'd get swept up in him, then days, weeks later suddenly look around, unnerved, wondering where I was, what time it was.

"You want to wait for our wedding night? Fine," he'd tease.

No wonder he never broke up with me, I thought later. *He wasn't missing out on anything at all.*

He had Kitten.

———

None of us had been back to Darrow, not even inside the Neverworld.

Arriving felt the way it always did, as if we were traveling back in time to a lost past of driving goggles, candlestick telephones, and people wearing tweed sprinkling their sentences with *grand* and calling good times a *gas*. Darrow had always been willfully old-fashioned, a quality the school went out of its way to proudly maintain, as if the place were not a school, but a sanctuary for some endangered bird. Classrooms had the same wooden tables as fifty years before, the chapel the same pews. Most of the teachers looked like walking daguerreotypes, with stiff necks and expressions suggesting great depressions.

I peered out the window, trying to ignore the nervousness in the pit of my stomach. Throughout the past year I'd wondered what I'd say to Vida if I ever had the chance to confront her, but now every scenario I had considered sounded pathetic and insecure. *What were you doing with Jim that night? Why did you suddenly vanish when he died? Did you love him? Did he love you?*

Ahead I could see the old white wood sign swinging in the torrential rain.

DARROW-HARKER SCHOOL. The bronze stag stood beside it. As we tore past I caught a fleeting glimpse of the antlers and eyes, FOUNDED IN 1887 flashing in the bloodred taillights before both sign and stage were swallowed by the dark.

"Don't worry, Bee," whispered Whitley, leaning her head on my shoulder. "I'll take care of everything."

"Every time you say that, child, someone loses an eye," said Kipling from the front seat.

She smiled primly. "I cannot vouch for the continued existence of anyone who messes with my best friends. They hurt Bee? They have to deal with unleashing the vengeful forces of the known universe."

129

"Well, Zeus, I'd pipe down if I were you," muttered Cannon, slowing the car.

Darrow's security gatehouse was ahead.

"What are we going to say?" asked Martha.

"Oh, the usual. We're former students. Kinda sorta dead? Stuck in a cosmic catacomb?"

"That sounds *so tedious*," whispered Whitley with a giggle, squeezing my hand.

Cannon pulled to a stop in front of the gate, unrolling the window. We watched in uneasy silence as Moses—Darrow's notorious security guard—took his time zipping his jacket, fixing his shirt collar, and opening a golf umbrella before ambling out. Grumpy, bent over like a question mark, he was whispered to have arrived on campus the same year the school was founded. He was a die-hard Christian, shoehorning God into most conversations, and a recovering alcoholic. Every Wednesday at midnight he secretly abandoned his post to attend an Alcoholics Anonymous meeting in the gym at St. Peter's, which meant there was a reliable two-hour window when you could stroll brazenly past the gatehouse, absconding from campus without getting caught, so long as you made it back before he returned.

"Evening," Moses shouted officially through the rain. "How may I help you?"

"You don't recognize us?" asked Cannon.

Moses peered closer, his bushy white eyebrows bunching together in surprise. "Well, I'll be. Cannon Beecham. Kipling St. John. Whitley. Beatrice. And little Martha. What on earth are you kids doing here on a soggy night like this?"

"We were in the neighborhood and wanted to take a quick drive around," said Cannon. "We won't be long."

Moses scowled in apparent consternation and checked his watch. When he glanced back at Cannon, he seemed uneasy.

"A quick look," he said, pointing at Cannon. "But no mischief, you understand me?"

Cannon nodded, waving as he rolled up the window, and we took off down the road.

"No mischief you'll remember tomorrow, old friend," he muttered.

——

"My goodness. This *is* a surprise."

Standing in the doorway, Mr. Joshua looked exactly the same. He was still trim, with sparkling blue eyes, rosy cheeks, and a flagpole posture, plus a penchant for sweater vests.

"To what do I owe such a treat? Come in. Out of this tempest."

He beamed with genuine warmth, causing me to feel a pang of guilt as the five of us filed inside, dripping wet.

"We're here to visit Vida," said Whitley, smiling. "Is dear Kitten at home?"

We'd already seen her car in the driveway, the red Nissan, the many lit-up windows, so we pretty much knew the answer to that question.

Mr. Joshua blinked, puzzled.

"*Vida*? Certainly. We're—uh—just having dinner. Come in. Come in. Please."

We moved after him through a quiet living room into the dining room, where we found Vida and Mrs. Joshua. Mrs. Joshua, wearing a yellow apron, was forking corn on the cob onto the three plates as Vida, seated idly at the head of the table, scrolled through her cell.

It seemed captivity had taken a toll on her, because she looked less intimidating than I remembered. She was stockier, with thinner, rattier hair. Though the five of us wordlessly assembled around her chair, she was totally oblivious, glancing up in apparent disinterest before returning to her phone. She was used to her father's students visits at all hours for guitar lessons and rehearsals.

"Peggy? Kitten? These are friends of Jim Mason's. You remember, Jim, my student? The, uh, wunderkind? One of the very best young lyricists I've ever come across." Mr. Joshua held up a finger, a soft smile. "He was going to go far. His musical about Lennon was one of the most gorgeous— A veritable tapestry of music and words . . ." He seemed to forget himself for a moment, blurting this with unabashed sadness. His face reddened. "*Well*. What brings you to our neck of the woods?"

It had never occurred to me to consider how Mr. Joshua had taken Jim's death—not until now, standing in the shabby taupe modesty of his house, the deafening rain pounding the roof, the faint smell of mothballs, acoustic guitars mounted on the walls hinting at some unplayed song. It had been Mr. Joshua, after all, who'd been Jim's biggest champion, coaching him about out-of-town tryouts and a Broadway run. It was Mr. Joshua who had taken Jim's dozens of demos, recorded on Logic Pro, and transcribed them into sheet music, Mr. Joshua who had pushed him to dream up cleverer lyrics, sharper characters, *more variety for the ear,* analyzing with him the ingenious phrasings and renegade words of Stephen Sondheim and Lin-Manuel Miranda and Tennessee Williams. It was Mr. Joshua who had arranged for a major New York producer to listen to Jim's demo of songs from *Nowhere Man.* The producer had loved what he'd heard, and a meeting, a lunch in New York, was being set up around the time Jim had died.

I found myself wondering if Mr. Joshua had been in love with Jim. Or was it something else? Had he seen himself attached to Jim's rising star—Jim, his one-way bus ticket out of town; Jim, his partner, pet student, meal ticket—all those hopes and prospects null and void now that Jim was dead?

"Vida definitely remembers Jim," said Whitley, grinning. She tilted her head, arching an eyebrow. "Kitten, dear? Now would be the optimal time to ask your parents to leave the room, unless you want them privy to all the gory details." She plopped easily into a chair at the head of the table, hitching one leg over the armrest, and helped herself to a green bean. "We want to know everything," she went on, nibbling the end. "Who started it? Who ended it? Where did the two of you sneak off to off campus? And why did you leave town the nanosecond Jim turned up dead?"

Vida only stared, her mouth open, incredulous.

"Please don't insult our intelligence denyin' it, child," drawled Kipling, waving his hand in the air. "For one? Beatrice doesn't lie. She's the kindest, most honest person you'll ever meet.

Her middle name's Good Witch a the North. And two, we don't have a lot of patience. We've been livin' this same day, known as a wake, over and over again? And it's made us all a little tense."

"A little impossible to deal with," added Cannon.

"Excuse me?" asked Mrs. Joshua. "What on earth is happening here? Paul? *Paul!*"

Mr. Joshua, standing beside her, seemed unable to move or speak, sort of like a wren hovering nervously around a park bench where a few breadcrumbs have just fallen.

"You people are nuts," said Vida in a hoarse voice. "I have no idea what you're talking about."

Smiling, Whitley grabbed a plate of food and launched it into the air like a Frisbee. It sailed across the room, chicken, corn, rice flying, crashing against the windows.

For a moment, everyone was too stunned to move. Then Mrs. Joshua dashed to the side table and grabbed a phone. She dialed 911.

"I'd like to report a home invasion."

"Tell her to hang up," Cannon told Vida, scratching his nose.

"We need the police. *Now.* There are children—teenagers—trespassing in our house—"

"Tell her to hang up if you don't like orange jumpsuits," said Whitley.

Vida glanced at her, startled.

"Or public showers," said Cannon, plopping easily into a chair.

"They're terrorizing us. My husband's former students. Please come at once."

"Hang up the phone, Mom," said Vida.

"One of my pet peeves is when girls don't support other girls," said Whitley. "When they just help themselves to someone's boyfriend like he's some free smoked gouda sample speared with a toothpick at Whole Foods. It's *so* unforgivable. And out-of-date."

"The Darrow School—"

"I'd call off your pit bull of a mom," said Cannon.

"Mom," said Vida sharply.

Mrs. Joshua didn't hear her. "Five forty-five Entrance Drive. Please hurry."

Vida leapt to her feet. She ran to her mother, shoving the woman aside as she wrenched the phone away and threw it across the room. It hit a small painting of a fox playing a violin, which immediately fell off the wall, revealing a bright rectangle of wallpaper spangled with black mold.

Everyone fell silent in total bewilderment.

Vida stood there gaping at us, wild-eyed, trying to catch her breath.

"What did you do this time?" Mr. Joshua asked her.

———

"I don't know how many times I have to say it," growled Vida. "We were *friends*. That's all. All he did was ask me for a ride. He wanted my help getting off campus. He hid under a blanket in the backseat of my car as I drove past Moses. And that was it, okay? I really don't know what the big deal is. You people are seriously insane."

"We don't believe you," said Cannon.

"That's your problem."

"Where did you take Jim?" asked Martha.

"I already *said*."

"Tell us again," said Whitley.

"I don't know. Some shopping center?"

"In Newport?"

"Yeah."

"Do you remember where it was? Or what it was called?" asked Martha.

"No."

"What *can* you tell us?" asked Cannon.

Vida shrugged. "It was some dingy section of town. Dollar stores. A pet store. The parking lot had some man in a chicken costume handing out heart balloons."

"And why did Jim want to go there?" asked Martha.

"Maybe he wanted to eat fried chicken and buy a pet iguana? I have no fucking clue."

"You must have drawn *some* conclusion," said Wit.

Vida shrugged, irritated. "I thought maybe he was trying to score some weed. There were these dime baggers loitering around the parking lot."

"What time was this?"

"Eight? Nine at night?" Vida sighed. "I offered to stay, give him a ride back to school, but he said he'd make his own way. And that was *it*, all right? I don't see what the big deal is, and I had nothing to do with his death. I mean, *please*."

For the past twenty minutes, contemptuous and huffy, Vida had been relating the same story over and over again: Jim had only asked her for a ride that night. That was all. There was nothing more to it. They had not been hooking up. They'd been accidental friends. She had not wavered in this explanation. And though I was inclined to believe her, listening to her was still like a knife through my heart, because even if it was true that there was nothing romantic about their relationship, it still meant Jim hadn't chosen to confide in me, that whatever he had been up to, whatever had upset him, he'd chosen to deal with it behind my back. And if he had lied to me about that, I couldn't help wondering what else he'd lied about.

"I find it pretty far-fetched that he'd ask you for a ride if you weren't more than friends," said Whitley.

Vida glared at her. "Like I said. We *talked*. Occasionally. He visited me at the art gallery and gave me advice sometimes. Jim was a card-carrying genius. He understood stuff. I talked to him about my issues, you know, and he gave me better advice in ten minutes than six years of Dr. Milton Yeskowitz with the goatee, the too-long thumbnails, and the bookshelf full of seventies self-help manuals called *Learning to Love Yourself*."

She said this with a scathing glance at her father, who stared back blankly. Both Mr. and Mrs. Joshua had been listening to their daughter as if she were speaking a strange dialect in which only every third word was comprehensible.

"Jim reminded me again and again that my life was alive and I had to tame it. That was why I decided to move to Chicago. I told him I had the opportunity to intern at the lab, and he said I had to go. I had to seize the day. Even if I was afraid. Jim said when there's a break in the path in front of you and you're freaked out, you take a running leap and trust that you'll reach the other side. He inspired me. And I helped him, you know. He was really stressed about his musical. He wanted it to be great. He wanted it to be up there with *Oklahoma!* and *Rent*. He aspired to greatness. More than anything, he wanted to go down in history. And he was going to. He showed me his notebook, and he'd written the most *insane* rhymes. He was a genius." She shook her head. "It's horrible what happened to him. But that's life, right? All the amazing people die too soon."

"When was the last time you saw him?" I asked.

"Don't you people *listen*? I *told* you. When I dropped him off at that mall."

"You didn't talk to him the night he died? He didn't tell you to meet him at Vulcan Quarry?"

She scowled. "What are you *talking* about? I haven't been out to that quarry in forever." She sniffed, shaking her head. "Soon as I heard what had happened, though, that he was not only dead but had been a major drug dealer or whatever? I went straight to the police and told them they were completely insane." She rolled her eyes. "Whatever drugs they found in his dorm? They definitely weren't Jim's."

"How do you know?" I asked.

"He told me who they belonged to."

"Excuse me?" asked Martha sharply, with a surprised glance at me. "What?"

"Oh, yeah." Vida nodded. "A couple of weeks before he died. It was all he could talk about. How he'd found out one of his best friends had been selling serious drugs to students for years."

"Did he say who it was?" asked Kipling.

"He didn't have to. As he was telling me, the friend called. 'Speak of the devil,' he said. I saw the name right there on his phone." Vida wrinkled her nose. "It was kind of weird. It was just one word."

"What was the word?" asked Cannon.

"Shrieks."

Instantly, a chorus of voices began to scream in my head: *No. No. Impossible.*

No one moved.

Whitley was gazing at the carpet, a blank look on her face.

"I gave the name to the police," Vida went on. "Told them everything. I said this person had something to do with Jim's murder. I was sure. Knowing their secret was about to come out? They had to get rid of him. Shut him up, you know?" She widened her eyes. "But the police didn't care. Or they'd eaten too many Krispy Kremes to peel their asses off their swivel chairs and *do* something, because I never heard anything about it. I wasn't surprised. No one does anything anymore. The only one who did, who went above and beyond for everyone, was Jim. And now he's gone."

She fell silent. There was a moment of uneasy stillness.

Then Whitley leapt to her feet and ran out of the house.

CHAPTER 12

We took off after her.

At the front door, as Cannon and the others barged into a downpour, I paused, taking a final glance back at the Joshuas, who were regarding each other sullenly, like three strangers held in a jail cell before charges were filed. Then I turned and sprinted out.

Whitley was already disappearing down Entrance Drive.

"Whitley!" shouted Kip.

"Come on!" yelled Cannon. "Where are you going?"

She ignored them, veering off the road and vanishing over the hill. When I caught up, they were far below, Whitley a dark figure flying past the tennis courts and soccer fields, Martha, Cannon, and Kip fanning out behind her.

"Hold on!" screamed Martha.

"Let's talk about this!"

"Whitley Lansing! Stop!"

I raced after them as fast as I could, faint police sirens erupting somewhere behind me. *Whitley? The White Rabbit?* How was it possible?

The rain was torrential now. Like ammunition blasting from the sky, it riddled my head and arms. It was hard to see where I was going. Tree branches cracked and thrashed overhead, thunder rumbling. I slipped and tripped my way to the bottom of the hill, where there was a swamp of thick, tarlike mud. My sneakers sank inches into the ground. I could see Wit and the others farther ahead, rounding the front of the girls' dormitories: Slate Hall, Stonington Manor, the Gothic arches hulking and dark, misshapen shadows stretching long and fingerlike under the yellowed lamps. I veered through the garden behind Morley House and nearly ran over Martha. Apparently she'd slipped and fallen facedown in the mud.

"Are you okay?" I shouted.

"Go," she gasped, waving me on.

I kept running. As I swerved around the front of the aquatic center, a hulking glass-and-slate building, I saw that one of the glass doors had been smashed with a brick. I opened the door and scrambled inside, disembodied shouts and footsteps echoing through the darkness in front of me. I hurried through the dark lobby, past the many display cases of trophies and first-place ribbons, black-and-white photographs of the swim team. I sprinted down the checkered corridor, my muddy sneakers slipping and sliding on the linoleum, and thrust open the double doors to the Olympic-sized pool.

Kipling and Cannon were inside. Whitley had dived into the water, and they were tracking her dark figure along the edge as she glided into the deep end.

After a minute, she surfaced, panting.

"What are you doing?" said Cannon. "We just want to talk to you."

"You can't outrun us, child," said Kipling.

Glaring at them, she only sank back underwater.

"She's going for the door again," said Cannon, running toward me. Sure enough, Whitley leapt up the ladder, shoving me aside so hard I tripped against a chair as she heaved the doors open, only to come face to face with Martha, who was covered head to toe in mud. Startled, Wit tried pushing past, but Martha was gripping one of the swimming trophies from the cases. She wheeled back and hit Whitley in the side of the head with it. Yowling in pain, Whitley fell to the ground.

"Behold the White Rabbit," said Martha, panting.

She slammed the doors and wedged the trophy between the handles to lock them.

"So it was you!" shouted Cannon, staring down at Whitley. "All along. How could you never say anything? How could you deceive me, day after day after— Unbelievable."

"I didn't mean to do it more than a few times," she muttered. She rolled upright, rubbing the side of her head. "My number started getting passed around, and the myth of the White Rabbit was born. It was impossible to stop."

"How could you?" I whispered in a low voice.

Whitley glared at me. "Yes, Bee, we all know that you'd never do something like that in a million years. That you're the good one. With a moral compass perfectly set toward sainthood. The rest of us aren't so lucky." She sniffed, staring gloomily at the ground.

We said nothing, reflections of the blued water of the pool trembling across our faces.

I couldn't believe how she'd lied. For years. I'd never suspected her. Neither had Cannon, given the enraged look on his face.

Yet it made a sort of twisted sense, considering that Whitley's mother, the Linda, ruled a pharmaceutical empire. It wasn't rare to hear Whitley talk about her mother's business acumen with awe—how she, armed with her mink coat, high school dropout's education, and Missouri-farm-girl common sense, could command New York City boardrooms and shareholder meetings, put macho bankers in their place with one of her perfectly timed ten-cent-gumball put-downs. *If stupid could fly, you'd be an Airbus A Three-Fifty.* The truth was—and it used to make me cry thinking about it, though I was always careful never to say anything to Wit—the Linda didn't love her daughter, not the way Whitley needed. Ever since Wit was a baby, she'd been shuffled between nannies and nurses and au pairs, summer camps and boarding schools and educational groups, like some lost suitcase. I somehow understood. Whitley had become the White Rabbit to prove to herself, or maybe even to her mother, that she was worthy.

I hadn't forgotten Vida's comment that unmasking the White Rabbit had possibly played a role in Jim's death. *I said this person had something to do with Jim's murder. Knowing their secret was about to come out? They had to get rid of him.* The comment nagged at me, glimmering with the unmistakable sheen of truth, though I didn't want to admit it.

"How did Jim find out about you?" I asked her.

Wit glanced up at me, sullen. "He caught me."

"When?"

"A week before finals. I always snuck out at three in the morning to do a drop. He was coming back from Vulcan Quarry and saw me entering the observatory. He followed me into one of the domes, watched what I was doing. And he went nuts on me. Made it into a bigger deal than it was. I mean, we were about to graduate. The White Rabbit was done. Jim started screaming about civic responsibility. Doing the right thing. He insisted that I confess to the administration."

"So you decided to frame him," said Martha. "You put your drugs in his guitar so he'd take the fall for you."

"No." Whitley adamantly shook her head. "That was an accident. I always kept my supply buried behind the old maintenance shed at the edge of Drury Field. You know that place everyone says is haunted? Well, it's not. It's just cruddy, with a lot of old athletic signs and banners. One day, I saw this general contractor inspecting it. I found out they were going to demolish the thing and build a greenhouse. That night at supper I excused myself and dug up my stash. I meant to keep it in my room, only they were painting the hallways that night. The place was crawling with maintenance. I was desperate. This huge stash in my bag? If I was stopped . . ." She shuddered. "I ducked next door into Packer, to Jim's room. I knew he kept his key under the carpet.

I shoved the stash in his guitar. I meant to go back and move it the next day. *Obviously*. But that was when they announced Jim was missing. By the time I had a chance to go back, the cops had already searched his room and found everything."

Martha stared at her. "Jim was reported missing Thursday morning. The police found him dead late Friday night. So when exactly did you hide the drugs in his guitar?"

Whitley glanced up, uneasy. "Maybe Wednesday?"

"Stop lying," said Martha.

"I'm not."

"Your story would have worked, if not for one little problem."

"What?"

"I had Jim's guitar."

We stared at her.

"He lent it to me so I could practice my song for Spring Vespers. I had it in my room for two weeks. They made the announcement Jim was missing Thursday morning. Late Thursday night, I returned the guitar to his room. That means only one thing. You knew Jim was missing when you put the drugs in his guitar." Martha looked at Wit, her face implacable. "You saw his disappearance as an opportunity to get out of the mess you'd made. You set him up."

Whitley glared at her.

"The night he died?" I asked, my voice breaking. "Were you with him at the quarry?"

"No." Whitley shook her head. "I swear. I swear, Bee. I loved him as much as anybody." As she said this, she began to cry. "Okay, fine. I set him up. I put the stash in his room. I was scared.

145

I thought he'd already gone to the administration and told them I was the White Rabbit. I did it to save myself. It was awful. But I had nothing to do with his death, I swear to God." She stared at me, her eyes red. "You have to believe me."

Abruptly, there was loud pounding on the door.

"Cannon Beecham, you in there?"

It was Moses.

"Please," Wit whimpered. "I didn't know anything about Jim's death. I *still* don't, I swear on—"

"Open up now. I got police with me."

"This is Warwick Police! You're trespassing on private grounds."

The door rattled but didn't budge.

"Let's get out of here," said Martha.

As the pounding continued, we sprinted to the opposite side of the pool, Whitley struggling to her feet and heading after us. There were bleachers. Girls' and boys' locker rooms.

No way out.

I was about to suggest we surrender and spend the rest of the wake at the police station, when Cannon grabbed the lifeguard chair and, spinning, launched it at the wall of windows. The glass only cracked.

"Open this door!"

Cannon picked up the chair again, hitting the wall a second time. I could see officers swarming outside. They were wielding flood flashlights. Another smash of the chair. Suddenly the glass shattered all at once. The five of us took off running, whooping and shouting at the top of our lungs, out into the night, exploding past the officers, their flashlights blinding us.

"Police! We command you to freeze!"

"Warriors!" whooped Kipling.

"Go to hell and back again!"

Somewhere behind me, Kip was howling. Whitley too. Cannon was singing. I ran blindly, weird, strung-out laughter hiccupping out of me as I willed the dark to swallow me. I could see one of the officers drawing his gun. I half expected him to shoot me out of sheer terror, thinking this was the beginning of some zombie apocalypse. I headed for the darkest part of the field, forcing my legs to go faster and faster, lungs tightening in pain, rain pummeling me. When I glanced back, I could see flashing red and blue police lights, figures swarming the aquatic center.

No one had followed me. I was alone.

I slowed to a jog, then a walk, rain needling my face. I realized I'd reached the edge of the woods. I crossed onto a hiking trail and headed down it. Soon my mind quieted and I was aware only of my footsteps and the mud. It was everywhere, gelatinous and black as tar.

Jim.

It was so dark, I could almost feel him here, strolling beside me.

I wanted so badly to scream at him, to demand the truth. *Why so many secrets?* Jim was the painting I'd always thought was a one-of-a-kind masterpiece. As it turned out, there were countless versions of the same work floating around, smaller watercolors and rudimentary pencil sketches, cheap poster reprints selling for ninety-nine cents in an airport gift shop. True, none of them had the beauty and detail of my painting, but they still depicted the same scene and thus rendered it a little less special. Vida had her version. Mr. Joshua his. Whitley hers. Even Martha—there had been something disconcerting about the way she'd announced it: *I had Jim's guitar.* Her feelings for Jim seemed to rise to the surface strong and strange, barely controlled, before sinking back into the depths.

The rain fell harder, thunder growling.

I walked on. Now and then, with a wave of revulsion, I swore I caught a glimpse of the Keeper, dressed in his gardener's slicker, hiking between the trees, but every time I stopped, my heart pounding, staring into the woods to be sure, there was no one.

Soon I could feel the leaden pull of the Neverworld taking hold, the now-familiar tingling grip starting at my feet, crawling up my shins.

The path had taken me to a clearing where there was strong wind and giant fallen trees all over the ground. Squinting, I saw a hulking oak teetering a few yards in front of me. Suddenly it fell with a deafening crack, the entire forest echoing with the sound.

I froze in alarm.

Another crack rang out right beside me. Turning, I realized it was another oak coming loose. I tried to move out of the way, only to realize my feet were stuck in the cementlike mud. I managed to wrench them free, blindly throwing myself forward as the tree thundered to the ground, missing me by inches, branches shaking and snapping, whipping my head.

What was happening?

I lifted my head and crawled away, tried to take another step but fell facedown in the mud.

The Neverworld blackout was descending. The end of the eleven point two hours had come. I managed to roll onto my back, gasping as I blinked up at the sky, the rain. It felt like being buried alive under the weight of a million poured coins, my body sinking deeper and deeper into mud. Soon I would feel my limbs breaking apart and dissolving.

Another tree began to tear loose a few feet away.

My final thought was panic: panic that I was going to die here with no solution to the mystery. The confessions of Vida Joshua and Whitley had solved nothing. Would I ever know what really had happened to Jim? How could I win the vote and get back to life?

At that moment, I realized a dark figure was standing over me with a cruel expression.

The Keeper.

"In the dark there grows a tree. A castle tower shelters thee. When will I stop, when will I see? There is no poison but for me."

I screamed as the oak tree fell on top of me and everything went black.

CHAPTER 13

I woke up, gasping, in the backseat of the Jaguar, Martha and Kip beside me.

My heart was still pounding from the massive tree collapsing on me, the swamplike mud, the sudden appearance of the Keeper, the insidious rhyme he'd recited.

I felt nauseous, but there was no time to think. Martha and Kipling were scrambling out of the car, running toward the house. I took off after them. Like me, they seemed worried that Whitley wouldn't be there anymore; that, humiliated by the revelation that she had long been the White Rabbit, maybe even scared that we'd hold her accountable for Jim's death, she'd fled.

Instead, we found her sitting with Cannon in the kitchen. I could see from their mutually subdued demeanors that they'd been having an intense conversation, perhaps even arguing.

Whitley looked red-faced and sullen. There was a hint of relief on her face.

"Whitley has something to tell you," announced Cannon.

She glanced up with a feeble smile. "I'm sorry. I'm sorry for what I did to Jim. To the other students. For lying to all of you. It was disgusting. And stupid. It could have ruined my life. It almost did. But I swear with every fiber of my being I had nothing to do with Jim's death. I understand you might not believe me now. But we will find out what happened to him that night, and you'll know I'm innocent."

Kipling and Martha, studying her, seemed to accept this. They nodded. I nodded too.

And yet, considering she'd lied to us for so long, I had to remind myself Wit was still capable of lying. Though I couldn't imagine her plotting to harm Jim, I also couldn't ignore what she was capable of in a rage, or the fact that she now had a motive. If Whitley had believed that Jim was going to expose her secret— that the administration and, most seriously of all, the Linda, were going to find out the terrible thing she'd been doing—it wasn't outrageous to think she would have done anything to prevent that from happening.

Abruptly, I was aware of everyone staring at me.

"What?" I blurted.

"We were wondering what you thought of Vida's confession," said Martha.

I shrugged. "I think I believe her."

"Me too," said Kipling with a wry smile. "A girl like Vida can't lie very well. How many times did she call Jim a genius? I'm surprised she didn't suggest he'd risen from the dead, like Jesus." He looked at me. "You know I loved Jim to pieces. But the way he collected admirers could get a little old. His ego, bless his soul, could be an insatiable baby."

"He didn't do it on purpose," I said. "People were drawn to him."

" 'Didn't do it on purpose,' " said Kipling. "*Sure.* That's like me holdin' up an iron rod in a football field during a storm and sayin' it's not my fault I got struck by lightning."

"She was especially impressed by Jim's lyrics for his musical," said Martha.

"Right. The sudden blast of brilliance. That *was* somethin'. 'Member how he had nothin' written for weeks 'cept a few bad rhymes straight out of MC Hammer? He kept complainin' that he was finished, dried up—torturin' us all, pretty much. Then, out of the blue, a masterpiece." Kipling waved his hand in the air, a drowsy gesture. "Strands of lyrics like pearls. One after the other. All about the immense pain of being young and alive."

"Those lyrics were amazing," said Whitley.

"The performance at Spring Vespers was a hit," said Cannon thoughtfully, interlacing his fingers. "The New York producer Mr. Joshua arranged loved the demo. Jim's destiny was teed up, on the brink, like he always wanted. So what happened?"

"Life," said Kipling dryly.

"Or," said Martha, "it had something to do with that ride from Vida Joshua." She gnawed a thumbnail. "I'm wondering if we can track down that shopping center."

"All Vida gave us to go on was a pet store and a fast-food restaurant," said Wit.

"When was the last time you talked to Jim?" Martha asked me suddenly, squinting.

"Tuesday afternoon." I cleared my throat. "The second night of Vespers. I confronted him about lying to me about the infirmary."

"So you didn't speak to Jim at all the next day? The day he died?"

I shook my head.

No one said anything, all of them doubtlessly thinking how tragic it must have been for me, for that argument about Vida Joshua to be our last conversation.

The truth was, Wednesday I'd exiled myself to Marksman Library, hiding out in the fourth-floor attic stacks in the History of South America section, which was seldom visited by students. It reeked of mildew and served as a shadowy breeding ground for a range of freakishly large moths. All day I sat hunched over my European history and English literature textbooks in front of the lone window with the dirty glass, Beats headphones blasting the soundtrack to *Suicide Squad* in my ears, forcing myself to focus on the French Revolution and World War II and *For Whom the Bell Tolls*. I kept my cell phone off all day because I didn't want to deal with Jim. The only time I exposed myself to the rest of campus was during my four-minute walk between the library and my room in Creston Hall around eleven o'clock.

I waited until I'd put on my pajamas and climbed into bed

at midnight before turning on my cell, whereupon I was hit by the torrent of texts. A few were from Kipling, Cannon, and Wit. Twenty-seven others were from Jim. They'd started at eight that morning, messages ranging from *?* to *come on* to *why are u bein like this* to desperate voice mails, his mood ranging from teasing to despair to anger, all of which sounded crazy and heartbreaking the more I replayed them.

Call me.

Call me Bumblebee.

We need to talk.

If you have any love left in your heart, call me.

Why are you doing this?

I need you. You know how I need you to survive.

I hate you. I hate you so much. Because I love you.

Don't do this.

I'm going to the quarry. Meet me.

That was the last text I ever got from him. Received at 11:29 p.m.

I deleted it. I deleted all of them.

When they found Jim dead, two days later, I expected the police to ask me about his texts. I'd tell them I'd remained in my room all night.

But they never did ask. No one ever even questioned me.

I was tempted to tell them that I knew Jim was going to Vulcan Quarry. But what if they didn't believe I'd stayed in my dorm all night?

I'd be damned to the Neverworld forever. I'd have no chance—none—of ever making it out of here alive.

"What if we went to the police now?" whispered Cannon.

"What?" asked Whitley.

"What if we went to speak to the Warwick police about Jim? We could get our hands on his case file. They have to have pulled his cell phone records. We get our hands on those reports. We'll know a lot about his final days—where he went and who he was with."

"The police never came up with anything substantial to make them think Jim's death was anything but suicide," said Martha.

"Unless the school forced them to cover up what they found," said Whitley.

"Or his family," added Kipling. "If Edgar Mason thought somethin' damnin' was about to come out about his beloved dead son? The apple of his eye? He'd do anythin' to stop it from gettin' out. Remember the safe house?"

We said nothing, all of us thinking back.

Christmas break, senior year, Jim invited us to his family

home in Water Mill, and we were shocked by the extreme security measures his family had adopted as totally routine.

Edgar Mason had always been paranoid. Hoover, Jim called his dad, a not-exactly-joking reference to J. Edgar Hoover, the fanatical wiretapping founder of the FBI. For years, Edgar Mason had employed a private security firm called Torchlight to safeguard his family, which meant for the entirely of Jim's life, two armed ex–Navy SEALs silently tailed him and every other member of his family when they left the house.

The Christmas visit revealed a new level of Edgar's obsession. Every inch of the Masons' many houses around the world was being recorded in HD, the feeds playing in a basement control room called the Eye. There was a cybersecurity team on staff in Washington, D.C., who monitored the family's servers twenty-four hours a day.

Then there was the safe house.

"For home invasions, terrorist attacks, and Zero Days," Jim said, pointing out the black bunker peering out, crocodile-like, over the hill on the edge of the property. "It has power generators, independent water supplies, a secure phone line that can call the director of Homeland Security in three seconds. When the end of the world happens, let's meet here."

The smile fell from his face, the lonely implications of such a structure hardly lost on him. He seemed reluctant to say more. After all, his dad's obsession with safety had everything to do with him. Edgar Mason had always been careful, but it was apparently Jim's boating accident the summer before senior year that had triggered this new level of mania.

"I say we go over there," said Cannon. "Ask around. See what the police know."

"Or are trying to forget," said Whitley.

"Bee?" prompted Martha.

Everyone turned, waiting for me to weigh in.

I stared back.

Taking a look inside Jim's police file could mean his final texts to me would come to light. I'd have a lot to explain. But what else was in that file?

The decision was really no decision at all.

CHAPTER 14

"Can I help you?" asked the police officer. POLK read his name tag.

"We'd like to speak to Detective Calhoun," Whitley said sweetly.

Calhoun had been the lead investigator on Jim's case. He'd given the few public statements and briefings. We had decided it was easy enough to start with him, with his thick gray beard and rodent eyes, his wan blinks at the news cameras as a gaudy rash of embarrassment seeped across his neck. One sensed he wanted nothing more than to get away from the glare of such a high-profile case and go back to working petty crimes like public bench vandalism.

"What do you want with Calhoun?" demanded another officer, now approaching. His name tag read MCANDRESS.

"We wanted to ask him about a case he worked on," said Martha.

"Which one?"

"The death of Jim Mason," I said.

"That case is closed," said a third officer.

After ten more minutes of hostile questioning—they seemed wary of outsiders—we made it to Calhoun's office, finding the man in question marooned behind a desk piled high with papers, like a giant bullfrog hiding in a bog.

I wasn't sure what I expected—maybe that movie scene where the grizzled old detective, asked about the cold case still haunting him after All These Years, begins to talk and talk.

Instead, Detective Calhoun was a concrete wall.

"Mason case was solved. Suicide," he belched.

"What made you rule suicide?" Martha asked, frowning. "Usually with suicides there's a ritual or preparation before the act. A note left behind. Glasses removed, as well as shoes and socks. Was there any sign of that with Jim?"

Calhoun flashed a grin that was really more of a sneer.

"That case is closed."

———

That case is closed.

The Warwick police station, located just off the highway, was a quaint banana-yellow bungalow with white shutters and a sign on the bulletin board that read LIFE IS BETTER WITH COFFEE.

The place seemed ill-suited for solving crimes, better for selling homemade muffins.

Little did we know how terrifying it would be—that our time with the Warwick police would be pandemonium.

There was no other way to put it.

We tried different tactics: warm, curt, nervous, sexy (Wit, wearing a low-cut red dress, perched on a desk). We tried surprising them. We tried a brazen arrival at Calhoun's private residence after his wife went to bed and Calhoun stayed up late drinking Harpoon IPA, eating gummy worms, and watching *Better Call Saul*. No matter what we said, and where, how, or what time we said it, Calhoun refused to tell us anything about Jim's case.

"Can't help you."

"You Nancy Drews get out of here."

"How dare you accost me at my home!"

"You kids get out of here, or I'll make sure every one of you spends the rest of your life flipping byproduct burgers at the local Mickey D's, because a fryolator and an automatic mixer to make a few watery milk shakes are all you'll be fit for after I get through with you. UNDERSTAND ME?"

We decided to give up on Calhoun and bribe the office manager, Frederica.

We waited for her to leave the station in workout clothes, watched her getting drenched in the downpour as her umbrella went inside out. As she fumbled for the keys to her Kia, Cannon ran to her, armed with a golf umbrella and a grin.

We watched from the Mercedes as he made his pitch: ten

thousand dollars cash to go back inside and steal the Jim Mason file. Frederica blushed, nodded, and power-walked back inside.

Cannon turned, grinning, giving us the thumbs-up. Then Frederica emerged with the entire Warwick police force in tow, eight officers hightailing it for Cannon.

"Get on your knees! Police!"

With a yelp, Whitley backed the car out, tearing through the lot to pick up Cannon, who, sprinting for his life, hurled himself into the backseat. We barreled through the grass, over a curb, and through a red light into a twelve-lane intersection, tires squealing, and nearly collided with a cement truck.

"Move!" Cannon screamed. *"Move!"*

———

We spent the next few wakes at Roscoe gun range learning how to shoot as we formulated our new plan. We would raid the Warwick police. We paid the owner of Last Resort Twenty-Four-Hour Pawn Shop fifty dollars for the name of a guy who sold guns without a license out of the back of his RV, called Big Bobby. Out of Big Bobby, we bought three guns: two Ruger LC9 strikers, and a Heckler & Koch HK45.

Our siege would take place at eleven-fifteen, when we believed all officers, apart from Polk and McAndress, had gone home for the night. We'd take them by surprise and lock them in the supply closet. Then we'd have the station to ourselves and we could find Jim's file.

The first time we attempted it, Officer McAndress—displaying moves apparently learned from a fruitful career moonlighting in mixed martial arts—struck Kip with an uppercut to the face, elbowed Wit in the ribs, then, spinning, back-kicked Cannon's stomach, sending him gasping to the floor. Meanwhile, Officer Polk had me pinned to the ground, his left foot gouging my back as he zip-tied Martha to a desk chair.

"The Warwick police aren't *actually* police," said Kipling with unabashed wonder the next wake. "They're the spawn of Satan."

He wasn't kidding.

How many times at midnight, at one, two, three o'clock in the morning, did the five of us storm that station? Was it a hundred times? Was it ten thousand?

How many different entry SWAT formations did we attempt, after finding on the Internet the *Ground Reconnaissance Operations Handbook,* a training manual for marines?

Single file, double file, double file advancement with variation, through front doors, back doors, barred windows, fire escapes, drainpipes, adjacent-building rooftops. We downloaded something called *The Criminal's Guide to Revelry* off the Deepnet, a hand-typed, poorly photocopied manual written by Anonymous Doe that detailed strategies for nullifying people who were aggressive, hysterical, or empowered by Superman fantasies, during any raid, heist, or robbery. How many terrifying masks did we try (clown, pig, *Clockwork Orange* droogs)? How many bullets did we shoot into the ceiling? How many threats and warnings did we scream?

It should have been easy to get our hands on one case file.

As the wakes went on, we transformed from disorganized teenagers acting out a makeshift version of *Mission: Impossible* into a real five-person platoon. We were able to advance without noise, reading each other's thoughts and movements with nothing but a look.

Wake after wake, we were thwarted.

This was due not to Officers Polk and McAndress, but to their wild card, Officer Victoria Channing, assigned to Traffic Safety. She was always in the women's bathroom, and she advanced on us out of nowhere, displaying an eagerness to kill that was psychotic.

"Take that, you little shitheads!" she screamed.

She was terrifying, even if we were immortal.

Though Cannon and Whitley had learned to nullify Polk and McAndress, Channing eluded them every time. She was able to slip like vapor through the back stairwell, the front stairwell, a panel in the ceiling, firing her Glock without warning into Cannon's chest.

Or Kip's stomach.

Or Whitley's forehead.

The time she shot Martha in the temple—as if blithely turning the knob on a gumball machine—I froze, stunned, staring down at her and the rest of my friends lying on the police station carpet, blood gurgling out of their foreheads and necks like water trickling from a hose.

"Hands up or you'll be joining them in hell!" screeched Officer Channing, aiming at me.

163

"Death feels like floating in a warm bath," said Martha, the next wake.

I was always the only one left alive. This was because I wasn't a natural warrior. I tended to freeze when I needed to act. As a result, Cannon had decided my job was to locate Jim's case file.

Find Jim's file. It was all I had to do.

The closed homicide cases were kept in the basement. It was an unnerving, neglected fish tank of a room: humming green fluorescent light, smells of mildew, pipes yowling with steam. Row after row of metal shelves extended, dreamlike, in every direction, floor to ceiling, packed with cardboard boxes. Each box was scribbled with a victim's name.

Appleton, Janice
Avery, Jennifer
Azella, Robert P.

At every break-in, no matter the hell being unleashed upstairs, I headed straight to the back stairwell and raced to the basement. I'd fling open the wooden doors marked STORAGE and sprint into the labyrinth of shelves, madly looking for the *M*s, my footsteps squeaking on the orange linoleum. Every time, Channing caught me and I spent the rest of the wake sitting in a jail cell hearing her tell the other officers a phony story about having to kill everyone else in self-defense.

And yet, each wake, while my friends were dealing with the mayhem upstairs, I was dealing with my own torment in that droning green basement, a trial that had nothing to do with Officer Channing.

It began when I accidentally kicked a box off a bottom shelf.

Hendrews, Holly

The box tipped over, sending a plastic bag marked *Evidence* spinning across the floor. Inside, there was a blood-encrusted Christmas scarf decorated with snowmen and reindeer, but what struck me—I stopped dead, blinking in alarm—was that the bag was spangled with black mildew.

The box was also leaking.

I kicked it closer, peering inside. An oil-like liquid had pooled in the corners, as if one of the evidence bags had leaked. Glancing up, I saw, stunned, that it wasn't just this box. There were others. At least four or five boxes had that same black liquid seeping through the bottom.

Then there were the shelves.

They were hulking and metal. Yet sometimes as I raced past them, madly searching for MASON, JIM, the slightest brush of my shoulder would send the giant shelf toppling over as if it were nothing but cardboard. It would land with a deafening clang, sending the one beside it over, the one beside that too, until all the shelves in the basement were falling around me like massive dominos, hundreds of boxes thundering to the ground. All I could do was scramble out of the way, press my back against the nearest wall, pray I didn't get hit until it was over.

Afterward I'd try to sift through the rubble for Jim's box before Officer Channing caught me red-handed, as she always did.

I never mentioned to the others what was happening. I was too scared.

"How's it going in the basement?" Cannon asked me. "Are you close to finding Jim's file? I heard a lot of banging downstairs this last time."

"There's a lot to sift through," I said. "I'm close."

The key, I'd found, was to sprint through the shelves as fast as I could, allowing them to fall after me as I kept running and running toward the row of *M*s at the very back of the basement. I had just perfected the optimal path through the maze when, once, barreling too fast, I missed the correct row and was forced to backtrack. I was careful not to graze the shelf as I made the turn and slowed to a walk, panting. Usually there was the sound of havoc upstairs, banging and screaming. This time it was quiet.

Too quiet.

Machinsky, Tina D.
Mahmoodi, Wafaa
Malvo, Jed

I spotted Jim's box on the top shelf at the very end. In a rush of disbelief, I sprinted to it, reached on my tiptoes, tried to jostle it down without sending the entire shelf clattering over.

"Gotcha, you little shit," a woman hissed. "Put your hands up and turn real slow."

Channing had stepped out from behind the shelves and was striding toward me, Glock aimed right at my head.

"Don't shoot. Please."

Her face was flushed. Her lips twitched. She pulled the trigger.

She never had before.

A giant match lit the wick of my brain. I hit the ground, rolling onto my back, accidentally throwing out my arms, which hit the shelf, sending it flying backward.

"What the . . . ?" Channing screamed in shock.

As the shelves fell, I blinked up at the fluorescent lights, green filaments flickering in mysterious Morse code. There was so much pain it spilled everywhere, then drifted away.

Dying was not as cataclysmic as I'd thought it'd be. Because even though I was in the Neverworld, my body and mind still reacted as if it were the real thing.

There was no white light. There was no tunnel.

Instead, as the shelves tumbled around me, there was a warm feeling of awe, as if, with the tearing away of my life from its attachment to earth, fragile as the connection of a leaf to a twig, everything permanent, factual, real—everything I swore was true— became the opposite of what I'd always thought.

My last feeling wasn't regret or pain. It was joy.

That was the most terrifying thing of all.

I get to see Jim now. That was all I was thinking before my life went out.

If I'm dead, I'll get to see Jim.

——

"Really don't feel like getting shot in the head today," sang Kipling merrily as we filed into Wincroft at the start of the next wake. "How 'bout we take a page from Momma Greer's Guide to the Good Life?"

"What's that?" asked Cannon.

"Can't beat your mortal enemy to a pulp?" He shrugged. "Throw him a party."

That was how we came to arrive at the Warwick police station armed not with our usual guns, but with identical Barry the Clown costumes rented from Gobbledygook Halloween World.

"May I help you?" asked Frederica at the front desk.

"We're from Big Apple Balloon-a-Gram," I said, smiling. "Where would you like us to set up for the surprise party?"

"What surprise party?"

"Detective Art Calhoun's surprise seventieth."

Frederica was astonished. So were Officers Polk, McAndress, Cunningham, Leech, Ives, and Mapleton, as well as Art Calhoun himself, who emerged from his office with a distrustful scowl. But we had moved fast. The wireless speaker was already playing "Margaritaville." Wit had already unveiled three dozen cupcakes, baskets of gummy worms, and party favors of gun Christmas tree ornaments. Cannon and Kip were standing on folding chairs, tap-ing up the tinsel Happy Birthday sign. Martha tossed bottles of Harpoon IPA into a cooler.

"Hold up. Just wait one . . ." Calhoun fell silent, eyeing the beer.

"What's happening here?" demanded Officer Polk.

I made an elaborate show of examining the phony invoice, which was really the receipt for our costume rentals.

"Elizabeth Calhoun hired us," I said with a frown.

"Lizzy did this?" whispered Calhoun, wide-eyed.

Liz Calhoun was his estranged daughter who lived in San Diego. She hadn't spoken to her father in three years, which meant there was little chance she'd take his call now, when he phoned to thank her for the unexpected party, even though his real seventieth birthday was over three weeks away.

That meant I had time to find Jim's file.

"Nothing better than cupcakes," said Officer Channing, grinning as she helped herself.

"And now, friends, let's start the entertainment!" shouted Kipling with a bow so low his red clown nose fell off and rolled under a desk. "If you could all gather round and join hands? Don't be shy."

That was my cue.

I darted into the back stairwell. I raced down the steps to the basement, heaved open the wood doors, and sprinted into the shadowed rows of boxes.

I raced along the back wall, slipping past filing cabinets and a copy machine, and veered into the Gs, the Js, the Ls, zigzagging in and out, careful not to graze the shelves, my oversized clown shoes making loud quacking noises, my balloon pants making me trip.

Eighth row. Far left. At the very top. MASON, JIM LIVINGSTON.

It was there. My heart pounding, I had to jump up three times to shove it off the shelf without sending the entire thing toppling over. I set it carefully on the ground.

"You found it?"

I turned, startled, to see Martha hurrying toward me.

She'd never appeared down here before. The knowing, even anxious look on her face seemed to suggest she had come because she didn't trust me, because she didn't want me left alone with the box. Or was it that she'd hoped I would never actually find it?

I ripped off the tape and pulled open the lid.

I stared inside for an entire minute, unable to speak.

No. No. No. Impossible.

"Are you kidding me?" whispered Martha in apparent shock, looking over my shoulder. "After *all that*? Getting shot dead a million times?"

Shaking her head, a hand on her hip, she took down another box.

"Maybe Jim's file got put somewhere else," she muttered.

I couldn't stop staring in, unable to breathe.

The box was empty.

There wasn't a single paper left except a coupon: *$5 off 1 bin of Honey Love Fried Chicken. Soul Mate Special!*

Upstairs, more singing and clapping had broken out. "For he's a jolly good fellow . . ."

Martha was madly thrusting more boxes to the floor, yanking off the lids. Every one was crammed full of papers, plastic evidence bags, black ink.

That ink was back, seeping through the corners again.

"How can anyone find anything in here? It's a mess. There's some kind of leak."

Martha was examining the ink between her fingers, wrinkling her nose, though when she caught my eye, the knowing expression on her face chilled me.

We spent another ten minutes going through boxes, Martha saying, "It has to be here somewhere."

The only empty box we came across was Jim's.

Martha knew something. That was clear. What it was, I had no idea.

CHAPTER 15

"Edgar Mason and Torchlight Security are behind it," said Cannon when we were back at Wincroft, sprawled across the couches in the library. "Who else could make an entire case file just *vanish*?"

"They had everything destroyed," said Kipling in agreement. "Which was why Calhoun and the other cops were always so touchy when we asked about the case. They've been paid off."

"But why?" I asked.

"Don't you see?" said Cannon. "Something in there was incriminating to Jim."

"Right," said Wit with a nod. "They didn't want it made public. So they sent some Torchlight ex–Navy SEAL into the station and he stole it."

"Which means the Masons know the truth," said Kipling.

"*And,*" Cannon continued, "if they haven't come forward to arrest anyone, if they've stayed silent, it means whatever they uncovered was damaging for the family."

As everyone fell silent, considering all this, my eyes caught Martha's.

She seemed skeptical, or her mind was somewhere else. I'd been unable to stop thinking about her sudden appearance in the basement and the look on her face when she'd spotted the ink. It made me wonder whether she suspected me somehow, whether she knew I'd received those texts from Jim asking me to meet him that night at the quarry.

"Out of all of us, Bee," she said suddenly, "you spent the most time with the Masons. Did they ever tell you what they thought happened to their son?"

I shook my head, shrugging. "We completely fell out of touch."

Countless times during the past year, I'd wondered how the Masons had handled Jim's death. I never found out. I never even made it to Jim's funeral. My parents, fretting about my mental well-being, begged me not to go. And while a few Darrow students—including Whitley, Cannon, and Kip—had gotten special permission to take the train to New York for the service, I decided to stay away. My absence, I knew, would come as a relief. His family had liked their modern art collection infinitely more than they'd ever liked me. Jim's mom, Gloria—a champagne flute of a woman, all ice-blond hair and long limbs, with a low voice—

always surveyed me as if I were a window with an airshaft view. Jim's father had to be introduced to me three times before he recalled who I was. And even then he called me Barbara.

"I say we pay a surprise visit to the Masons," said Whitley.

"We'll probably have to waterboard 'em to get 'em to talk, child," said Kipling. "But count me in."

"There's a problem," I said.

"What?" asked Martha.

"The wake."

"What about it?"

"It's only eleven point two hours. That's not enough time."

"What do you mean?" asked Kip, frowning. "We fly to East Hampton. We'll be outside the Masons' Water Mill estate in less than two hours."

"They're not in Water Mill. The Masons spend every summer on Amorgos, an island in the Aegean Sea. It takes eleven hours by plane. Plus a three-hour boat ride. Then you have to hike up a mountain to reach the house."

They seemed skeptical, so I dialed the Masons' Fifth Avenue apartment. The housekeeper who answered confirmed the family was away.

"Are they at Villa Anna Sofia on Amorgos Island?" I asked.

"That's right. Would you like to leave a message for Mr. and Mrs. Mason?"

Jim called his family's compound in Greece the Milk Shake for the way it oozed down the cliff overlooking the ocean. Much to my parents' irritation, I'd spent five days there with Jim the summer before junior year. Although the time had passed in a sunburnt blur of bleached-white beaches and outdoor feasts, sunset boat rides and Greek folk music, Jim working relentlessly on his musical, that island and the Masons' vertigo-inducing compound remained one of the most surreally beautiful places I'd ever seen.

"We could try Skyping them," suggested Kipling. " 'Hi, we're Jim's old friends phoning from purgatory. We command you to tell us everything about your son's death.' "

"I guess that's that," said Whitley gloomily.

"Not exactly," said Martha.

I turned to her with a shiver of dread.

"It's time you guys learned the truth."

"What are you talking about?" asked Whitley.

Martha cleared her throat.

"The Neverworld is more complex than you think. I mean, none of you have noticed anything strange?"

"Oh, no, this is all perfectly routine," said Kipling, smiling.

"Strange things like what?" I asked.

"Unusual disruptions. Magnetism. Instability."

Instantly I thought of the mold, the peeling wallpaper, the tumbling trees, the collapsing shelves, the exploding snow globes, that black ink soaking through all the case files.

Martha appeared to know what it was, what it meant. She was fumbling in her heavy black bag, pulling out a small black notebook.

I recognized it. It was the one I'd spotted her carrying in the early days of the Neverworld, when she stopped to hastily scribble in the pages before moving on.

" 'Sighting, six thirty-nine p.m.,' " she read. " 'One mysterious purple-feathered owl perched atop a maple tree, unknown species.'" She turned the page. "'Overheard. Variety of eighties songs by the Cure in every passing car and every surrounding house.'"

Martha closed the notebook, surveying us.

"Remember what the Keeper said. 'Imagine if each of your minds was placed inside a blender, and that blender turned on high. The resulting smoothie is this moment.'"

"Okay," said Whitley, nervous.

"He was talking about the physics of the Neverworld. I'm very excited to tell you that it's based in part on J. C. Gossamer Madwick's groundbreaking masterpiece. And it's my fault."

"What are you talking about?" asked Cannon.

"I wrote a two-hundred-page thesis on the novel. I tracked down every rare book about it. Every obscure blog. I interviewed professors, experts, and scientists. I even went to visit Madwick's daughter on Bello Costa Island in the Florida Keys, rowing out to this tiny, falling-down beach house in a remote cove swarming with alligators. She let me inspect Madwick's notebooks, which have never been seen by anyone outside the family, not even the people at Harvard who've been bullying her to donate them to their archives. I read all eleven notebooks, translating them from Lurroscript, the language Madwick made up."

She stopped her mad outpouring of words to take a deep breath.

I realized she was talking about *The Bend*, the fantasy novel she'd been obsessed with, the one no one had ever heard of except her and a bunch of geeky fanboys on the Internet.

"My preoccupation with the book made it our reality. I lived it. Breathed it. Now it's in the Neverworld."

"But what does that mean, child?" Kipling asked, faint shrillness in his voice. "We're all about to float out into outer space? Become androids?"

Martha tilted her head and grinned, the lenses in her glasses flashing in the light.

My heart plunged. Whatever she was about to tell us, I knew I couldn't trust it.

I also knew that in this world stuck on repeat, everything we knew was about to change.

CHAPTER 16

"Well, for one thing," Martha said excitedly, "it means rather than waking up at Wincroft, we can wake up anywhere in the past, present, or future."

"And how do we do that?" asked Cannon.

"We climb out the unlatched window."

We could only stare, baffled.

She sighed. "*Right*. Okay. I got way ahead of myself."

She took another impatient breath.

"Lesson One. J. C. Gossamer Madwick was a science fiction writer. He wrote just one book, called *The Dark House at Elsewhere Bend*. *The Bend* for short. It's this amazing adventure story and alternative world, different from anything you've ever read. It was never published. Just photocopied over and over again, bound using a hole-puncher and garbage bag zip ties, passed hand to hand by anonymous travelers, student backpackers, and disaffected youths in hostels. The thing you have to do once you finish *The Bend*? You sign the dedication page and leave it for the next lucky person on a park bench, bunk bed, airplane seat, or train compartment. For the longest time the only copies to be found were in ancient bookshops and on eBay, some with hundreds of thousands of signatures. The ones with famous names of the readers, like Marilyn Monroe and Leonard Bernstein and Frank Sinatra? They went for as much as four, five grand. Now it's an official cult classic, steadily in print, and even random people like E.S.S. Burt have copies."

To my surprise, Martha raced over to the shelves and pulled out a hulking silver hardback book. Returning to the couches, she handed it to me. The cover featured a collage of birdcages, steam trains, men and women wearing top hats, masquerade masks straight out of Victorian England.

> *The Dark House of Elsewhere Bend* by J. C.
> Gossamer Madwick.
> *The legendary cult saga of future pasts.*
> *Present mysteries. An undying love at the end of*
> *the world.*

I flipped to the back flap and stared down at the author photo.

It was grainy and black-and-white. In a rumpled suit, Madwick was a man few would look twice at: hound-dog face, extravagant ears, an apologetic slouch suggesting he was more comfortable ducking out of a room than entering one.

Jeremiah Chester Gossamer Madwick (December 2, 1891–March 18, 1944) was an American novelist from Key West, Florida. His only work, the posthumously published The Dark House of Elsewhere Bend, *won the Gilmer-Hecht Prize for Fantasy in 1968. For 37 years he worked as a bus driver for the Key West transit office, driving passengers to and from Stock Island by day, and writing his 1,397-page masterpiece by hand on hotel notepads by night. At age 53, he was found dead in the doorway of Hasty Retreat Saloon, a harmonica, a tin of tobacco, and the final paragraph of his novel in his pocket.*

"Madwick died penniless and unknown," Martha said. "Now he's considered one of the greatest fantasy writers who ever lived. Harvard has an entire class about him: Hobos, Strangers, and Vagabonds: The Literature of Madwick. He even has a cult following in the real-life physics community due to his theory of time."

She paused to hastily draw something in her notebook. It was a sketch of a train.

"Which brings me to Lesson Two," she said. "Time travel. Madwick viewed time not as linear, or an arrow, or even a fabric, like Einstein. He saw it as a locomotive. To time travel in *Elsewhere Bend,* you climb out the window of your speeding train compartment and scale onto the roof, like a bandit in an old western. Then you carefully move toward the *front* of the train, the future, or the *back* of the train, the past. It's vital not to move too quickly in either direction because that will cause instability. Like, the train can jump the tracks, or crash, or separate compartments, or veer suddenly onto a *wrong* track heading clear in the opposite direction."

Shuddering in apparent horror at the thought of such a scenario, Martha took a deep breath and tucked her hair behind her ears.

"In the event of such disasters, you, the time traveler, are doomed. Because you'll never be able to get your train back running on the original track, much *less* on time, much *less* climb back to the compartment in which you began. Although technically you can live the rest of your life in the past or future, the carriage where you were born, the original present, is where you belong. *Always.* That's where life will be the smoothest journey for you. Where things work out and love lasts. A life lived at any other time will be restless, rough, ill fated. You can visit the past and the future, but you can't stay there. Not if you want any chance at happiness."

"What does this have to do with the Neverworld?" asked Cannon, uneasy.

"We want to interrogate Jim's parents? I believe we can. We just have to choose a day in the close past or the future where we can reach them in the eleven point two hours of the wake. Then we find the open window in our train and climb out. And this open window . . ." She nibbled her fingernail. "It's somewhere here. I don't know where yet, but it's a collision of life and death.

It tends to be suicidal. In *The Bend,* the protagonist uncovers it by accident in Chapter One when he tries to commit suicide. And obviously none of us has ever committed suicide."

I shook my head. So did Whitley, Cannon, and Kipling.

"So that rules *that* out," Martha said gloomily. "We'll have to locate the open window by some other means. Which brings me to Lesson Three."

She cleared her throat. "The Neverworld was created not only by me, but by each of you. *My* biggest contribution is Madwick's *Dark House at Elsewhere Bend*. But what about you? The closer you study the Neverworld, the more of yourself you'll find. Your darkest secrets. Your worst nightmares. Your fears and dreams. The embarrassing thing you never want anyone to learn. It's all here, buried, if you look close enough."

An uneasy chill inched down my spine.

There was something threatening in the way she announced this. The others looked uncomfortable too. Whitley sat on the couch, motionless. Kipling looked pale. Cannon stared her down, completely absorbed.

Martha surveyed her notebook with a faint smile. "Kipling." She cleared her throat. "I meant to ask you." She held up a page where she'd drawn a red wasp. "The scarlet-bodied wasp moth. Native to Louisiana. I've spotted three at Wincroft. Two crawled out of the attic upstairs. Another from a radiator. They shouldn't exist this far north. Do you recognize it?"

"How did you . . . ?" blurted Kipling. He chuckled nervously. "Momma Greer used to catch them in mason jars. Kept them all around the house. Pit fiends, she called them. Said the sting was lethal and she'd put them on me while I slept if I didn't sit still during church."

Martha nodded blankly, unsurprised. She turned the page.

"Cannon. Surely you've noticed all the Japanese larch?"

He sat up, nervous. "The . . . what?"

"The Japanese larch and silver birch trees growing around Wincroft. If you look closer, they're dead. A bunch of tall, spindly black tree trunks sticking out of the ground. Those trees aren't native to Rhode Island. They're indigenous to the Chubu and Kanto regions of Japan. If you go up to one and dig down about six inches, chalky blue water pools everywhere." She beamed. "You know what I'm getting at?"

Cannon only stared.

"Blue Pond?" she suggested. "Cannon's Birdcage? The bug you discovered in Apple's OS X operating system sophomore year? The accidental combination of keystrokes that crashes your hard drive, delivering the photo of Blue Pond wallpaper to your screen? The photograph is an almost surreal picture of a bright blue lake, dead snow-tipped trees growing right out of it."

He was confounded. "Okay. What about it?"

"That photo is embedded in the Neverworld's landscape. Everywhere."

Cannon said nothing, only slipped to his feet, crossed the library to the window, stared out.

"Then there's Whitley," Martha went on officially. "There's a volatility in the Neverworld's weather because of you."

"*Me?*" said Wit.

"Gale-force winds. Constant rain, thunder, lightning. It's your temper."

Whitley glared at her.

"The night we went back to Darrow," Martha went on. "How we got chased by the police. I watched wind overturn every car in the parking lot. It was because of your confession about being the White Rabbit."

Whitley huffed in apparent disagreement, but her eyes flitted worriedly to the windows.

"These details go for all of us," Martha went on. "The closer we get to the truth, the root of who we are, the more unstable this world will become. Which brings me to Beatrice."

She turned to me, her expression stony. My heart began to pound.

"I have no clue."

Everyone frowned at her—and then at me.

"Your contribution is here. Somewhere. But I haven't figured it out yet."

I swallowed. What was Martha attempting to do? Intimidate me? Scare me? If so, it was working.

She sighed. "One thing I do know is that if we try changing the wake, we have to stick together."

"Why is that?" asked Cannon.

"We don't know how we're going to react. The past hooks you like a drug. The future jolts you like an electric chair. Reliving beautiful memories can be just as devastating as reliving the terrible ones. They're addictive. Given that time travel in *The Bend* is so dangerous, and that inside the Neverworld there are elements we can't anticipate—the things *you* are each contributing—we have no idea what will happen if we even attempt this." She shook her head, her voice trembling with so much emotion, she reminded me of an evangelical minister on a public access channel, lecturing a rapt congregation about the end of the world. "It could be a complete disaster. We could accidentally end up in different train compartments on different trains speeding in different directions. That means it'll be impossible to ever make it back here. To Wincroft. Together. *To vote.* Then we really will be trapped here forever."

The rest of us eyed each other in alarm. No one spoke.

I gazed down at the hulking book on my lap. I couldn't breathe.

What was she up to? Was Martha actually trying to help us? Or was this new revelation only the meticulous and conniving arrangement of her chess pieces on the board, some ingenious trap we would all fall into, which would somehow result in everyone voting for her?

What I *did* know—or at least strongly suspected—was that she knew what my contribution to the Neverworld was. I could tell by the way she looked at me, by her flat, implausible explanation: *I haven't been able to figure it out.*

Martha always figured everything out. For whatever reason, she'd decided not to disclose this piece of information.

Not yet.

CHAPTER 17

For the next couple of wakes, we stayed in the library at Wincroft, studying *The Dark House at Elsewhere Bend*. We wanted to understand everything Martha had told us.

We downloaded the audiobook and spent hours listening to all 1,322 pages, curled up under mohair blankets, drinking tea as the narrator—some young British actor from the Royal Shakespeare Company with an opera baritone and a schizophrenic ability to sound like completely different men and women, young, old, poor, aristocratic—told the futuristic tale of love and loss. It was a bewitching story, one of the best I'd ever heard, a heart-pounding mystery unfolding against a future world, fascinating and terrifying plot twists you couldn't see coming.

The book took place far in the future. The main character, Jonathan Elster, was a bumbling, absentminded professor at a university for outcasts in Old Earth. He taught a popular alternative philosophy course, Intro to Unknowns, which covered, among other things, the nuts and bolts of time travel. For years, Elster had been in love from afar with a mysterious woman named Anastasia Bent, who taught in the history department. When she accidentally stumbled upon a cover-up about the history of the universe and vanished—a fisherman witnessing her wandering a cliff walk suggested she committed suicide, though her body was never recovered—Jonathan set off on a perilous quest across space and time to find her.

All of us grew silent and sullen as we listened. The violence at the Warwick police station had brought us all together, opened up the roped-off rooms in the sprawling, lavish mansion that had once been our friendship, flung the sheets off the furniture, turned on the lights. Now it seemed Martha's disclosure had us taking refuge in our separate rooms again, disappearing up winding staircases, holing up behind closed doors, the only hint of company an occasional creak of the floorboards overhead.

I didn't know what they worried about. They chose not to confide in me or, it seemed, in each other.

My own anxiety had everything to do with Martha. Those bombshells she'd dropped—J. C. Gossamer Madwick, the physical laws of the Neverworld being tied to each of us—had prompted me to scrutinize her every knowing glance and comment even more closely than I had before. To my shock, I realized that somewhere in the time since I'd found her at Brown with Professor Beloroda, she'd managed to quietly seize control of the entire group. For years, her status had been peripheral. She was the tagalong sidekick, Jim's friend, the oddball you could count on to react to PETA commercials with some jarringly cynical comment like "Such propaganda," or, when any couple ended up together at the end of a romantic comedy, "Another horror movie with a high body count." Martha had always made us roll our eyes and chuckle. Now, incredibly, impossibly, she was the one the others looked to for guidance, for expertise and reassurance. A few times I tried confiding in Kip, Whitley, and Cannon, hinting that I didn't trust Martha or this new direction she was urging us toward. They didn't share my suspicion.

"What do you mean, she's up to something?" Kipling asked me, frowning.

"I don't know. It's just a feeling."

"But it's good old Martha. Rain Man. She's not conniving. She's too honest and goofy."

"I don't think so."

"Oh, come on."

"I'm serious. She knows more than she's letting on."

"Does it really matter?" whispered Kipling. "What else can we do, Bee? I don't know about you, but I need something to change. Anything. Even if it means . . ."

"Even if it means what?"

He shrugged, his expression bleak, the meaning behind his unfinished sentence obvious.

Even if it means we never get out of here.

———

Our evenings passed in heated discussions about how to change the wake and get to the Masons.

In *The Bend,* Jonathan Elster discovers time travel accidentally when following in the footsteps of the missing professor Anastasia Bent, who the police believe committed suicide by jumping off a seaside cliff. As Jonathan follows suit, jumping from the exact spot where Professor Bent was last seen, plummeting a hundred feet toward certain death, he finds himself crashing not into the rocky cliffs, but into the Thames in London in the year 2122.

"The open train compartment window for time travel always exists on the verge of death," said Martha, "which is why so few people ever find it. You have to think you're facing your death in order to reach it. So how do we find it here, in the Neverworld? I know I already asked you guys this, but have any of you ever tried to commit suicide?"

Again, we all shook our heads.

Martha seemed perplexed by this response, though she only nibbled a thumbnail thoughtfully, saying nothing more.

Another critical fact to remember was that for everyone to arrive at the right place and time—the same train compartment in the past or the future—we had to make sure it was the final thought in our heads right before the moment on the verge of death.

"We'll aim for Villa Anna Sophia on Amorgos Island one day in the past," Martha announced. "Yesterday. August twenty-ninth. That's where we'll start."

"Why the past and not the future?" asked Cannon.

"You never know what tomorrow will bring. The future could hold a natural disaster, terrorist attack, alien invasion. The past has already happened, so we know what to expect."

"But if we're going into the past," I asked, "why not just go straight to Vulcan Quarry on the night Jim died? Then we'll know everything."

"She's right," said Cannon.

"No," said Martha, shaking her head. "No *way*. We're not ready. In *The Bend*, the train gets shorter and shorter with each leap in time. That means our wakes will get shorter. It'll cause too much instability. It could mean we won't have enough time to come to vote with a consensus. We have to start out slowly."

I didn't buy her explanation—she seemed too quick to condemn my suggestion—but the others appeared to accept her answer. So I decided not to challenge her. Not yet.

No one had been to Amorgos except me. Only I had visited Jim that summer. So the others could vividly envision the time and place, I showed them photos from the trip on my phone and told them what I remembered: The island's scalding brightness. The open-air Jeeps the Mason family drove around the island, tearing down the dirt roads like an occupying army. Edgar Mason, shut away at all hours in his space-age office, from which he'd abruptly emerge like Zeus coming down from Olympus (if Zeus was tanned to the color of whiskey, had spiky hedgehog hair, and rose every day at four a.m. to practice Ashtanga yoga while whispering into an earpiece). Jim's younger siblings and their respective friends stampeding up and down the house's staircases like herds of antelope. Jim had two younger twin sisters, Gloriana and Florence, and two adopted brothers from Uganda, Cal and Niles. Much to my amazement, they had a Swahili tutor living with them ("A cultural attaché," Jim said). Jim and I had spent most of our time alone, reading aloud from John Lennon biographies, diving off the dock, exploring the coastline in a blue skiff called *Little Bird*. We snorkeled and ate grilled fish doused with lemon that squirted into my eyes and stung. We fed dinner rolls to the packs of wild dogs that patrolled the night streets like gangs, and stayed up into the early morning at drunken family feasts at gangplank tables under a blue night sky, chains of yellow paper lanterns bobbing overhead.

Though Jim had invited me to spend the entire summer with him, my parents only agreed to let me visit for five days. To get them to agree to even that took State Department levels of persuasion. Those five days passed in the blink of an eye, each tinged with a blinding, far-fetched sheen, which made me feel at once uncomfortable and bewitched. Jim's world was so vivid, so improbable. As suddenly as I was thrown into it, I was tossed out, marooned back in sleepy Watch Hill, distracted and gloomy as I worked alongside my parents at the Crow, leaving milk shakes too long in the mixer, preparing egg salad sandwiches for customers who'd ordered turkey and Swiss. I was haunted, like Wendy by memories of Neverland and Peter Pan. I spent the rest of the summer tabulating in my head the seven-hour time difference so I could picture what Jim was doing, and roared through the house like a caged lion tossed a fresh carcass to seize the phone in time whenever he called.

Per Martha's instructions, I described as best I could a single room in the house: the main living room, with its dreamy gauze curtains, whitewashed furniture, and scalding view of the Aegean. This was so they could feel as if they'd been there too, could have it be the very last thought in their heads before the moment on the verge of death—whatever that turned out to be.

———

When the five of us weren't holed up in the library hashing over *The Bend,* I'd grab an umbrella and head into the storm, hiking the property alone.

As I walked I could hear Martha's voice in my head, her unnerving whisper: *Your contribution is here. Somewhere.*

It was during one of these solitary walks when, heading down the narrow stairs to the dock, I noticed the trees writhing with an intensity that wasn't normal. The ocean was rough, whitecaps licking the inky water. The sailboats moored far out in the cove clattered and bobbed. Ropes had come loose from the masts, thrashing like snakes. A buoy clanged somewhere out on the ocean, the sound mournful, deathly.

Suddenly I heard a woman's sharp scream.

The moan of the wind made me think I'd imagined it.

Then I heard another cry. This time it was a man.

Two people were arguing. Sensing that the voices were coming from behind me, I closed my umbrella and hurried off the dock and out of sight, darting into the foot-wide space between the bank and wooden steps.

Moments later, I heard them again. I realized they weren't

coming from Wincroft at all, but from one of the sailboats out in the harbor. Dark figures were moving along the deck of one anchored close to the dock of the property next door.

Andiamo, it was called.

I remembered hearing Whitley mention it belonged to E.S.S. Burt. A tiny gold light was shining from the bow.

Then it came: another scream.

I waited. Minutes later, I heard a motor. A skiff was approaching. Peering through the steps, I saw Whitley. She was alone. She docked the boat, hastily knotting the ropes before climbing onto the pier, running up the steps. Her face caught the light as she barreled right past my head. She looked angry.

I waited. When there were no further voices, I headed back to the house. I knocked once on the library doors, and opening them, I saw Whitley, soaking wet, sitting with Martha on the couch. They jolted upright as soon as I entered, startled looks on their faces. My first thought was of two teenagers surreptitiously smoking pot in a living room, suddenly interrupted by a parent.

"What's the matter?" I asked.

"Nothing," said Whitley.

Martha smiled. "Could you give us a minute, Bee?"

I stared at Whitley. Never had she preferred to confide in Martha over me. *Never.* Hadn't our friendship come back to life after all this time in the Neverworld? Weren't we friends again? But she only stared back at me, sullen.

I left with a sinking feeling in the pit of my stomach, closing the door.

Almost immediately I could hear Whitley, her voice low and muffled, her words indistinguishable.

What the hell is going on?

I headed upstairs. Searching the bedrooms, I found no sign of Cannon, or Kipling either, which seemed to suggest they'd been aboard the boat too. Had they held some kind of secret meeting purposely behind my back? Why? What were they doing? I grabbed the umbrella, headed back outside, and hiked down to the dock.

There was no obvious movement on the sailboat and there were no more voices.

I stayed there for another hour, watching. When nothing happened, I decided to hike back to Wincroft, and as I hurried up the path I noticed the Keeper.

Immediately my throat constricted. The last time I'd seen him had been in the woods at Darrow. He seemed to have vanished for a time. Now he was back, a dark figure in a black raincoat, hunched over, drenched. He was digging with great exertion, his whole body contorting with each fling of dirt.

I veered off the stone path to avoid him and sprinted through the trees. When I reached the house, I couldn't help turning back to look at him.

He hadn't noticed me. He was still digging what I now realized were four muddy holes in the earth. Four graves.

But that wasn't the strangest thing.

He was wearing the black glasses of a blind man.

━━━

I didn't have time to ruminate on what the Keeper had been doing, or what it meant, because the very next wake the answer to the mystery of the sailboat argument and Whitley's private conversation with Martha came to light.

"Kipling has something to tell us," announced Martha as we all assembled in the library. "Whitley brought this to my attention late last wake, and I think it could help us."

"You didn't," Cannon said angrily to Whitley.

"I had to," she answered.

He glared at her, livid.

"Oh, *please*. Stop the policeman act. You want to get out of here, don't you? I mean, don't you want to find out what really happened to Jim?"

"It wasn't your secret to tell," he hissed.

"If it affects our ability to change the wake, it is."

"It's all right," said Martha, placing a hand on Cannon's shoulder. "You can tell us."

That was when I noticed Kipling. He was crying. *Truly* crying, in a way I'd never seen him before—the kind of crying that was more of a wringing out than normal tears. He was seated on the couch, head in his hands, tears streaming down his chin.

"I call it the Black-Footed Sioux Carpet," he blurted suddenly, staring at the floor. "It's a form of self-harm. 'An unsuitable attempt to solve interpersonal difficulties.' That's what the shrinks all call it. Momma Greer invented it. She coined the term from some crazy-lookin' rug she'd filched from an antiques store. We did it together. Mother-son bondin'. Sometimes we did it multiple times a week. She'd drive me out to a country road on a Friday night when she decided there was nothing good on TV. The first time I was five. We'd lie down in the road side by side, holdin' hands, waiting for a car. 'Roll out of the way when I say bingo,' she told me. 'We'll see how much God likes us. If he wants us to live. Cuz I'll only say bingo if God tells me to. That's the deal.'" Kipling shuddered. "I pissed myself I was so scared. I hadn't said my prayers. Good God. I mean, did God even know I existed? Did He like me? He couldn't like me *that* much if He'd given me *this* face to go through life with. *This* body. I'd squeeze Momma Greer's hand. She was my lifeline. Then the car. You always felt it first in the pavement underneath you. It'd take Momma Greer a year to yell bingo. But it always came. I'd squeeze my eyes shut and roll out of the way. The tires would miss me by centimeters. By the time I opened my eyes Momma Greer would be up dancin' on the side of the road, whooping and hollerin', yankin' off all her clothes. 'See that? God loves us. He loves us after all.' She was always in a good mood after that. If I was lucky, it lasted a whole week."

He fell silent a moment, rubbing his eyes. I could only stare. While I had known Momma Greer was dangerous, this was by far the most terrifying thing I'd ever heard she'd done.

"It became an addiction," Kipling went on. "The rush of it. I never stopped. Every few months, whenever things got out of hand or hopeless, I'd find a way to do my Black-Footed Sioux Carpet. I'd sneak off campus. Immediately felt better. I did a big one junior year, right before Christmas break, when Rector Trask told me I couldn't return next semester. I was kicked out. I was the sort of student—*how* did he put it?—who needed an environment with 'less vigorous expectations.' Like, he thought I'd do better in Sing-Sing. My Black-Footed Sioux Carpet after *that* nearly got me made into an egg-scramble sandwich by a Folger's truck." He glanced up, sniffing. "It certainly would have given new meanin' to their slogan 'The Best Part of Wakin' Up.'"

I gazed at him, speechless. Kipling had always been a rotten student. While I knew there had been cliffhangers at the end of every school year as to whether he was passing, I'd never known he was actually kicked out. His poor academic record had changed senior year, when he managed to focus on his studies. By the time we graduated, he had done well.

"It was Cannon who saved me," Kip said with a faint smile. "He saw what I was tryin' so hard to hide."

"You weren't that good at hiding it," said Cannon, grinning. "You were walking with a limp and winced when you sat down."

Kipling looked at me. "Remember how I missed two months of school due to a 'family emergency'?"

I nodded. Vaguely I remembered him telling me a vibrant and long-winded story about his aunt's heart condition.

"It was all lies. I was at a treatment center in Providence, doin' tai chi, watercolorin' fruit bowls, and developin' a middle path to manage my unrestrained patterns of thought. It was Cannon who checked me in. Cannon who came during visitin' hours. Coordinated with the shrinks on my progress. Lobbied Darrow to give me one last chance. He helped turn my grades around. Got my college applications ready. Sat up with me all night helpin' write my essay about Momma Greer. 'Mommy Bipolar.' Otherwise known as 'How to Survive in the Custody of a Complete Lunatic.'

That got me into Louisiana State. I'd be encrusted right now in the front tire treads of a UPS truck if it weren't for Cannon."

My mind was spinning. I thought back to senior year, and though I recalled Cannon as always quite busy, coming and going abruptly with his backpack and an armful of textbooks, never had I suspected what he was up to. But it made sense. He was the silent problem solver. "The steady trickle of water that always finds a passage," Whitley used to say. Still, I felt hurt that they hadn't wanted to confide in me, that there had been an entire history happening right before my eyes about which I'd had no clue.

"Why did you never say anything?" I asked Kipling.

He glanced at Cannon, and I saw pass wordlessly between them some fleeting shadow of understanding that was gone almost as soon as I recognized it.

Kipling shrugged. "There comes a point where your personal pile of crazy gets to be a bit much. Even for your best friends."

"That's not quite the whole truth," prompted Whitley expectantly, tilting her head.

Kipling looked sheepish. "Yeah, well." He cleared his throat. "My eleventh-hour streak of Cs and Bs, revealin' me to be a decent student who'd only been *pretendin'* all that time to be abysmal? That wasn't real."

"What are you talking about?" I asked.

He seemed unwilling to go on.

"Cannon hacked Darrow's network for him," blurted Whitley. "All senior year. Kipling had every test from every teacher ahead of time. Including midterms and finals."

"Not every teacher," said Cannon.

198

She glared at him. "It was still cheating."

"It was assisting a beloved friend," he said stonily.

Whitley huffed. "You could say the same thing about what I was doing as the White Rabbit. Everyone thinks *I'm* the bad person? Look at what you guys were doing."

Cannon said nothing. For years he had assisted Darrow's notoriously backward IT department. It wasn't unusual for him to be summoned from class to help with some bug or networking error. And though he was glaring at Whitley now in obvious annoyance, he didn't appear to feel in the least bit guilty about this disclosure.

"How did you do it?" I asked him.

Cannon shrugged. "Social engineering. The weakest component in any given network is always the human. I sent a faculty-wide email, a required update for Darrow's intranet. For Kipling's teachers I included a RAT. They downloaded the trojan and I became root. It was as easy as untying a shoelace."

He frowned at the look of disbelief on my face.

"Come on, Sister Bee. You of all people should understand. Darrow-Harker was an obstacle in the way of Kipling's bright future. Kicked out junior year? He'd have to start over at some second-rate institution. Away from us. It'd look like shit on his record. And anyway, Kipling can't be measured by such blunt objects as As, Bs, and Cs. No. Kipling is an experience. I had to help him in the best way I could." He shrugged. "There are the rules of this world, and there is what you do when life comes crashing down around you."

Cannon stared at me with such a penetrating look, I felt chills inching down my arms. I'd forgotten how intense a presence he could be, how when he focused, he seemed more energy than flesh and bone.

"So that's it," said Kipling. "That's the two-headed monster in my closet who can't stop drooling."

"The question is," Martha whispered, looking him, "will your secret help us change the wake?"

She fell silent, frowning, lost in thought. For a minute no one said a word.

That was what Martha did sometimes—let a question dangle for minutes, sometimes even an hour, before suddenly blurting the answer when everyone else had forgotten the problem.

"I have an idea," she said.

CHAPTER 18

That was how we came to be parked in the wild beach rose along the empty coastal road at 4:47 in the morning, four minutes before the end of the wake.

Directly across the street was where we'd had the accident—where, according to the Keeper, one Mr. Howard Heyward, age fifty-eight, of 281 Admiral Road, South Kingstown, had smashed his tow truck into our car, condemning us to the Neverworld, where somewhere, in some other dimension of time more real than this one, we were lying inside a totaled car inside a single second waiting to unlock.

Martha knew the exact spot, a hairpin curve twisting one hundred and sixty degrees through dense pine trees. She admitted she'd come back here to inspect it in the Neverworld.

How had it happened? I could hardly remember. Aggressive

flashes of headlights blinding me. Hedges of beach rose trembling in the torrential rain. Windshield wipers waving as if in warning. Liquid night. Our drunken laughter spilling everywhere. Honking. Spinning. The car bouncing off the road, leaping into the dark. A loss of gravity.

"He's a drunk," Martha said. "He sits in the Raccoon and Hound Saloon in Warwick and drinks twelve Coors Lights. *Twelve.* Then he climbs behind the wheel. He can hardly stay awake. Nearly crashes into a telephone pole. In the Neverworld, he drives straight past the spot where he hits us. But that marks the end of the eleven point two hours of our wake."

Rain hammered the roof. The windshield and windows were fogged. I felt as if we were sealed inside a submarine at the bottom of the sea. The radio stuttered classical music.

Only one car had passed us, a blue pickup. Spotting us nestled in the bushes on the side of the road, it braked and backed up. Martha unrolled the window.

"You guys got a flat?" asked a middle-aged man in a hunting vest. "Need a hand?"

"No, thanks," said Martha. "We're fine. We're looking for our lost dog."

He frowned, baffled by the sight of five teenagers dressed in green hooded ponchos smiling stiffly. With a perplexed grimace and nothing left to say, he drove off.

"Three minutes," said Martha, checking her watch.

I felt like I was going to be sick. Kipling and Cannon's revelations, shocking as they were, had elicited more questions than answers. For one thing, everyone was acting strange, though it was difficult to put my finger on why. They were irritable and out of it. Twice, when they weren't aware I was watching, I saw Kipling and Cannon exchange long, knowing glances, the meaning of which seemed vaguely ominous. *What was going on?* What were they planning?

And though Martha was coaching us, assuring us it was going to be fine—*August twenty-ninth, nine-thirty-five a.m., Villa Anna Sophia, Amorgos Island, Greece, that's all you have to remember, okay?*—the fact that she of all people was in charge of this operation only made it worse. What was she up to? Was she pushing us to follow in the footsteps of characters in *The Bend* so she could condemn us somehow, trap us in some train compartment of time? Or was it only about the vote for her?

The vote. The vote. *The vote.*

Now, hunched beside Whitley in the backseat, I could feel the wake coming over me, that familiar ocean-wave immensity pressing down on my feet, inching into my shins. Abruptly, the radio belched with static, then began to cough and stutter "Boys Don't Cry" by the Cure.

The rain grew louder, as if the volume had been turned way up.

"I don't feel so swell," said Kip, pressing a hand to his throat.

Martha turned to him. "I feel it too. And it's not just the wake. It's the open window. It's happening."

She was filled with excitement—as much as someone as deadpan as Martha *could* be filled with excitement.

"Can you feel it?"

I did. There was an electrical charge in my hands, as if I'd just shuffled across a heavy carpet in socks. I held my hand an inch from the steamed window. It made a print. I waved it back and forth, and it magically wiped the window clean. I held my hand a few inches behind Whitley's hair hanging outside the hood of her poncho, and the gold strands leapt right into my hand like the tentacles of some strange sea creature.

"Two minutes," said Martha. "Let's move."

She nodded at us and scrambled out, Cannon and Kipling taking off after her without a word. I opened the door and was instantly drenched by a blast of rain. Whitley grabbed my arm.

"I can't do this, Bee," she whimpered. "I can't keep it straight in my head."

"What?"

She was crying. Never in my life had I seen her so afraid.

"I'm going to get lost in the past. I know it."

"No. You're not." I grabbed her by the shoulders. "Listen to me. August twenty-ninth. Nine-thirty-five a.m. Villa Anna Sophia. Say it."

"Villa Anna Sophia."

"Remember the sea. The sky. The pristine white beauty of it all. The curtains. The smell of oranges."

"Oranges. Right."

"You've got this."

She blinked at me, unsure. I held out my hand. She grabbed it. Then we both climbed out of the car into the downpour.

I hadn't anticipated how chaotic it would be. The rain felt like nails. There was a gravitational pull intent on thrusting us back to the car. My thoughts turned to liquid, splattering the inside of my head. All we had to do was approach the spot of the accident and lie down in a Black-Footed Sioux Carpet the way Kipling had explained it. So far only Martha had made it. She was lying on her back along the faded yellow line. I headed toward her, trying to drag Whitley after me, but I was dizzy, and every step was like lifting four cinder blocks tied to my feet. Kip was standing in the road, turning in a circle like a cork caught in a toilet flush, and Cannon was on all fours, trying to crawl. I forced my thoughts to slow. I took big steps, one at a time, squeezing Whitley's hand. Finally we reached the spot and lay down beside Martha. A minute later Cannon arrived with Kipling.

I blinked, raindrops pounding my face. I couldn't see. The rain was falling too hard, so I closed my eyes. The wake had crept up to my knees, pushing me into the pavement.

August twenty-ninth. Nine-thirty-five a.m.

I could picture the rocky, windswept cliff, the modern white house poised there like an eagle's nest, nothing in the windows but a reflection of the sea.

"Fifty seconds!" bellowed Martha.

Villa Anna Sophia.

"I can't do this!" Whitley screamed.

Someone scratched me in the face. I moved my arm to shield my eyes, realizing it was a giant oak branch torn off a tree. It had careened over us before cartwheeling down the road.

Whitley was sobbing, trying to scramble to her feet. Cannon held her in place.

"Stop it!" he shouted.

"Let go of me! I can't do it!"

"Calm down!" shouted Martha.

"I can't! I keep thinking of other things! I can't stop my thoughts!"

I heard the roar of the approaching engine. Howard Heyward, age fifty-eight, drunk and half asleep, was seconds away now. My entire body was shaking. I squeezed my eyes closed, my fingers gripping the pavement, trying to hold on.

Amorgos Island. Greece.

Someone else was screaming now. Kipling.

"Stop it! Stop it!"

"Don't you see? We're going to lose each other!"

"It's a trick! It's a trap!"

Thunder exploded like an atom bomb. My ears blew out, squeals and whines ricocheting strangely around my head. The wake was pressing down on my heart now, so strong it took a moment for me to realize something was viciously stabbing my neck. I cried out in pain, my cold, numbed fingers fumbling to see what it was. I felt something small, hard. I yanked it out of my neck, screaming.

It was the bumblebee pin, the one Jim had given me, the one stolen from me.

The rest happened at once. Headlights sliced through me. The truck was honking, careening toward us. Raindrops fell in slow motion. A howl of brakes. Someone was still screaming. I opened my eyes, catching a fleeting glimpse of a figure in a green poncho sprinting away, vanishing into the woods. Clanging metal. The

206

truck was jackknifing, massive tires sliding on the wet pavement right toward my skull. A smell of scorched rubber. And hell.

One . . . two . . .

Bumblebee pin.

Jim.

PART 3

PART 5

CHAPTER 19

When I opened my eyes, it was daylight.

I was facedown in the grass. I lifted my head, heart pounding, feeling an overpowering wave of nausea. I was sick to my stomach, my body spasming. It took a minute to catch my breath. I wiped my mouth, looking around, my eyes stinging in the light.

I was not on any coastal road. I was not being run over by Howard Heyward's tow truck—at least, not anymore. I was in no physical pain.

I also wasn't in the back of the Jaguar. For the first time in a century it wasn't raining. The sun was shining. I was lying on the ground—dead leaves, dirt, surrounded by trees. It was brisk out, a bite in the air, the sky hard blue. I held out my hands, opening them.

They were empty.

The bumblebee pin. Where is it?

I looked around. I definitely wasn't near Villa Anna Sophia or on any Greek island.

I was in the middle of a forest. I stared down at my clothing.

The burgundy Ann Taylor wool coat my mother had picked up years ago at a secondhand store in Woonsocket. Black tights. Black wool dress. Scuffed black leather pumps.

Puzzled, I stumbled to my feet. My shoes were too tight, my dress scratchy. I lurched forward, staring through the trees at a grassy clearing. There was a lake littered with small white sailboats, people milling around the perimeter. I stumbled toward it, wondering if I looked like some deranged lunatic. But as I stepped out of the woods and down the bank, no one gave me a second glance. There were at least twenty sailboats out on the lake, children and a few teenagers operating them by remote control.

I understood where I was: Central Park. The Conservatory Lake. I'd visited here a long time ago with Jim.

"There you are."

Hearing his voice was like having the floor drop out under my feet. I couldn't breathe. I closed my eyes, my mind jelly. I was falling through a hole a mile deep.

"Where'd you go? Are you already trying to get rid of me?"

He was alive. He was right behind me, his hand on my shoulder. He smelled the same: peppermint soap, wind, and fresh laundry.

"I came out here all the time as a little kid. Once, the remote control broke and my sailboat got stranded in the middle of the lake and my father said, as I cried, 'If you want it, go get it.' I had to wade out there and retrieve the thing. Clearly it was some survival-of-the-fittest, free-market personality test he'd learned in business school and— Hey, what's wrong?"

He spun me around to face him.

What's wrong? How can I begin to answer that question?

"Look at me."

I opened my eyes.

The sight of Jim Mason inches away from me—sun blazing behind him, birds chirping, kids squealing in delight—was so unfeasible, my head turned inside out.

This wasn't real. It couldn't be.

But it was. It was Jim. He was the same, but he wasn't. As I stared up at him, it struck me how no one ever really sees anyone. Memory turns out to be a lazy employee, intent on doing the least amount of work. When a person is alive and around you all the time, it doesn't bother to record all the details, and when a person is dead, it Xeroxes a tattered recollection a million times, so the details are lost: the freckles, the crooked smile, the creases around the eyes.

"Come," Jim said. "We can't be late."

He tucked my hand into the crook of his arm. I'd forgotten how he always did that. He escorted me down the path, past women wheeling babies in strollers—all of whom glanced at him with varying degrees of admiration—and a man pushing a shopping cart filled with plastic bottles.

It seemed the wake had brought me to one of the occasions when I'd visited Jim's family in New York.

It wasn't Christmas. And it was too chilly for spring break.

So when was it?

I could ask him what we were going to be late to, but it was a daunting prospect to speak. Every time I looked at Jim, I felt jolts of disbelief. I wanted to annotate everything about him, every blink, sniff, and sideways grin. I was terrified too. There was a lump in my throat like a giant wad of gum, threatening to dislodge. If it did, I'd end up crying or rambling on madly about the Neverworld, the fact that he was dead now.

You're dead, my love. You have such little time.

Biting my lip, I let him escort me across Fifth Avenue. We rushed into his building—*944 Fifth Avenue* read the elegant script on the green awning—its lobby pungent with hydrangea and roses from the colossal flower arrangement on the table, asteroid-like and silencing. Jim casually waved at the doorman.

"Hola, Murdoch."

Then we were alone in the elevator. Jim leaned back against the wood-paneled wall, surveying me. I had forgotten the way he studied people as if they were priceless pieces of art.

"Don't be nervous," he said.

He was clutching my hand again, grazing his lips against my knuckles as he pulled me, walking backward, into his apartment. I had forgotten how grand it was, echoing like a museum, iron sculptures of birds and oil paintings of stark faces, spindly furniture more giant praying mantises than viable places to sit. Looking down, I noticed the scuffs on my Mary Jane pumps, the lint balls on my old stockings, and felt that familiar cringe of embarrassment. As we moved into the living room, slipping through the crowd, I noticed everyone was wearing black—black dresses, black and white and red silk scarves, blue suits—and I understood where I was.

Freshman year at Darrow. Five years ago. A weekend in late September.

Jim had invited me to come home with him for his great-uncle Carl's funeral. I barely knew Jim back then.

He'd only introduced himself a week before.

——

"Jim Mason."

He was sitting behind me in English. He pulled his chair over, so close I could feel his peppermint breath on my cheek as I tried to work out a rhyme for a song I was writing.

"Whatcha doing?" He frowned at the notebook I was scribbling in. "What's *Fenfang's Chinese Laundry Meltdown: An Original Soundtrack*?"

Embarrassed, I slid the book under my laptop.

"Nothing."

"That didn't look like nothing."

I cleared my throat. It sounded like a swamp.

"I create fake album soundtracks for movies that don't exist. It's just something I do. Don't ask me why."

"I see." He nodded matter-of-factly. "So, when's the commitment to the mental institution happening? Next week? Next year?"

I laughed.

He extended his hand. "Jim Mason. Really delighted to make your acquaintance before they cart you off to your padded cell."

"Beatrice Hartley."

He winked. "I'm a mad poet too."

I smiled. There was a stretch of awkward silence, during which Jim did nothing but sit back and survey me. I turned to my laptop, trying to stop blushing, pretending to type something important. I assumed he was about to return to his desk and leave me alone.

Instead, he started to beatbox, not even trying to be cool about it.

"There was a fetching girl in my English class / Wary as a bluebird, radiating class / I'm scared to look away from her, in case she flies away / Congress needs to declare her a national holiday."

Everyone in class went silent, a boy behind me snickering.

Little did I know that this was how it would always be, that being the subject of Jim's attention would be like having a bomb go off in my face: unexpected, shocking, accompanied by a fall-out of popular girls suddenly approaching me with long, swingy mermaid hair and doubtful glances.

"How do you know Jim Mason?"

"*You're* from New York?"

"Did you go to Spence?"

"I'm from Watch Hill. No, I went to Watch Hill East. I—I don't know Jim."

That was how I met Whitley. She was friends with Jim from some exclusive Native American camp in the Blue Ridge Mountains.

"Jim Mason has a crush on you." It was the first thing she ever said to me.

I hurried along the hallway, clutching the strap of my backpack like it was my floatation device and I was drowning.

"No, he doesn't."

"Yes, he does." She peered at me, frowning. "He calls you 'haunting.' He said you're old-fashioned. And innocent. Like you're from the 1940s or something, and have been transported here by time machine."

"Thanks."

"It's a compliment."

The next day, suddenly Jim was strolling beside me down to the athletic fields. My heart flopped like a freshly caught fish.

"Did you grow up on an Amish farm milking cows at sunrise?" he asked.

"Um. No."

"You look like you did."

"Okay."

"Want to come home with me this Sunday?"

He asked it like he was offering me a bite of his sandwich.

I said no. Sunday was Family Sunday, which meant Darrow's students either went home for the day or signed up for a field trip to a museum. I hadn't seen my mom and dad in a month, and they'd planned an elaborate lasagna dinner. Of course, the truth was I said no because I was terrified by Jim's attention, the brash, drenching spotlight of it, both blinding me and causing everyone else to stare.

Little did I know, *no* to Jim was simply a yes that hadn't happened yet.

"Beatrice!" he shamelessly rapped at the start of English, causing our teacher Mrs. Henderson to regard me with irritation. "She's a realist. With secrets. A conscienceless realist who leaves me sleepless. And speechless. Oh, Beatrice."

He left notes in my locker. *Say yes (jump off a cliff with me).* He recorded a theme song about me. It got passed around the entire school.

" 'The Queen's Neck'? *Please,*" I heard a girl hiss during chapel.

"Say yes!" Jim blurted when he passed me in the hall. ("Yes to *what*? Having his babies?" the varsity volleyball captain snarked to her friends.) Jim called my parents to formally introduce himself, discuss train times to and from Penn Station, give them his word that I'd be safe with him, that he was a gentleman.

This deluge of attention would have been too much coming from anyone who wasn't Jim Livingston Mason, Jim of the thick, tangled black hair, the chocolate eyes, the sideways grin.

"He sounds so adorable and kind of quirky, actually," said my mom.

Back then she'd been naïve about the old-moneyed jungle of Darrow and Jim's lionlike position inside it.

"It's wonderful you're already making some interesting connections," said my dad.

The Sunday trip to Jim's house for the funeral—*this very trip*—would end in disaster.

Fast-forward five, six hours? I'd be taking a train home from New York early, alone, the reasons for which Jim and I always argued about afterward. To this day I found it difficult to recall what had really happened. What had I been so upset about? I could never separate my shyness, my self-consciousness at being painfully underdressed and awkward, from the truth. During the post-funeral buffet, held in some relative's Gilded Age apartment on Park Avenue, I remembered Jim disappeared for what felt like a torturous period of time. I'd grabbed my coat off the hall rack and snuck out without a word to anyone. I cried the whole ride back to school. I vowed—unreasonably, because even then my feelings for him felt as inevitable as seawater in a rowboat full of holes—that this would be the end of my friendship with Jim Mason.

That Monday morning, however, during English, he placed a red Cartier box on the notebook I'd been drawing in.

"Forgive me."

Inside the box was a diamond-encrusted bumblebee pin.

———

The bumblebee pin.

Thinking of how it had mysteriously gone missing from the sock drawer in my dorm room, then abruptly reappeared all these years later, jammed in the side of my neck as we lay in the middle of the coastal road, sent a fresh wave of shock through me. Clearly it had been meant as a means of sabotage, a surefire way to get rid of me, make me think of Jim, thereby pulling me into some compartment of the past. Whoever had done it had meant to hurt me, purposefully destroy any chance we had of voting and leaving the Neverworld.

Which one of them had done it?

"Cookie?"

I jumped, startled. I realized dazedly I was in the Masons' living room staring out the window at Central Park, which from this height looked like an architectural rendering of a park with pipe-cleaner trees. One of Jim's adopted siblings—Niles, nine or ten years old—was offering me a stack of cookies held between his thumb and forefinger.

I took one. "Thanks."

He squinted. "You're Jim's latest girlfriend?"

"No. I'm a friend of his from school."

"Well, take care you don't go"—the little kid crossed his eyes, making a deranged clown face—"like all the others."

I laughed.

"Whoa— Did you see that?"

The kid moved to inspect a large red Rothko, which had just fallen clean off the wall, revealing a dark square of what appeared to be mold.

"That was totally *Poltergeist*!"

I smiled stiffly, moving away as Jim led his mother over.

"Mom. This is the girl I was telling you about. Beatrice Hartley."

"Hullo there."

Mrs. Mason was beautiful, her black suit sealing her like an envelope. She extended her hand like it was a gift. I'd forgotten how chilly she could be: the boredom in her smile, the flick of her eyes over my shoulder, as if somewhere behind me something more charming was always happening, like dolphins leaping out of the sea.

"Darling, did you speak to Artie Grossman about the Currin?"

Mr. Mason stepped over. He was short and tan, with spiky hair and the tense stare of all moguls. His teeth were big and artificially white, hinting they'd glow in the dark during a blackout.

"Dad," said Jim. "This is Beatrice."

Mr. Mason smiled warmly, shaking my hand.

"Just started Darrow-Harker with Jimmy, is that it? How are you finding those old-school traditions and Kennedy smiles?"

"Fine."

"Wonderful. Wonderful. Glory, did you talk to Artie?"

"I'll do it right now," said Mrs. Mason.

She was smiling again, drifting away. "Lovely to meet you," she said unconvincingly over her shoulder.

I couldn't help staring after the two of them, wondering how they had reacted to Jim's death. What had they done, all these polished, perfumed people? Had any of them screamed and lost their minds as I had, or had life simply floated on?

Jim was dead now. He was lying in a coffin underneath a gravestone that read *Life Now Forever* in Sleepy Hollow Cemetery. In this sunlit apartment with the thick walls and marble floors, the idea was unfathomable.

Jim smiled after them. He appeared to mistake my stare for admiration.

"They met on the R train when they were twenty years old. Still madly in love after twenty-eight years. Completely unforgivable. Come."

He clasped my hand again. We slipped through the crowd, past mute housekeepers in gray uniforms, a waiter holding a tray of triangular sandwiches like little starched pocket squares. He whisked me out of the living room, past three siblings playing Wiffle ball in the foyer ("Totally inappropriate!" Jim shouted at them), a wood-paneled library with a ladder to retrieve the thousands of first-edition leather-bound books, a dining room with a modern steel chandelier that looked like a giant tarantula. In two years I'd eat Christmas dinner there and his mother wouldn't say a word to me the entire meal. His father would call me Barbara.

Jim pulled me through a door and closed it behind me. It was his bedroom, a shadowed, chaotic rock star's lair with electric guitars mounted on the wall and sheet music covering every flat surface, handwritten quarter notes and half rests spangling the bars. Synthesizers. A McIntosh stereo. Three laptops. Piles of notebooks burping up pages where song lyrics were taking shape in terrible handwriting. *Lost Little Blue*. A biography of Janis Joplin. *Sweeney Todd: The Complete Score*. A framed copy of a Bruce Springsteen Madison Square Garden set list signed with a note: *Love you, Jimmy. Keep hearing the music. Bruce*. Rumpled boxers and T-shirts and rolled-up posters swamped the corners of the room.

Jim was rifling through a bookshelf, looking for something.

"Okay, so, I have this song I wrote about a girl I haven't met yet," he said, pulling out a notebook. " 'Immortal She.' It's about the love you have for someone that can't die, no matter how far apart you are, even if you're separated by death or time. That's what I'm searching for."

The lump in my throat was there again, a pile of rubble.

He began to read the lyrics, as he would countless times after this. I came to know that song well. It was one of the best he ever wrote. I'd sing it for him on a picnic blanket at school during finals week. He'd sing it to me some nights at Wincroft as I fell asleep.

I remembered this exact moment. I'd related it to Whitley a dozen times, because it was the classic chorus refrain of "The Ballad of Jim and Bee," an old standard. This was the first time we were ever alone together, our first deep conversation. Our first kiss was seconds away. Having it before me again made me feel paralyzed, out of control. As he read, stumbling over a word here and there, pausing to scratch his nose, he seemed so beautiful and so young—younger than I ever remembered. He raised his chin and strained his voice a funny way on certain words, as if they were spears he was launching blindly over a wall.

"It's beautiful," I said when he finished.

He had a funny look on his face. He carefully set the book on his desk and sat beside me.

"I was going to wait to do this, like, weeks, and be this total gentleman and woo you like a knight in medieval times? But I'm punting that plan. I'm not a knight. I'm not even a gentleman. But I am devoted. Once I decide I'm with you, it never goes away. I swear to you that, Beatrice."

He kissed me. There was a whole world in that kiss. Every moment of pain, regret, loneliness I'd felt since he'd died fell away. I'd missed him so much, how much hit me only now. As his hands slid down my back, I knew I was going to tell him about the Neverworld, the Keeper, the vote, his death. Would he be able to tell me why he died if I asked him? Couldn't we run out of here, get into a car, and go live out the wake at a highway motel where the light was gold and the carpet full of vending machine crackers?

Tomorrow we could do it again.

And again.

And again.

I didn't have to be without him anymore. I'd tell him everything. He, of all people, would understand. It'd be like it was before, before his strange moods, his anger, his lies.

When he pulled away, I was aware of a rapid popping noise behind us. Jim looked stunned.

"How weird."

He stood, moving to the guitars mounted on the wall. He widened his eyes, mystified. "All the strings just broke. Every single one." He grinned. "It must be your effect on me."

I smiled weakly.

———

My decision to tell Jim everything set off some gangster-movie escape scene from the funeral, wavered, and stalled the moment he took my hand and we rejoined his family.

There were so many uncles, cousins, women wearing black mink coats and stilettos with toothpick heels, swirls of blond hair like sugar garnishes on thirty-four-dollar desserts. We made our way outside, a glamorous black-clad procession up Madison Avenue into the Frank E. Campbell Funeral Chapel.

"Last time I was here it was for Allegra de Fonso," a woman told me.

The funeral service was long, filled with sniffling people quoting Dylan Thomas and Bob Dylan, "Let It Be" by the Beatles. There was a speech from a red-eyed woman who couldn't stop clearing her throat. Children snickered over an ancient man in the front row announcing too loudly, "It smells like cat piss," before a nurse escorted him out. Jim smiled down at me and squeezed my hand. I found myself staring in wonder at a photo of the dead man: Great-Uncle Carl, memorialized in a laminated poster propped on a brass easel beside the casket. He had mottled red skin and an oblivious yellow smile. Had he ended up in some kind of Neverworld? I was closer to Great-Uncle Carl's state than any of these people could imagine.

I had to tell Jim.

However, once the service ended and the crowd spilled onto the sidewalk—black Cadillac Escalades lined up eight deep, everyone shaking hands and muttering condolences and observations about Carl, how he "did it his way" and was a son of a gun—every time I was about to tell him "I need to talk to you," some new person tapped his shoulder and gave him a bear hug, asking how he'd been, when his first musical was premiering on Broadway. Jim was amiable and kept trying to make his way back to me, but before he could, someone else would approach. When he finally rejoined me, he had two girls in tow. He knew them from grade school.

"Beatrice, meet Delphine and Luciana."

I'd always recalled the girls as intimidating and otherworldly. Seeing them now, they weren't as jaw-dropping as I'd remembered, though they had waist-length hair, which they tossed out of their eyes like ponies, and a bored manner that could be mistaken for expertise. Jim kept putting his arm around me as he talked, but after a while, as I stood listening to stories about Millicent, Castman, and Ripper—whether these were people, a law firm, or impossible-to-get-into nightclubs, I couldn't tell—I began to feel like a giant old L-shaped couch that had been carried out to the sidewalk and left there.

The feeling continued when we piled into an Escalade. We were a large group. Jim was forced to sit in the back next to Luciana. I sat next to an elderly woman wearing red taffeta who reeked of alcohol.

"Here we go again to do what we do," she mumbled.

We were dropped off at Jim's great-aunt's apartment on Park Avenue. Jim deposited me on a love seat by a porcelain pug and disappeared on a mission to find me a Coke. After forty-five minutes with no sign of him, I stood up and roamed the dense crowd, perusing bookshelves and photographs, slipping down crowded hallways as if I knew where I was going. I peered into the kitchen, where caterers were sweating over ovens and trays, and a guest bathroom where the wallpaper looked like twenty-four-karat gold. It was all coming back to me, how desolate I'd felt, adrift in a place I didn't belong. I'd wanted nothing more than to be away from these people, back in Watch Hill, eating lasagna with my parents, hearing my dad talk about a new BBC David Attenborough program on Netflix.

Now, five years later, inside the Neverworld, I wasn't nearly so sensitive, but I was still bothered by Jim's absence. Where had he gone? He'd told me he'd gotten stuck talking to relatives, and I'd believed him.

The question gnawed at me.

I snooped in room after room, searching for him in bedrooms that resembled hotel rooms, offices that looked like libraries, an echoing marble gallery filled with aviation antiques behind glass. Jim was nowhere. Neither, worryingly, were the two girls. At one point, when I opened a closet filled with nothing but Japanese puzzles and board games, Jim's father, Edgar, stepping out of an office, spotting me, and doubtlessly noticing how awkward I looked, beckoned me.

"Jessica," he said to me, smiling warmly, slipping what appeared to be a small black flash drive attached to a rubber bracelet over his wrist. I caught a glimpse of a series of digital numbers flashing along the side before he pulled his shirtsleeve over it.

"Can I get you a drink, my dear?"

"No, thank you, Mr. Mason."

"Edgar. Come meet my partner, Craig, and his daughter,

Greta. Greta just returned from Sri Lanka, where she was a visiting neurosurgeon at the District Hospital in Colombo."

Obviously, high-powered Craig and his neurosurgeon daughter didn't want to be saddled talking to a mute high school freshman, so it was a matter of seconds before they turned to greet someone—"Bertrand? Is that you?"—and I slipped away.

I couldn't call Jim. I didn't have a purse with me, much less a phone. I could wait where he'd left me. Eventually he'd come back. Wouldn't he?

Another hour went by. With each passing second my plan to confess, run away with him, began to grow stale and sag. When I was jostled for the third time by a woman toting a giant alligator handbag, and Mrs. Mason slipped past me with a cardboard smile, Martha's words of warning suddenly leapt into my head.

We don't know how we're going to react. The past hooks you like a drug. The future jolts you like an electric chair. Reliving beautiful memories can be just as devastating as reliving the terrible ones. They're addictive.

Maybe it was shock at being forgotten by Jim again, the nagging question of his lies about Vida Joshua, or the understanding that one of my friends had tried to destroy me, deliberately sticking me with the pin to send me to back to some other moment in time, doubtlessly believing I'd be too smitten with Jim to ever leave his side again, trapping me here forever.

I leapt to my feet, barging through the crowd. In the hallway I snatched my burgundy coat off the coatrack. It abruptly collapsed, sending piles of minks to the floor. I threw down my old coat, seized the fattest, most unwieldy fur I could find, and shrugged it on, hit by a wave of perfume. I ran down the hall, my heart pounding, pressing the down button for the elevator. It splintered under my finger. I wheeled around, shoved open the door to the stairs, and raced down each flight, lightbulbs in the lamps overhead shattering as I passed each landing. I charged out into the lobby, the doormen gawking.

How could I have forgotten where I was, and what I had to do?

Didn't I want to live?

I sprinted outside. The wind was strong, too strong, the green awning chattering and flapping in the gale. I ran to the sidewalk, about to hail a cab, when I heard a girl's shrill laughter. Wheeling around, I saw Jim.

He was perched on the wrought-iron railing in front of the building next door, Delphine and Luciana beside him. They were talking to a doorman, cracking up over his comical impression of someone, what looked like Marlon Brando in *The Godfather*. They were all howling so hard they couldn't stop.

I stood there, frozen, willing Jim to look up and see me.

But he didn't. Staring at his grinning face, I realized then. I saw it as plain as day. I hadn't even crossed his mind.

Maybe I never did.

I wanted to shout his name. I wanted to scream like some vengeful witch in a fairy tale, causing clouds to fast-forward across the sky, wiping the smiles off their faces: "Jim Mason, in four years you'll be dead!"

He leaned back so carelessly, hooking his arm around Luciana's neck and nuzzling her ear, my heart felt freshly sliced in two.

I'd been so stupid, so blind.

Tears sprang to my eyes. I veered around and ran out into the street, nearly getting hit by a taxi before the driver slammed on the brakes, honking.

I climbed in.

"Honey, are you okay? What the—? *Jesus!*"

The driver blinked, mystified at the sight in front of him. The green awning to Jim's apartment building had come entirely free in the wind, detaching from the sidewalk. It was barreling down Fifth Avenue, clanging and swooping; it collided with the rear windshield of a town car before soaring straight up into the air, gold poles flying out, bystanders shouting as it was flung through the sky like some strange soaring monster.

I'm anything but okay.

——

Martha had said to meet back at Wincroft in the event of an emergency.

Always go back to the original wake. If we have that as our meeting place, there remains a hope we can all eventually convene there across space and time. To change the wake again, go back to the coastal road if you can and do the exact same thing, okay? If you can't get to the coastal road, find a suicide.

I took the train back to Newport. When I arrived it was after ten. I climbed into a waiting cab at the station, asking the driver to take me to Narragansett. It was a half-hour drive, and I didn't have money, but I figured I'd be able to think of something at Wincroft.

The gate was open. The lamps were lit. As the cab accelerated down the drive, I could see the driver sit up and glance at me curiously in the rearview mirror, wondering if I was an heiress. The house lights were on. There were eight gleaming cars in the driveway. As the cab waited, I went running up the steps and rang the bell.

When the door opened, I found myself face to face with E.S.S. Burt. He wasn't as creepy as I remembered. In fact, he looked like any rich man in a pastel sweater. There were voices coming from the dining room, glasses clinking. Apparently I had interrupted a dinner party.

"Can I help you?" he asked.

"I'm looking for Whitley."

"She's not here. She's up at her boarding school. Darrow-Harker."

"We were supposed to grab dinner tonight."

He was surprised. "Did you try calling her?"

"She's not picking up." I went on to explain that unfortunately I didn't have enough money to pay the forty-eight dollars for the cab. Blinking in bewilderment, Burt pulled out his wallet, jogged down the steps, and paid the driver.

"I guess I'll go back to my hotel and try Whitley later," I said.

He nodded, puzzled. "What did you say your name was?"

"Beatrice."

Burt didn't know what to make of me, a gawky girl in a black mink bulky as a killer whale. I waved to him and took off on foot down the driveway. He watched me, then disappeared back inside, apparently too preoccupied with his party to wonder, if the cab had driven off, how I was going to get anywhere. I circled back to his vintage-car garage, typed in the four-digit security code. Thankfully it was the same code as five years later, and the door rose with a groan. I hurried to the key stand in the back and unhooked the keys to the Rolls.

Driving out to the coastal road, I expected sirens. None came. My heart began to pound. I could feel the wake coming on. Checking the time, I realized in surprise that this wake had shortened. It had been barely eight hours. I could feel the crushing heaviness pressing into my legs. I floored the gas, engine roaring. The prospect that I might end up with Jim again, back in Central Park, if I didn't make it into another wake willed me to drive faster and faster. My legs went numb. As I rounded the curves, the car seemed to fly out from under me, tree branches scratching at the windshield like an angry mob. When I reached the hairpin curve, I veered into the bushes, narrowly missing a tree. I barreled out, lurching into the middle of the road, the strong wind shoving me down across the yellow line.

I rolled onto my back, gasping. The sky was a deep night-blue, freckled with stars.

I had no idea whether this plan would work. Would the open window even be here anymore? I slowed my thoughts and closed my eyes. *August 29. Villa Anna Sophia. Amorgos Island. Greece.* I waited for a car to come, but there was only the deafening wind in my ears, the shrill hiss of crickets, the distant whoosh of the sea, even as a metronome. I heard a piercing whistling, growing louder. A bicycle. It came at me suddenly, the rider swerving to avoid me, losing control, crashing into bushes on the side of the road with a clang of metal, shouting. The biker was uninjured. After a moment of gasping and swearing, he lurched to his feet.

He stared down at me, faceless in the dark.

"What the fuck?" he whispered as his head jerked up in surprise, headlights of an oncoming car illuminating him like a flash camera.

He threw himself out of the way as my world went dark.

CHAPTER 20

When I opened my eyes I was lying on my stomach on wooden planks. Instantly, streaks of vivid blue tore into my vision. It was the ocean. I raised my head, blinking. I was wearing cutoff jean shorts and a faded pink Captain's Crow T-shirt. I was lying on a dock, barefoot. I turned my head and saw the white wooden staircase zigzagging up the sheer rock face, at least a hundred feet high.

Villa Anna Sophia. I'd actually made it.

Light-headed with relief, I lurched to my feet, only I was so woozy, I stumbled and was sick, nearly falling into the water. Catching my breath, I lurched to my feet.

I headed up the stairs. With every step I took, pebbles and rocks loosened under the planks, bouncing, plummeting down the cliff into the ocean. I kept moving. I didn't look down. When

I reached the top, panting, the house—a wild architectural marvel of glass and steel—sat before me, totally silent. It looked deserted. I hurried past the pool, an inflated swan raft drifting leisurely in the center, and tried one of the glass doors. It was locked, the windows shaded. I was just wondering if I'd gotten the wrong day when I heard a woman scream. With a pang of unease I tore down the stone path, past the olive trees, to the front, where I saw Kipling outside the massive double-oak doors. He appeared to be keeping watch.

I was so relieved to see him, I threw my arms around his neck.

"Thank goodness," I whispered.

"*What*—my—how did you manage it, child? Martha said we'd lost you, maybe forever."

I pulled away. There was no point going into what had happened, not yet. Blinking up at Kipling, though it hurt me to think it, I reasoned he could have very well have been the one to stick me with the pin. Yet he seemed genuinely relieved to see me.

"I made a mistake," I said. "Where is everyone?"

"Inside." He made a face. "We've tied the whole family up and we're tryin' to extract information. But it's not going well." He shrugged, visibly nervous. "We *tried* the nice way. Arriving casually, announcin' we happened to be on vacation, and were friends of Jim's, and we wanted to know about his death, and so on. But they're slippery eels, the Masons. They served us grilled octopus and basil sorbet and invited us for a dip in their pool. Before we knew it, four hours had passed. We were all drunk on ouzo, and we hadn't had one *real* conversation about Jim. Whitley got fed up. So these last few wakes, she's gone nuts on these people. The deluxe Whitley special, you know, with the screamin' and the punchin' of walls and the throwin' dishes." He sighed. "Edgar Mason has his twenty-four-hour security detail, but they switch shifts at noon and they're lazy, so that's when we strike. We've got two tied-up guards at the end of the driveway."

I frowned. "But how many wakes have you had?"

"Five. Each one lasts about five hours. How many have *you* had?"

"One."

This had to be what Martha meant about instability, trains speeding in different directions at different speeds, the risk of never being in the same place at the same time to vote.

There wasn't time to worry about it, not yet. Kipling had opened the door and was beckoning me inside.

There on the couches sat Mr. and Mrs. Mason, tied up along with their four children, their eyes red from crying. They were watching Whitley in mute horror. She looked like a South American guerilla, bandana wrapped around her head, T-shirt knotted in a crop top around her waist, a mad glint in her eyes. She was holding a gun on Mr. Mason. The side of his face was swollen. It was a shock seeing Jim's family like this, when at the last wake they were crisp as fresh flower arrangements, floating around, air-kissing people at Great-Uncle Carl's funeral.

Spotting me, Whitley widened her eyes in surprise. She raced over.

"Beatrice," she said, hushed. "Where the hell did you come from?"

I gave her an abbreviated version of what had happened, how I'd accidentally returned to a different date but managed to get back to the coastal road to change the wake.

"So you're all right, then?"

I nodded. "Where's Martha?"

"Trying to log on to Edgar's computer. Not having much luck."

"What about Cannon?"

"He's gone."

I stared at her. "What?"

She shook her head with a bleak look. "He never arrived. We have no idea where he is. One second he was there, and the next? Nowhere."

I recalled the person I'd seen sprinting into the woods. Cannon.

"Hello? Oh, my God. Is that *you*?"

Mrs. Mason, sitting on the couch, craned her neck to get a better look at me. I'd never seen her so forlorn. She was almost unrecognizable. Her face was red; her blond hair, usually so immaculate, had wilted like a plant left too close to a radiator.

"Who? Who are you talking about?" asked Mr. Mason.

"That little girl Jim went with in school. *You* know. *Her*." She glared at me. "*You're* involved in this? You let us go right now. We have no information about Jimmy."

I grabbed the gun from Whitley and pointed it at Mrs. Mason. She gasped.

"Tell me what you know about Jim's death," I said.

She glanced at her husband, terrified, then back at me. She began to whimper. It was an odd sound, like a beach ball losing air through a tiny hole.

"Leave her alone!" bellowed Edgar suddenly. "Gloria has nothing to do with this, you little con artist!"

I pointed the gun at him. "What happened to Jim?"

"I've told you people countless times now," he said, spitting. "We know nothing."

"That's impossible."

He shook his head. "The police told us it was suicide."

"Jim never would have done that. And you know it."

"I don't. I *don't* know it." Mr. Mason appeared to be crying, staring at the floor.

That was when I remembered.

I stepped behind him, inspecting his wrists, which were bound with zip ties. I yanked up the cuff of his shirtsleeve. Mr. Mason knew what I was after, because he immediately began to contort himself, trying to move his hands away.

"No! Don't you dare—"

It was the black rubber bracelet I'd seen him wearing. He still had it on, five years later, though this one seemed an even more sophisticated version, with digital letters and punctuation with the numbers. I couldn't pull it off his wrist, so I went into the kitchen, returning with a knife.

"Don't you dare! Don't you *dare!*"

I sliced the bracelet off his wrist.

"Now you've done it. Good for you. Bravo. Kiss your future

goodbye, missy, because you'll be spending the rest of your life in a hole so foul you'll *beg* to be sent to prison."

"I should be so lucky," I said.

I turned to Whitley, who was blinking at me in shock.

"What got into *you*?" she whispered.

"I'll be in Mr. Mason's office," I said, racing up the spiral staircase.

———

Martha was stunned to see me.

"Oh, my God. What happened?"

"It's a long story. But I'm fine."

I raced into the all-glass tower, pulling a chair alongside Martha behind the hulking desk. She couldn't seem to stop staring. Naturally it made me wonder if she had been the one to stab me with the bumblebee pin. But there was no figuring it out. Not yet.

"I've been trying to log on to Edgar's laptop," she said, indicating the screen. "It's impossible. There are three prompts for encrypted passwords."

I stared down at the shifting line of numbers, symbols, and letters on the bracelet. They reset every fifteen seconds. I typed the displayed sequence into the three password boxes.

The computer unlocked.

"Are you kidding me?" whispered Martha in awe. "Like *that*? How did you—?"

"I'll explain later."

Before I clicked into the desktop, I placed a piece of tape over the webcam. I didn't know what would happen when it became clear that there was a security breach, but I knew we'd have to work quickly. Edgar Mason had a personalized email interface called Torchlight Command. As soon as I opened the program, a timer recording my activity appeared in the upper right corner of the screen.

The first thing to do was to search for emails from Jim.

We couldn't find one. Searching for the names of his brothers and sisters turned up countless emails, but there was not a single message either to or from Jim.

"He's been wiped from his father's email," whispered Martha. "Why?"

"Maybe he wrote something inflammatory."

She shrugged.

On the hard drive, there were over two thousand folders on a cloud server called Torchlight Library. I searched for *Jim Mason*. Nothing came up. We found a trove of financial records, listings of obscure holding companies with names like Redshore Capital America and Groundview Fund, with addresses in the Cayman Islands and Panama City. There were trade receipts and wire transactions from a bank in Turkey to another in Switzerland, some of which listed dollar amounts so enormous they looked like typos. If any of it was illegal, or tied in any way to Jim's death, the truth was buried under layers of names, numbers, and symbols, none of which could be easily excavated.

"Maybe Edgar's committing fraud," said Martha. "Sweatshops. Child exploitation. Maybe Jim found out about it, and they had a major falling-out."

"If Jim had found out something like that, he'd have been devastated, yes. But he wouldn't have killed himself."

She shrugged. "What if Edgar hired someone to kill Jim?"

I stared at her, surprised. "His own son?"

"If he thought he was going to lose the empire he built? Why not?"

Suddenly she sat up, frowning, pointing at the glass walls. I realized in horror that every pane was breaking. All around us thin cracks were spidering through the glass, branching out, one after the other.

"The instability of the Neverworld," whispered Martha.

I nodded and hurriedly clicked back into the in-box. I certainly didn't want her to wonder what the destruction meant, if it was all being caused by me. I leaned forward, squinting at the screen.

"Most of Edgar's emails are from this woman named Janet," I said, clearing my throat. "His executive assistant. They have a system where she reads his emails and summarizes them."

" 'Chris Endleberg, president of Princeton, called,' " Martha read slowly. " 'He appreciates the way you handled the matter re S.O. They'll hold off on disciplinary measures.' Huh. Okay. What else?"

We scanned the emails in the weeks leading up to Jim's death.

There was nothing unusual. A board member was problematic. *Patrick has to go.* A real estate broker wanted to show Edgar an off-market listing for an estate in Bedford worth $48 million.

Sick pad, man. Someone involved in a fast-food restaurant wanted another loan. *I hear your concerns, but it's time to expand on the line of frozen fried chicken dinners with romance-related flavor names.* In the days following Jim's death, there were emails about funeral arrangements and flower deliveries, the West Side Boys Choir, lists of who was attending and who would speak. It was oddly cold to read through. Just like that, Jim's death was another action item in his father's in-box. My name was buried among three hundred others.

"I don't get it," whispered Martha, frowning at an email she'd just opened.

"What?"

" 'S.O. wants to change his dormitory, FYI.' " She glanced at me. "This is from Janet. 'He needs you to call the Princeton dean and make it happen, as this isn't freshman policy.' Bizarre."

"What's bizarre?" I asked.

"Another email from Princeton. Who in the Mason family goes to Princeton?"

It was a good question. Jim was the oldest. His other siblings were in grade school.

"Who is S.O.?" I wondered.

We did a search of the initials. One more email appeared. As I opened it, the wall of broken glass in front of us spontaneously fell away, millions of shards sliding across the roof and down the side of the house. A powerful gust of wind billowed through the room, sending the gauzy curtains flying out and stacks of papers swirling off Mr. Mason's desk.

"We don't have much time," I said hastily. "The system is about to lock us out."

Martha nodded, biting her lip, and peered closer at the email.

S.O. wants lunch tomorrow to discuss a business opportunity. Booked 1 p.m. Jean-Georges.

"Try searching the keyword *Princeton*," Martha said.

I did, and one more email appeared.

Chris Endleberg of Princeton wants to thank you personally for your donation. Invited you to dinner 2/24. I declined, as you'll be in Buenos Aires.

"S.O. could be a cousin," I suggested. "Maybe Edgar pays for his education?"

"Or S.O. is his Emotional Support Animal, wearing a yellow vest, which he takes with him on planes, trains, and automobiles."

This appeared to be her attempt at humor, though you could never tell with Martha.

"Or S.O. is his imaginary childhood friend," I said.

"Or S.O. is his *sixth* personality, as he has secretly suffered from schizophrenia for years."

We smiled at each other, though unsurprisingly, the moment ended as soon as we realized what was happening: we weren't on edge in each other's company.

That was when another three walls of glass dropped away and a strong gale barreled through again, papers exploding around the room.

At that moment, Whitley stuck her head around the doorframe.

"The wake is three minutes away—" She frowned. "What the— What's happening in here?"

Martha leapt to her feet. "It's the Neverworld. We have to go. *Now.*"

They hurriedly explained their plan. We needed to head back to Wincroft to find Cannon. The Masons were impossible to break. It was better for the five of us to get back together than to keep interrogating them. Our questions were eliciting no new information about Jim.

"Use the cliff for the wake," Martha ordered cryptically before ducking out.

I remained where I was, searching Edgar's laptop as the wind howled around me, and papers cycloned, every glass wall falling away. Not a minute later, the desktop speakers sounded an alarm, and I was locked out, the screen going black. I leapt to my feet, and as I hurried past the open spaces overlooking the backyard, I spotted Martha, Kipling, and Whitley running out of the house and past the pool toward the cliff.

Use the cliff for the wake.

I watched, stunned, as they stood side by side at the very edge.

They joined hands. Then they jumped.

———

When I returned downstairs, the Masons looked terrified.

They'd seen what I'd just seen. They believed now that we were all crazy.

I questioned them for another hour. Mr. Mason's cell rang incessantly. So did the landline. A printer wailed in a room upstairs. It was doubtlessly Torchlight Security trying to alert Mr. Mason of the security breach. Holding the gun on him, I said I wanted to know what he and Jim had argued about in his final days alive.

"What are you talking about?" he wailed. "My son and I didn't argue. We never argued."

"Who is S.O.?"

"S.O.?" He looked confused.

"The freshman at Princeton."

He sneered. "It's a colleague's son. What does *he* have to do with— You truly are a troubled young woman, my dear. If you have any sense, you'll untie us all, go back to your dingbat life, and hope—no, *pray*—my fleet of attorneys doesn't decide to spread you on a cracker and serve you as an hors d'oeuvre."

I tried setting a few more verbal traps for Mr. Mason to fall into, telling him Jim had confessed to me all about his financial fraud. I tried to see whether he looked uneasy or afraid. Unsurprisingly, my blind fishing elicited little more than confounded stares and indignant comments from the family that they'd always thought I was a good girl, which made my involvement in this nightmare all the more disappointing.

"There's no need to pretend," I said. "You never liked me. And my *name,* in case you were wondering, is not Jessica, or Antonella, or Barbara, or Blair. It's Beatrice Hartley."

I shot the gun into the ceiling. Instantly, minute cracks fanned out through the plaster, spreading into every corner, then moving down the walls.

"We'll give you any amount of money," whimpered Mrs. Mason, worriedly eyeing the ceiling.

That was when I felt the wake coming on. I set down the gun and left without a word, leaving the Masons staring after me, uncertain, afraid. As I raced past the pool, I saw two police cars inching up the vertiginous drive. One emerged, shouting at me in Greek.

I ran to the edge of the cliff.

As I stood there, the rocks and dirt began to loosen and tumble under me, as if I were the weight of a building, as if I weighed ten million tons. Boulders were pulling out of the ground. I leapt into the air, shouting, just as the ground dropped out. I was plummeting fast, upside down, breath sucking from my lungs. Blue sky spun overhead. I squeezed my eyes shut, trying to quiet my mind as I thought of Wincroft the day I'd first arrived there, though almost immediately something else slipped into my head.

A connection. It was barely remembered, an itch at the back of my brain.

I'd seen it before. Twice.

I tried to ignore it. Spiky grass, bushes, and cypress trees were spinning past me. Screaming, I opened my eyes to catch sight of the entire cliff through the dust, then the house dismantling behind me, a roaring mass of shattered glass and steel and rock coming for me as we all fell toward the sea.

It was too late.

CHAPTER 21

"Hon? You okay?"

Someone was shaking my shoulder.

My eyes opened. I jerked my head up, shouting.

A large woman with red hair and heavy eye makeup stared down at me, visibly freaked out. She was wearing a pink visor emblazoned with a cartoon chicken, a heart on its chest.

"Sorry, hon, you can't sleep here. Do you need me to call someone?"

I looked around. I was in a wooden booth in a cramped fast-food restaurant. People around me were eating fried chicken and fries and drinking milk shakes. The walls were covered with heart wallpaper, photos of couples kissing or holding hands. I blinked at the paper mat in the tray in front of me.

Alonso's Honey Love Fried Chicken. One Taste and You're Lovestruck.

"Where—where am I?" I blurted.

"Newport. I can call your mom for you, hon. Or a shelter?"

I shook my head and lurched to my feet. I realized dazedly that I was wearing my old Darrow uniform: a white blouse, green tartan skirt, black tights, the beat-up black Steve Madden ankle boots that had seen me through four years of school.

"Seriously. I can call someone."

I pressed a hand to my throbbing head, and stumbled away from the woman.

What had happened? Why hadn't I made it to Wincroft? Then I remembered the thought that had slipped into my mind as I'd been falling.

It was what Vida had said, about the ride she'd given Jim.

Some dingy section of town. Dollar stores. A pet store. The parking lot had some man in a chicken costume handing out heart balloons.

"Why did Jim want to go there?" Cannon had asked her.

Maybe he wanted to eat fried chicken and buy a pet iguana? I have no clue.

Fried chicken and hearts had turned up again in the coupon inside Jim's empty case file.

$5 off a bin of Honey Love Fried Chicken. Soul Mate Special!

Finally, it had appeared in an email I'd read in Edgar Mason's in-box. A restaurant owner had been asking for another loan. *I hear your concerns, but it's time to expand on the line of frozen fried chicken dinners with romance-related flavor names.*

248

I staggered past the cashier, blinking at the laminated advertisement on the counter.

ALL-NEW! Honey Love Fried Chicken Organic Chicken Dinners, now available in the frozen-food aisle at a supermarket near you. Try our original flavor! Honey Love Mesquite.

"May I take your order, miss?"

The teenage boy behind the cash register was staring at me. With a fitful smile I shoved open the door and moved outside, steadying myself on a *Newport Daily News* vending machine. After a moment, I realized I was staring at someone wearing a yellow cartoon chicken costume passing out heart-shaped balloons to passersby. The strip mall was exactly as Vida had described it. There was a handful of people loitering around the parking lot.

I leaned down to check the newspaper date.

Friday. May 14. Last year.

I'd managed to get it right. After all, I remembered the night I'd watched Jim drive away with Vida as if it were yesterday.

An elderly man was pushing a shopping cart loaded with shopping bags past me.

"Excuse me?" I asked. "What time is it?"

He checked his watch. "Twelve-forty-nine."

Vida had said she'd dropped Jim off around eight or nine o'clock, which meant I had nearly eight hours to kill until he appeared. I hoped the wake would last that long. If Jim even *did* appear. It was a long shot. It also wasn't the worst connection to make. Whoever had confiscated the papers from Jim's case file at the Warwick police station hadn't looked twice at the coupon, but what if it had been actual evidence? What if it had been stuck in Jim's file because the detectives had been tracking his movements during the final days of his life, and they'd discovered he'd come here to this complex, to this restaurant?

My head was still pounding. I slipped along the covered sidewalk, past a liquor store, a Dollar Mart, a pet store called Man's Best Friend. I had to change my clothes. If Jim did come here, the restaurant was small. He'd spot me immediately. But I had no money to buy clothes. I watched the people come and go, men in faded T-shirts racing into the liquor store, women hauling toddlers, an old woman bent over ninety degrees pushing a cart. When I spotted a smiling woman leaving a stationery store walking a Pomeranian, I approached her.

"Excuse me, ma'am? I'm hoping you might help me. I need a change of clothes—"

She picked up her dog with a horrified look and climbed into her car.

I ended up going into every store at the shopping center, striding brazenly through Employees Only swinging doors into back storerooms, janitors' closets, and cargo unloading areas, to see if I could find some kind of spare uniform. I managed to steal a pair of khakis from Man's Best Friend, a hoodie from a manager's closet inside the Stop & Shop. I asked an old man pulling a pint of Ben & Jerry's out of the freezer if I could have his baseball cap. There must have been something totally desperate, or strange, or otherworldly on my face, because he handed it to me without a word and quickly wheeled his cart away.

I hurried into a Chinese restaurant, Fu Mao Noodle, and changed in the bathroom, grabbing a handful of fortune cookies by the register as I left. I sat eating them on a bench outside the pet store facing the parking lot, a feeling of dread in my chest. *Small opportunities are the beginnings of great enterprises. You are the architect of your fortune. Big journeys begin with a single step.* I had to change benches three times, because every one I sat on, the wood began to splinter and crack under me. One even collapsed in half.

The longer I waited, the more afraid I was that I'd been right to track Jim here, that he'd actually appear. Was he meeting some other girl? What had preoccupied him, been so shameful that he couldn't tell me about it? *What had he been so afraid of?*

At five minutes after eight a beat-up red Nissan pulled into the parking lot, a For Sale sign in the back window. It slinked up to Honey Love Fried Chicken and the passenger door opened. Jim climbed out. Black T-shirt. Jeans.

I could see Vida behind the wheel. Jim entered the restaurant. Vida waited a moment, as if to make sure he wasn't coming back. Then she drove off, exactly as she'd said.

I waited another minute. Then I darted along the covered walkway, ignoring the fact that every column was spotted with black mold.

I peered through the glass door. Jim was standing at the counter, his back to me.

I quickly slipped inside and took a seat at an empty table by the window.

"Call him again," I heard Jim say. He sounded angry.

The woman he was speaking with—the one who'd shaken me awake—was mystified.

"I just did. He said he'd be right out—"

"Call him again."

Frightened, she grabbed the phone, dialing.

"He says he'll be right out."

Seconds later, a Hispanic man with a thick mustache appeared from a back room. He was slight, midforties, a kind face.

"Jim. It's been too long. How are you?"

"We need to talk."

"I'm about to jump on a conference call. Why don't you come back after closing?"

"We're going to talk *now*."

Disconcerted, the man beckoned Jim to follow him. I slid to my feet, watching them disappear through the back door. I waited another minute and headed after them, pausing to hear another door slam before I darted inside. The kitchen was in front of me. Beyond that, there appeared to be a back office. The door was closed, but it looked thin, and hurrying up to it, I could make out the voices easily enough.

"I'LL ASK YOU ONE MORE TIME. WHO IS ESTELLA ORNATO?"

"What are you talking about?"

"ESTELLA ORNATO!"

"She—well, yes, she's my daughter—"

"And?"

"And?"

"Four years old. She died last year. That jog your memory?"

"Jim, please, let's not do this here—"

"DO NOT PICK UP THAT PHONE OR I SWEAR—"

"Jim—"

"FOR ONCE WOULD SOMEONE TELL ME THE TRUTH?"

"Who told you? Where is this coming from?"

"Your brother wrote me a letter. ESTELLA DID NOT DIE IN A CAR ACCIDENT—"

"Jim. *Jim*. Now, hear me out—"

The voices quieted. Abruptly something large smashed against the door.

"TELL ME THE TRUTH OR I SWEAR TO GOD—"

"Excuse me," said a woman. "You're not authorized to be here."

I turned. It was the redhead. She was indignant, hands on her hips.

"I have an interview with your manager," I blurted.

She squinted at me, puzzled. A second deafening crash from inside the office was disturbing enough that she quickly forgot me and went hurrying back to the kitchen to confer, wide-eyed, with the teenager behind the cash register.

"DID MY FATHER PAY FOR THIS? AND THIS? AND THIS?"

There was a high-pitched cry, followed by a moan. Alarmed, I pushed open the door, barging in to see Jim throwing a bag of golf clubs on Mr. Ornato, now cowering on the floor in a fetal position. Jim started kicking him in the stomach.

"Jim," I said.

He turned, startled. The redhead barged past me into the office. "Oh, my God. Mr. Ornato. Are you okay? I'm going to call the police."

"No, no, it's all right." Gasping, he rolled upright, his face sweaty, his hair standing on end. "There's no need. It's just a misunderstanding. Let's get back to work."

Jim wiped his face in the crook of his arm, dimly surveying the demolished room.

Then he began to sob. I stepped toward him and put my arms around him.

"Let's get out of here," I whispered into his ear.

——

We sat on the curb outside Fu Mao Noodle. We watched the cars speed past in the closing day, the sky going blue and black, traffic lights changing from red to green to yellow. We watched small black birds land on telephone wires and fly away, heard the giggling wheels of shopping carts. All that ordinary life—vending machines belching up sodas, stock boys taking cigarette breaks, cars backing in, backing out.

I watched it all as Jim told me everything.

I listened in shock. It made perfect sense—his father's obsession with security, Jim's distraction and moodiness, his decision not to tell anyone, not even me. If he had told me the truth before, would it have changed everything? Would he still be alive?

It had to do with the boating accident. Jim and a friend had taken out a speedboat on Mecox Bay, and they'd crashed into a fisherman in a skiff. When Jim woke up in the hospital, he heard the story from his family and the police—all corroborated by articles in the *East Hampton Star*. No one except Jim was hurt.

The fisherman happened to be none other than Alonso Ornato, the owner of Honey Love Fried Chicken. But this wasn't the whole truth. Alonso had had his four-year-old daughter, Estella, in the boat with him. She was killed on impact.

This should have resulted in a charge of manslaughter against Jim, which meant, as a minor with his father's connections, at most, given that he'd been drinking, he'd have gone to a juvenile facility for a few months, maybe even weeks, and would have been released on probation.

That wasn't good enough for the Masons.

Instead, they decided the incident shouldn't have happened at all. So they decided to erase it from history and redesign the past. They struck a deal with Alonso Ornato. They would take care of him and his family for the rest of their lives—monthly allowances, new houses and cars, Ivy League educations for his other kids, bottomless loans for his business—all in exchange for erasing Estella from the boat that day. She would die in a car accident instead.

Mr. and Mrs. Mason arranged the whole thing with the assistance of Torchlight. They drove Alonso's car into a tree, artfully inflicting the right kind of damage so the police wouldn't ask any questions.

"Wipe the spill off the kitchen counter," said Jim. "Remove all signs of rot. Fumigate the foul odors seeping through the basement. All for me. So I'd suffer no shame. No heartache. No pain. I could continue my life guilt-free, like a diet drink. I could soft-shoe toward my golden destiny." He stared blankly at the pavement. "They don't realize they've destroyed me."

I touched his arm. "That's not true. You can still do something."

You are such a liar, whispered the voice in my head. *What can he do now? He's dead.*

"Like what, Bee? It's gotten inside my head. It's why I've been sick, why I can't write a goddamn decent note anymore. I'll never pick up another instrument. Because their poison is inside me." He hit the side of his head scarily, over and over. I grabbed his hand to make him stop. "They've killed me, don't you see?"

"You should contact a newspaper. Turn them in to the police."

He laughed bitterly. "Sure. I'll turn them in. That'll solve everything. My family will be destroyed. My brothers and sisters will have convicts for parents. The whole world will loathe us. We'll become poster children for all that's depraved. All to placate my guilty conscience. What good would it do? That girl will still be dead. That's the worst part. I can't *do* a goddam thing. I've gone over it and over it."

He began to cry again, head in his hands.

I stared out into the parking lot with a strange feeling of desolation and calm. Jim was right. Even if he were alive and this moment were real, what could he do? Start a foundation in Estella's name? Write a musical about it all? The awful thing was, what the Masons had done was like toxic gas, pervading everything.

We stared ahead in silence, holding hands. It felt as if we'd both removed our glasses, and now we saw for the first time that the world had never been as beautiful as we'd always thought. It was a vision lost, never to come back.

"At least I have you, Beatrice," said Jim, squeezing my hand. "You save me."

But you don't have me. I'm not even alive. Neither are you.

We're ghosts. We're air. We're approximations.

I felt a painful lump in my throat. I wanted to cry, for him, for myself. My legs were growing heavy. It was the wake. I didn't know how much time I had left. It seemed to be moving through me faster now. My head felt as if it were melting.

Jim frowned, surveying me. Perhaps he was wondering how I'd known to follow him here. Then I realized he had noticed the black mildew covering the cracked curb we were sitting on, and the pavement quietly splintering under our shoes.

I lurched to my feet, staring down at him. There was one last thing I had to know.

"You wouldn't, because of this, do something terrible, would you?"

He squinted up at me.

"You wouldn't throw your life away."

"You mean commit suicide?" He looked insulted.

No.

"I have to go."

I turned and took off running, though when he began shouting my name, asking where I was going, I threw back my head and turning, laughing crazily, I shouted, "I love you, Jim Mason. I always have."

I ran out of the parking lot into the six-lane highway. Cars honked. A woman in a passing car rolled down the window and started to scream at me. "Get out of the way! Honey, what are you doing out here? *Honey?*" I could hear Jim calling me, but I stepped in front of a cement truck and closed my eyes.

———

August 30. Wincroft. 6:12 p.m.

"Beatrice? Bee! Beatrice!"

CHAPTER 22

Martha, Kip, and Whitley were waiting for me in the library.

There was no sign of Cannon.

"You made it, Bee," said Whitley, hugging me.

"What happened after we left?" asked Kipling.

I didn't answer. Instead, I slipped past them, heading straight to an upstairs bedroom. Minutes later, returning downstairs, my suspicions confirmed—I'd found what I'd been looking for—I explained where I'd gone. I told them about the connection I'd made between the man in the chicken costume handing out heart balloons, whom Vida had mentioned, the Honey Love fried chicken coupon left in Jim's case file, and the email in Edgar Mason's in-box.

I told them about Estella Ornato.

No one said a word for a long time. Whitley opened her laptop and Googled the name, then read aloud the only information that appeared about Estella's death, a four-sentence mention in the *South Shore Sentinel*.

"'Officials have released the name of a four-year-old child killed Wednesday night in a car accident in Water Mill,'" she read.

"S.O.," I said to Martha. "I think it's Alonso Ornato's son."

Sure enough, a search of *Ornato* and *Princeton* turned up a Facebook page belonging to Sebastian Ornato, about to start his sophomore year. On his page there was a photograph of him sitting in Firestone Library wearing a Princeton sweatshirt, grinning and making a goofy peace sign.

"Poor kid thinks he got into Princeton on his own steam," said Kipling.

"I can't believe it," said Whitley, solemn. "I knew Jim's family was capable of anything. But erasing the existence of an *entire person*? Designing a new death that's more elegant and acceptable to all involved? And getting away with it?"

"It proves Jim's suicide, doesn't it?" suggested Kipling, taking a deep breath. "Jim probably felt so alone. Lost. So he rode his bike out to Vulcan Quarry and jumped."

"I don't think so," I said.

They turned to me in surprise. I told them what Jim had said in the parking lot.

"Well, if it wasn't suicide," said Whitley, "then what happened?"

I dug in my pocket and pulled out the bumblebee pin, placing it on the coffee table.

Kip widened his eyes. "What is that, child?"

"The gift Jim bought me freshman year."

"Oh, that's right," said Whitley.

"Didn't someone steal it from you?" asked Martha.

I nodded. "I just found it upstairs in Whitley's jewelry case."

Wit stared at me, her face pale.

"You stole it from me. I know you did. It was one of your notorious thefts. Wasn't it?"

"Bee, I'm so sorry—"

"You never think. Little do you know how your most haphazard gestures inflict such pain. It hurts to be your friend. It always has. But I still love you."

Ignoring Wit's astonished face, I went on to explain how I'd been stuck in the neck with the pin moments before the wake, which had sent me plunging back into the past with thoughts of Jim.

"I didn't do it, Bee," said Whitley. "I swear."

"I know. It was Cannon."

Everyone gaped at me.

"He knew you'd taken it, so he stole it out of your jewelry case the first night we changed the wake. He wanted to throw me off track, send the rest of you into a state of perpetual limbo. He doesn't want us to find out what happened to Jim. He doesn't want to ever leave the Neverworld."

"You think he had something to do with Jim's death?" asked Martha.

"I don't know yet."

"Bee does have a point," said Kipling with a dubious expression. "Cannon knows if anything goes wrong he's supposed to meet us here. So where the hell is he?"

"He's hiding somewhere in the past or the future," I said. "There's really only one way to get to the bottom of what happened to Jim."

No one spoke for a minute, all of us doubtlessly thinking the same thing.

"No," said Martha, shaking her head. "No. It's out of the question, Bee. *No.*"

"It's not as dangerous as you think," I said.

"Yes, it *is.*"

"I did it already. I went back even farther, five years by accident. The crazy thing about the past is that you never meet yourself. There are no doubles. If you arrive there, your past self exits on cue to make room for you."

Martha looked furious. "How long are your wakes now?"

I shrugged.

"Ours are only *four hours.*" She shook her head. "They're getting shorter and shorter. And it's getting worse. Every time we go into the past or future, it makes the possibility of a unanimous vote even more impossible. *Don't you get it?*"

She snapped this at me so furiously—eyes bulging, glasses going crooked on the end of her nose—I could only stare back in shock. We all did.

She fell silent, seemingly embarrassed by her outburst.

Kipling turned to me. "How long is your wake now?"

"Six hours?"

"It's enough time to try, isn't it?"

Martha said nothing, staring sullenly at the floor.

"If we arrive at Vulcanation at one in the morning," I said, "even if your wake is four hours, or three, I'm almost positive it will give us enough time to see what happened to Jim."

With a pang of queasiness I thought back to his last text. Sent at 11:29 p.m.

I'm going to the quarry. Meet me.

They still didn't know about the texts from Jim. I wasn't going to tell them.

"Let's do it," said Whitley.

As the rest of us talked about the logistics of changing the wake, Martha stayed silent, slumped way down in the couch cushions, her expression a mixture of resentment and hopelessness. It appeared my suggestion of venturing once and for all to Vulcan Quarry was flying in the face of her grand plan. It had made her lose control of the group, though what she was so anxious about, and what this meant for the vote, I could only imagine.

CHAPTER 23

When I woke I was staring at a clear night sky filled with stars, the deafening screech of crickets in my ears. I was lying in thick grass, the long, razorlike blades slicing my bare arms. I was wearing my Darrow uniform. I lifted my head, realizing with a rush of relief that I was outside the quarry, though almost immediately relief gave way to suffocating dread.

The rusted chain-link fence was only a few feet away. I checked my watch.

It was 1:02 a.m.

I crawled to my feet, dizzy, and looked around.

There was no sign of anyone.

I groped my way along the fence, kicking back the grass, the gnarled coils of brambles sharp as barbed wire. Ahead I could see the rusted yellow sign: NO TRESPASSING. Somewhere near was the hole we'd always used. I bent down, forcing aside the weeds, fumbling along the ground. I found the hole and crawled through.

Far ahead, suspended in the sky, I could see the Foreman's Lookout. I shivered, trying to ignore the nausea rising in my throat. The old wood tower looked like an abandoned space station in the dark.

"Bee!" hissed a voice behind me.

I whipped around. Whitley was waving at me from the other side of the fence. Kipling was behind her, his head barely visible above the ocean of grass. I directed them toward the opening, and within seconds they were beside me.

"Where's Martha?" I asked.

"Missing," said Kipling, scrambling to his feet.

"What?"

"She bailed."

"One second she was there," said Whitley, shaking her head. "The next, nowhere."

"She never wanted to come," said Kipling. "So she *didn't*."

We eyed each other, unsettled at the thought. Where had she gone? Was she hiding out like Cannon somewhere in the past or future, terrified of what we were about to discover?

There were so many questions, but there was no time to figure them out. Not now.

"We need a hiding place," I whispered. "There's that cement pipe in the grass next to the entry to the mining shafts. We could stay there."

Whitley frowned. "What about the old mapping office right beside the road?"

I shook my head. "Too obvious. Jim might see us. Then we'll have interfered with the past, and we won't find out what actually happened."

"Cement pipe it is," said Kipling, with a cryptic grin.

We took off, fighting our way through the grass to reach the quarry road. Little was left of it, apart from bits of rock and gravel, and the grass there was only knee-high. As we headed down the path, I noticed after a minute that Kipling was lagging far behind, an oddly bleak look on his face. When he saw I was waiting for him, he glanced up, feigning a smile.

"Are you all right?" I asked.

"Oh, *sure,* child. Splendid. It isn't every day I get to watch one of my friends get murdered."

I put my arm around him for reassurance, pulling him beside me as we trudged on, fighting back the fronds, the wail of the crickets so deafening, it sounded like a million knives being sharpened in my ears. Yet the question blinked glaringly in my mind: *How did he know Jim was murdered?* He'd blurted it without thinking.

As if he *knew.*

As we walked on, Kipling seemed unconcerned about his disclosure, which made me wonder if it had actually been one. Did he know something? Or was he only giving voice to his suspicion that someone came out here tonight to kill Jim?

Within minutes we had reached the center of Vulcanation, where the old quarry road made an elongated U past the mapping office, the outhouses, the Foreman's Lookout. The Lookout was held aloft by four massive steel legs reinforced with crisscrossing beams, the wood ladder stretching up the center like an old, arthritic backbone. There were a few more structures dotting the road—lodging for the miners, little more than heaps of rotten pine logs—and a collapsed crane, which looked like the remains of a great blue whale.

The three of us paused, looking around, apprehensive. It was totally overgrown and wild, more than I remembered. The tempo of the crickets' screeching began to quicken as if it were the pulse of the night itself, terrified, on edge.

There didn't appear to be anyone here.

Not Jim. Not anyone.

Suddenly, a wave of nausea came over me, and I was sick all over the ground.

"Poor Bee," said Whitley, brushing away the hair stuck to my cheek. "Maybe we should forget all this and go back."

I shook my head. "I'll be fine."

Ignoring her worried glance, I stepped past her into the grass. It took a few minutes for us to find the cement pipe, some thirty feet long, only a few feet from the edge of the quarry. As I stepped toward the precipice, I was afraid the ground would start to crumble underneath me, but it held. I stared out, my chest tightening from the shock of how abruptly the ground gave way to total nothingness.

It was a three-hundred-foot drop, the crater stretching out, a stadium of rock, a vast sky littered with stars, and far below the lake, dark water glistening in the moonlight.

"Sister Bee," whispered Kip, stepping up beside me. "I have a funny feeling death will be like this."

His voice, eerily flat, sent a surge of fear through me. I wondered numbly if he was about to push me in.

"It'll feel like falling, but on and on, never stopping. You know?"

He was staring at me with a thin little smile. I swallowed, barely able to breathe.

"Look," said Whitley.

Turning, I saw she was leaning against the pipe, pointing at something. High in the wooden tower of the Lookout, a tiny green light was visible in a window. It belonged to the oil lamp some student had smuggled up there years earlier.

None of us spoke. The conclusion was obvious: Someone had been up there. Or they were up there now.

"I'll go see who it is," said Whitley.

"No," I said.

"Why not? I want to see if it's Jim—"

"He'll *see* you. If you interfere, we won't know what really happened—"

"Then let me just see if I can find his bike."

"Don't." I grabbed her arm.

"Bee, what's the matter with— *Stop* it!"

She yanked it loose, about to take off, but suddenly the sound of someone yards away fighting a path through the brush made her stop dead.

None of us moved as we watched the top of a dark head bobbing toward us.

It was Jim. A wave of horror choked me.

The grass trembled and shook. Martha stepped out.

We gaped at her. Her neon-blue hair was gone. She was her old self from Darrow, dark hair in a careless ponytail, oversized Oxford shirt.

"What hole did you just crawl out of?" asked Kipling.

"We thought you ditched us," said Wit.

"Yeah. Sorry about that." She adjusted her glasses. "For *some* reason—I think it was because I was thinking of the map of the entire quarry before the wake—I ended up waking not by the south fence with you guys, but by the *east* fence behind the Pancake House. I had to hike the mile along the quarry road to get here." She took a deep breath. "Seen anything yet?"

"Only that light," said Whitley, indicating the Foreman's Lookout.

Martha squinted up at it. She seemed unsurprised.

"Did you see anyone along the road?" I asked her.

She shook her head.

It was then that I noticed she was drenched in sweat. Her shirt clung to her. Her hair was plastered to her forehead. Walking along the quarry road wouldn't have exerted her to that extent. She was lying.

Noticing my stare, she smiled thinly and slipped past me to the pipe, wiping her forehead.

"Now what?" she whispered.

"Now we wait and see," I said, moving beside her.

—

269

The car arrived at one-thirty.

We heard it coming before we saw it. A loose hubcap. Radio blaring. The four of us fell silent, standing shoulder to shoulder along the pipe. Gold headlights swept across the grass. Then a red Nissan slowly rounded the quarry road, bouncing and clanging along the uneven ground before stopping right beside the Foreman's Lookout. I couldn't see who was driving, though I could make out a For Sale sign in the back window.

"Vida Joshua?" whispered Whitley, incredulous.

The engine idled, white moths whirling in the headlights. The radio switched off. There was a moment of silence. Then the driver's door opened, and someone climbed out.

When I saw who it was, chills electrocuted my spine.

Cannon.

He dressed in jeans, his old gray hacker's hoodie. He fought through the grass and disappeared into the old mapping office, a sagging shed with a tin roof, though after a minute he reemerged, agitated. He clambered back to the car, texted someone, waited for a response, crossing and uncrossing his arms. As I watched him, I wondered how Cannon of all people had come to be driving Mr. Joshua's car, a car that usually remained parked behind the music school when Vida wasn't using it. Then I remembered how he and Whitley had always stolen things around campus. He had stolen the car to drive out here to meet someone.

"Hello?" Cannon called. "Anybody here?"

No one answered.

He moved to the front of the car and sat on the hood, staring meditatively into the headlights. Another ten minutes, and he was furious. He looked around, scowling, then seemed to give up and climbed behind the wheel, slamming the door, radio blasting heavy metal. He tried to pull away, but the wheels were caught in the grass, the tires spinning. He put the car in reverse, and it bumped backward a few feet. He hit the gas harder and the car roared back, hitting something. Cannon inched the car forward, then reversed again. The car jerked, smashing whatever it was, bouncing over it and stalling.

Cannon climbed out. He crouched down to check under the tires.

He stood up immediately. Then he bent down again. Then he stood up.

He bent down a third time.

"No. No. No. No. *No.*"

Cannon threw his head back and began to howl.

"No. No. No."

Bewildered, I glanced over at Martha, Kipling, and Whitley watching the scene in silence beside me. They seemed as puzzled as I was.

Muttering something, Cannon bent down once more, seemingly trying to wrench whatever he had run over out from under the tires. For minutes, all we could see were shaking grasses.

When he stood up again, he was making a strange noise, as if he was crying. That was when I caught sight of what was in his hand.

A tweed cap. It was Jim's.

No. This can't be happening.

Cannon was back behind the wheel. After a few tries, he

managed to back out, doing a three-point turn. He was about to drive away, it seemed, only he had second thoughts, because the car jolted to a halt and he climbed out again.

He stood frozen for a moment, as if in a trance.

Then he stepped over to what he had pulled out from under the wheels; what I could see now in a rush of disbelief, of horror, as I scrambled on top of the pipe for a better look, was no log. It was Jim, my Jim, lying on his side. His jeans were streaked with blood. Cannon was cradling Jim's head in his lap. Cannon bent over him, whispering something, and then he was on his feet again, on the phone.

"Call me. I need you to come. I need you to help me. *Now.* Please call me back. Please. Please."

He said it over and over, his voice a high-pitched whine. It was terrible to witness. Cannon's resolute action, his ease with problem-solving, his unflappable tenaciousness—all of which had come to define him in my mind the way waves define the ocean, clouds the sky—it was gone now. He was a different person.

"I need you. I need you now. Please come. *Please.*"

Whoever he was calling, no one answered. Cannon climbed into the driver's seat again, sitting in pitch darkness, engine running, radio on.

Fifteen minutes later, when he finally emerged, he had a plan. He was his old self, the fixer. He grabbed Jim's ankles and began to pull him brutally through the grass, cursing as Jim lost a loafer, crying out in disbelief, in despair, before wiping his face in the crook of his arm and continuing on.

He reached the quarry's edge. It was yards away from where we were watching.

He threw Jim into the quarry without saying a prayer, without hesitation.

There was the hushed whir of the body falling, knocking against rocks, and then nothing, the muted splash of Jim hitting the water lost in the shriek of crickets.

Cannon stared after him, immobile, his blank face hollowed by shadows.

I wondered if he was considering going in with Jim, ending it all, right then and there.

Instead, he turned with an empty stare, climbed into the car, and drove off.

—————

It was a moment before any of us could move.

I was standing on top of the pipe in the dark, my heart pounding, my mind short-circuiting. Too late, I realized the cement was cracking under my feet. Abruptly, with an angry belch, the entire thing collapsed, Martha and the others jumping back into the grass as I was sent plummeting into the pile of rubble.

Wit helped me, gasping, to my feet.

"What the hell was that? Are you okay?"

I nodded, climbing out, dusting myself off.

We stood silently in a circle for a moment, eyeing each other in shock.

"But who did Cannon call?" whispered Wit with a hint of indignation. "Because it wasn't me. I never knew any of this."

"He called Kipling," said Martha.

We turned to Kip. He eyed us stiffly, guiltily, his arms held at odd angles at his side.

"She's right," he whispered. "The devil called, and I answered."

He said it flatly, with a hint of relief, and I remembered with a shiver of shock the meaningful glance I'd seen Kip exchange with Cannon back in the Wincroft library, when they were confessing how Kipling had made it through Darrow. They hadn't been thinking about the arrangement Cannon had made, or the cheating. They'd been thinking about this very night, and the secret they kept.

"I helped him throw Jim's body into the quarry," said Kipling.

We stared at him.

"How can that be?" asked Whitley. "We didn't *see* you."

"Chapter Thirty-Nine, *The Bend*," whispered Martha. "You never run into yourself in the past or the future."

Kipling nodded. "I had to come here. I had to watch. I had to know, once and for all, if it had been my idea to throw Jim into the lake, or Cannon's. Would it happen if I wasn't a part of it? I had to know who was the bad one, and who was worse."

"Did Cannon tell you why he had come here?" Martha asked, and bit her lip.

"He did."

"What did he say?"

Kipling smiled demurely. "Why don't you ask her?" He nodded at Whitley.

She glared at him, livid. For a moment, I thought she was about to start screaming, unleashing one of her rages. Instead, she sighed.

"Cannon was my best customer," she said.

"What are you talking about?" I whispered.

"Adderall. The White Rabbit gave him his boundless supply. He popped them like Tic-Tacs. He still does."

"All that time during school, he never knew you were the White Rabbit?" asked Martha.

Wit shook her head. "Not until Vida. I was too scared to tell him."

I thought back to Cannon's reaction when he'd learned Wit was the White Rabbit. He had been livid. Now I understood why. It was because she had known his secret all along, and had never told him hers.

"So let me get this straight," said Martha. "On the night Jim died, Cannon called the White Rabbit for another stash of Adderall, and you sent him out here."

Whitley nodded, sullen.

"Why here?"

Wit shook her head. "Jim had found me out a few weeks before. He was watching me constantly, telling me I had to stop. I was afraid to do a drop on campus. So I decided out here was perfect. It was remote. I texted Cannon as the White Rabbit, telling him he could find his supply inside a desk in the mapping office. Only I couldn't make it out here in time. I got caught talking to Mrs. Lapinetti about my Italian final. I raced back to the quarry and did the drop, but I had no further contact that night from Cannon."

"When did you make it back here?" asked Martha.

"It was three in the morning. I didn't see anything or anyone, I swear to God."

"You must have just missed them." Martha checked her watch. "When Jim turned up dead at the quarry, you must have suspected Cannon. After all, you knew he'd come out here."

Wit nodded. "But I knew he'd never willingly hurt Jim."

Martha turned, staring up at the Foreman's Lookout.

"So the only question now is . . ."

She fell silent, nibbling a fingernail.

"What?" prompted Kipling.

"How did Jim appear so suddenly under that car?"

She turned on her heel, resolved.

"Come," she ordered.

Beckoning us to follow her, she vanished into the grass.

CHAPTER 24

When we caught up to Martha, she was crouching underneath the Foreman's Lookout. Staring overhead, I saw in astonishment that the ladder to climb up was missing. I realized then that what remained of it was strewn all over the ground.

"Incredible."

Martha gasped in shock over some revelation, then stood up, shaking her head.

"It's really the most impossible sequence of events."

"What?" asked Kipling.

"Momma Greer was right."

"About?"

"The freak possible."

Martha rolled one of the pieces of wood under her sneaker, then gazed up at the landing suspended high over our heads.

"Poor Jim."

She looked at me, and instantly I felt chills inching up my arms. What was she aiming at? What was she trying to do? It was dark, but her eyes sparkled behind her glasses, alert, alive.

"It happened right here," she said. "Jim was undone over Beatrice confronting him about his lie, the night he went off with Vida. He was also distraught over Estella Ornato. His perfect life had fallen down around him, so he escaped here, as he often did, to be alone, to write music. He started to climb up to the Foreman's Lookout, but the ladder gave out. He managed to grab a few supporting beams, trying to save himself, but they didn't hold."

Martha bent down to inspect a piece of the wood, showing us that the underside was completely rotten.

"He fell. It was a considerable distance, five, six stories, a drop that would have killed most people. Yet Jim survived."

"How?" I whispered.

"He was drunk. It's why drunk drivers survive car accidents. Drunks don't tense up on impact. They relax. That saves their lives. He was unconscious for an hour. Maybe two. Then he woke up." She squinted out at the quarry road. "He must have heard the car, or seen the headlights. Or maybe he was just trying to get to his bike."

Martha hurried to the other side of the road and dragged Jim's bike out of the grass, throwing it at our feet with the flair of a magician whisking a rabbit from a hat.

"He crawled from here to here." She pointed toward the road. "That's eight, ten feet? He was trying to get help. At that point, Cannon had climbed behind the wheel again. If Jim called out, it was lost in the crickets, the engine, the radio. We couldn't hear a thing, or see much in the dark. Neither did Cannon. Cannon, assuming the White Rabbit stood him up, has to get back to school, drive the car back before Moses returns to the gatehouse after his AA meeting. Frustrated, he puts the car in reverse, hitting Jim. He realizes what's happened, and he goes crazy. He calls Kipling, who is in his debt. Kipling arrives, and together they decide that the only way out of this unimaginable turn of events is to throw Jim into the quarry and pray the police think suicide."

Kipling nodded. "We hoped the cops wouldn't notice the difference between injuries sustained from a car hitting you and injuries from a three-hundred-foot fall."

"The police probably would have looked closer," said Martha, "if not for the Masons. They were worried the business about Estella Ornato was about to be exposed. They didn't know what Jim had told people. Given the level of his anger, they probably weren't so sure Jim *didn't* commit suicide, having learned the truth about what they'd done. What *he* had done. So they stayed silent. And probably applied some pressure on that little police station. Whatever other pieces of evidence the cops unearthed—Jim's visit to Honey Love Fried Chicken, Vida's tip-off about Shrieks being the real White Rabbit, cell phone records? They stopped pursuing it."

"The Masons confiscated the contents of Jim's case file, don't forget," said Kipling.

"Exactly."

"But there's blood here," whispered Whitley. She was using the light on her cell to illuminate the area where the Nissan had been parked. "It wouldn't take much effort for police to see that something brutal had happened right here."

"We cleaned it up," said Kipling. "I noticed the blood, and we spent an hour tearing up the grass with bloodstains. I shoved it into my backpack and spent more time at school flushing it down the toilet."

"There you have it," said Martha. "The freak possible."

There was nothing to say, nothing to do except to consider the strange history Martha had just related like a professor illuminating to her students some new law of gravity. For a while, I was aware of nothing but my own shallow breathing, and the orchestra of crickets, and the night, gasping and alive all around us.

Never had I imagined a truth like this.

"It's too extraordinary," whispered Whitley, crossing her arms, shivering. "When you think about it, we all killed Jim. I sent Cannon here. And Cannon hit Jim with the car. And Kipling helped him cover it up. All of us are guilty, right? All of us except Martha and Beatrice. You're the good ones."

"That's not true," I blurted, tears burning my eyes, a lump in my throat.

"It's time to get out of here."

Martha whispered this, frowning thoughtfully as she stared overhead. Bewildered, none of us moved. Then she was pushing us and I realized, stunned, looking up, that without even being aware of it, I'd been standing too close to one of the tower's steel legs, because the entire thing was tottering. The wood was groaning and splintering.

Suddenly, with a thunderous moan of metal and glass, the entire Lookout was tipping over, rusted nails and screws and wooden beams raining down on us as we took off across the quarry road. I threw myself into the wall of grass, fighting back blades as they slapped and whipped my face. I ducked and covered my head as the entire structure collapsed around me with a roar, Kipling and Whitley shouting somewhere behind me. I felt myself tossed forward.

When I opened my eyes, I was on my stomach, the immense pressure of the ending wake pressing against my legs. I managed to heave myself onto my back, blinking up at the sky.

I heard voices, and then Martha and the others were bending over me.

"She's at the end of her wake," said Martha. "We don't have much time. We have to find Cannon."

"I think I know where he is," said Whitley, her face grave.

When she told us the location, no one spoke. Of all possible places in space and time, this one seemed the most frightening, and the most impossible.

"No," said Martha. "No way. It's too risky for Bee." She was helping me to my feet, pulling me toward the edge of the quarry. "We should go back to Wincroft."

"We need Cannon for the vote," I said. "I'll go. I'll get him and bring him back."

Martha looked anxious. But there wasn't time to argue. I could feel the wake traveling up my neck. I knew what to do. I stared down at the quarry and the lake, so far below.

This was the same journey Jim had made. My Jim.

"I'll see you there," I whispered.

They were watching me, afraid, but there was no time and nothing to say to reassure them. I squeezed their hands, one by one.

Then I jumped.

CHAPTER 25

When I opened my eyes, I was submerged in freezing water.

Milky blue liquid floated before my eyes. I kicked, barely able to feel my legs. I couldn't tell which way was the surface. My lungs throbbing in pain, I blew bubbles, watching dimly as they floated in the opposite direction of where I'd thought to go. I kicked after them into murky darkness, the water growing icier, shadowed fish circling me, their cold, gelatinous skin brushing my toes and fingertips.

I wanted to scream.

I kicked again. Suddenly, I breached the lake's surface, gulping in the icy air.

I looked around. Dense white fog swirled everywhere, chalky and crystalline. A thin layer of ice on the pond's surface splintered around my shoulders. I dog-paddled in a circle, groping for something to hold on to, but there was nothing. It was impossible to see more than a foot ahead. Dead white tree trunks rose out of the water around me, retreating into the whiteness overhead.

It was where Whitley had told us to go. Blue Pond, Cannon's Birdcage, at 3:33 p.m. on his birthday last year. It was the real-life place in the photo inside the bug Cannon had discovered in Apple's operating system sophomore year at Darrow. It was a dreamlike setting of chalky mist, and thin black Japanese larch and silver birch trees growing straight out of an icy blue lake.

There was nothing else here.

"Cannon?"

My voice, hoarse and unsteady, ventured only a few feet in front of me before giving up. My legs were so frozen, they felt unattached to me. The cold was like knives in my back.

"Cannon!"

A boat motor roared behind me. Startled, I turned to see the paint-chipped bow of a skiff blasting out of the fog, heading straight toward me. I caught a glimpse of faded blue words, *Little Bird,* Cannon hunched over the motor, his bearded face red, his hair long and matted. The boat hit my head. White pain exploded through my skull. The water silenced my shocked scream as I was dragged under.

Everything went black.

——

When I opened my eyes again, I was submerged in freezing water.

It was silent.

Blue water clouded my eyes. I could see debris floating around me, seaweed, bits of shell, and mud. Long, dark fish with overbites and bulging eyes drifted around me. They looked dead until I touched one and it shot into the shadows.

I wasn't in pain, apart from my lungs. I blew bubbles, kicking after them. Within seconds I had blasted through the surface, gasping.

It was the exact same scene, the Blue Pond, Cannon's Bird-cage.

A motor grunted. I whipped around to see the skiff heading for me again.

I dove back down into the water, madly kicking through the explosion of bubbles as the boat missed my head by inches. My left foot burst with pain as the propeller's blade sliced it. When I resurfaced, Cannon had circled the boat around and was aiming for me again.

I dove under again, swimming away a few feet before coming up for air.

"Cannon, please, just wait a minute—"

"You shouldn't have come here, Beatrice."

"We need to talk."

"There's nothing to say."

"What about Jim?"

He scowled at the mention of the name, killing the engine.

"Cannon. Please. I just want to talk to you."

I held out my hand.

He leaned over the boat, smiling reluctantly, extending his hand to help me aboard. As I grabbed it, however, he pulled an

284

oar out and struck me with it on the side of the head, my vision exploding into whiteness.

I screamed. I could feel my body sprawling, coming apart, cold water in my mouth, an oar on my back as he pushed me down.

No matter how hard I fought, that oar remained on my shoulders, keeping me underwater.

He was drowning me.

There was no reasoning with Cannon anymore.

The Neverworld had driven him mad.

———

When I opened my eyes again, I was submerged in freezing water.

The quiet was deafening.

I realized with a stab of panic exactly what was happening: I was reliving the same wake over and over again. Cannon was killing me, whereupon I remained dead until I was pulled back to the wake. How long did it last? An hour? Minutes?

I could hardly think. I was nauseous with fear. I had to stay calm. Trying to ignore the pain in my lungs, I kept swimming. Blinking up at the surface, I could see the underside of Cannon's boat amid large chunks of ice. He was hiding between the trees, waiting. I dove deeper, ignoring the dark fish with their flaking skin shooting around my legs. When I couldn't hold my breath any longer, I swam to the surface, trying not to make noise as I gulped down air.

Cannon's boat was yards away. He didn't see me. He was standing in the skiff, looking around.

"Beatrice!" he called. His voice sounded calm, even friendly. "You out here?"

I ducked back under and swam away, the water growing dark and murky, the rotten roots of underwater trees, yellowed and tangled, wafting what looked like chimney soot. I could no longer feel my feet or hands. My thoughts were cloudy and strange. As I swam past the debris of a sunken skiff, the faded words *Little Bird* barely visible, I felt the pull of an undertow. I tried to fight it, but the current was too powerful. As soon as I recognized the deep thundering drone of a waterfall, it was too late; I was plunging through the air. Spray blasted me like a fire hose. Rocks knocked my head and scraped my hands, branches clawing my face. White trees. Blue sky. They flipped over me and under me. I kept waiting to hit the ground, for it all to go black, but the end refused to come.

I was falling, falling for what felt like an hour, every inch of my body freezing, stiffening.

Then I hit a boulder. Life left me like light from a bulb with the flip of a switch.

——

When I opened my eyes, I was submerged in freezing water.

How many times had I been here before? Four times? Four million?

Fish swirled around me like murderous thoughts. I swam into them and they scattered.

I floated deep under the water until I spotted his boat. The water was getting colder. A thin layer of ice was forming on the surface, growing thicker by the minute. I could see Cannon, searching for me. Grabbing a submerged piece of driftwood, I swam directly underneath the hull, clinging there, breathing through a hole in the ice around the boat's edge. I yanked off my pink T-shirt and let it drift to the other side. Cannon, thinking it was me, bent over to pull it out, and as he did, I surfaced and jammed the wood in his back as hard as I could. He cried out in surprise, pitching forward, losing his balance, somersaulting through the ice. I climbed into the boat, nearly capsizing it. I yanked the cord to start the engine. I pried off Cannon's hands gripping the side and veered the boat away.

"Beatrice!" he howled, waving at me. "Come back!"

I ignored him. His old gray hoodie and a red flannel blanket were folded up around a thermos in the hull. I yanked on the sweater, wrapped the blanket around my shoulders. I unscrewed the thermos and drank. It was tea, so hot it scalded my mouth.

I drove on. It was impossible to see where I was going. The fog disclosed only inches of the world at a time. Blue water, driftwood, blackened tree trunks—they appeared suddenly, ramming the sides of the boat, causing the engine to stall. After a while I could hear the deafening roar of the waterfall and Cannon far behind me. He was crying.

"I'm freezing. I'm going to die here. Help me, Beatrice."

I wasn't sure how far I'd gone when I spotted a coil of long blond hair under the ice, ice at least three inches thick. I smashed it with the oar, realizing in shock that it was Whitley floating there. She was barely conscious. A few feet away, trapped under the ice, were Martha and Kipling.

One by one, I heaved them into the boat. They were half dead, heads lolling. I placed them in the stern, pulled off their boots and jeans and T-shirts, pulled the blanket over their legs to get them warm, poured tea into their mouths.

Soon they showed signs of life.

"What is happening?" asked Martha.

I told her. She asked to see Cannon, so I turned the boat back, steering between the trees until we stumbled upon him. He was clinging to a trunk, so much ice encrusting his beard it was completely white.

He was dead. His lips were blue. He had pulled off all his clothes.

"His wake must be years if his hair is this long," whispered Martha, touching a frozen strand. She turned to me. "We have to keep at this, but next time, keep him alive. It's up to you, Bee. We don't arrive in time. So get control of the boat, restrain him, but keep him alive until we get here. Then we can vote."

Cannon's not himself anymore. How can he vote?

I wanted to ask this, only I realized as the boat jerked backward suddenly that we were getting pulled into the waterfall.

I grabbed the oar, trying to fight it. Martha grabbed the other paddle. Whitley tried to grab hold of passing tree trunks to stop us. Kipling could only stare out at the fog, petrified. It was futile, of course. In less than a minute, the skiff was swinging into the throes of the current, water pounding us. We were rocketing past boulders, ricocheting against trees, overturning into the white-out. The last thing I saw was Whitley reaching out to try to grab my hand as the boat fell out from under us and we fell.

———

The vote. The vote. *The vote*.

How long did it all go on? The fight for the skiff. Cannon's rescue. Binding his ankles and wrists. Hauling my friends out of the ice.

I did it over and over again, in the freezing cold, trying not to drown.

I tried different tactics every time. Cannon might have been half mad, but he was on to me. He was a strange, terrifying foe, at times vicious, other times childlike. He was the worst person to have to capture alive, because I knew him from before. There were times when he was his old self again, funny and kind and sensitive, vocal about wanting to help me, to do everything in his power to make it better. Inevitably, though, he'd cast this persona off like a Halloween costume, revealing someone upended by rage and regret. I understood then that Cannon had always lived his life with his future glory in mind, that every moment of his every day and every act of kindness had been because he was expecting that at some future date he would be somebody at last. Now that he had no future, he didn't know how to exist.

He'd shout his grievances into the fog.

"I was duped. Swindled. First there was the nightmare of Jim. And now this? *Are you kidding me?* It isn't supposed to be like this. I'm supposed to grow up! I'm supposed to have another seventy years! I never made an impression. It's like I was never even here. Was I here? Was I even here, Beatrice? *Beatrice!* Where are you?"

Sometimes, when Cannon gave me trouble, I was too late freeing the others from the ice. When I found them they were all dead except Martha. She was always semiconscious, deliriously whispering the same two words over and over again.

It's you.

After a while, I had a map of the entire Blue Lake in my head like a blind man who's memorized every inch of his neighborhood. I knew where every dead tree stood, where every boulder sat, when every spray of water would firework over the rocks into oblivion.

The chance for the vote inched closer. Faster and faster I restrained Cannon. This had as much to do with his increasing fatigue, his resignation, as with my speed and resolve. I bound his hands and ankles with a yellow vine ripped from the bottom of the lake, pulling him up into the boat, leaving him sulking in the bow. Faster and faster I revived the others.

The remainder of my wake was eleven minutes. Eleven minutes between the time they were warm and under the blanket and the moment I rigged the boat to the trees so we wouldn't plunge into the waterfall. Eleven minutes to vote.

"I'm not voting," Cannon always said.

"Yes you are," said Whitley.

"No."

"Then you'll drown here."

He laughed. I'd grown used to his mad cackle by then, but it still scared the others.

"Drowning? You think I'm scared of *drowning*? Drowning for me is shaking a hand. It's saying 'Have a nice day!' It's saying 'Would you like an Egg McMuffin with those hotcakes?' It's saying 'Welcome to Home Depot, can I help you select a Weedwacker?'"

"Please stop," whispered Whitley, trying not to cry.

The vote. The vote. *The vote.*

We had no pen and no paper. I pried a piece of splintered wood off the skiff's bottom boards and we used that to cut the first initial of our chosen survivor into our palms.

Over time, strange things began to happen in those eleven minutes. The dead trees began to topple and crash into the water, creating waves that surged and flooded the boat. The fog retreated, revealing a gray sky, clouds roiling like potion in a witch's cauldron. Swarms of red insects like the ones Martha had drawn boomeranged around us like tiny squalls of rain, emitting a high-pitched hum, colliding with our foreheads and ears and getting tangled in our hair, making us scream. A single fat fly appeared too, buzzing around our heads. We all knew it was Pete, the imaginary friend who'd lived inside Cannon's boyhood computer, the one he'd told us about. Ice encrusted our hair and eyelashes. It thundered and snowed and hailed. In the eleventh minute, the skiff even began to disintegrate under us, blue water seeping up between the beams until the wood began to blacken and crumble to mud.

I understood what was happening, though I didn't say a

word. No one did. It was the decision, the slow settling in on the single name. It was the death of our dreams, our youth, of possibility. There had always been hope here in the Neverworld, no matter how terrifying things got.

Now even that was disappearing.

Cannon ignored our entreaties to vote. He stayed slumped against the side of the boat, staring out, singing "Just Like Heaven" by the Cure under his breath, repeating the phrase "You, soft and lonely" over and over again.

Then, one wake, he actually snatched the wood from Kipling, and gnashing his teeth in frustration, he too carved what appeared to be someone's initials into his hand. He did it rashly, blood oozing between his fingers as he collapsed back, staring out, exhausted.

That was when Whitley sat up, pointing into the fog.

It was the Keeper. He was rowing a boat toward us, wearing his dark suit and tie. He maneuvered alongside us. In spite of the hail, his boat jerking and bobbing against ours, the spray of water, he was remarkably dry.

"Congratulations," he shouted, his voice scarcely audible over the thunder. "There is a consensus."

"What?" gasped Whitley.

The Keeper only smiled, gripping the sides of the boat so as not to be tossed out.

He cleared his throat, straightening his tie, though almost immediately the wind flung it back over his shoulder.

"Life does not belong to you. It is the apartment you rent. Love without fear, for love is an airplane that carries you to new lands. There is a universe in silence. A tunnel to peace in a scream. Get a good night's sleep. Laugh when you can. You are more magical than you know. Take your advice from the elderly and children. None of it is as crucial as you think, but that makes it no less vital. Our lives go on. And on. Look for the breadcrumbs."

I think we were only half listening. We were all stupefied.

"It's been a pleasure." He bowed.

And just like that, he took up the oars again and rowed away.

The change was immediate. The water stilled. The storm tapered off. The roar of the waterfall faded to a whisper. The sun emerged out of the blue sky, glaring and hot. In fact, the scene so quickly transformed to a calm, serene lake with shimmering water that the memory of all I'd endured these past twelve wakes—or twelve million—seemed as hazy as some half-remembered dream.

It grew hot. Whitley and Kip stripped down to their underwear, and whooping and shouting, they cannonballed into the water as if it were the final hours of summer camp. Cannon, with a deadened look, threw himself headfirst over the side, and though I stood in alarm, calling out his name, he only kicked away from me on his back, his eyes closed. He seemed so tired. He seemed to want peace.

That left me with Martha. I had something important to say to her, and I might never have another chance.

"Martha."

She was watching Whitley and Kipling laughing about something. She turned.

"We've never been friends. I just want to tell you that I understand why. And it's okay."

She stared at me.

"I was his girlfriend. Everyone was in love with Jim. It wasn't so hard to imagine that you were too. I just wish we'd gotten to know each other better."

She tilted her head, frowning.

"Jim? You think I was in love with Jim?"

I nodded. She smiled.

"I never loved Jim. It was you. What you did for me. You saved my life."

She said it faintly. I wasn't sure I'd heard her correctly.

"Do you remember that night freshman year, during the snowstorm? The night of Holiday Dance. The power went out, and you ran back to the dorm to change your dress. You found me reading in the common room. You laughed because I hadn't noticed the window was wide open, and there was a snowdrift on the carpet. You stayed and talked with me, even though Jim was waiting for you."

I remembered. It was the one time we'd had a good conversation.

"It wasn't an accident the window was open."

I stared at her.

"I'd been planning it for weeks. I'd done the math. Sixth floor. Larkin Hall. A simple acceleration due to gravity across seventy-six feet. Even landing in a snowdrift, my chance of survival was less than one percent."

I couldn't breathe.

"It was stupid. One of those dark spells of loneliness that I thought meant everything. Little did I know, it meant nothing.

These monumental moments of our childhood, they're just one bend in the river, a tight curve filled with boulders so you can't see beyond. The river roars on across distances we can't even imagine. I was about to jump when I heard someone coming. It surprised me, so I hesitated, threw myself on the couch, grabbed some random book, pretending to read. You came in, and you saved my life. So here, in the Neverworld, I had to save yours."

I opened my mouth to say something, but no sound emerged.

"I thought for sure you were on to me," she said, shaking her head. "Like, back at the Warwick police station, how I suddenly appeared downstairs with you. You knew I was the one who removed the papers from Jim's case file, right?"

"What?" I whispered.

"It wasn't the Masons. It was me. I hid the files in another box so they'd never find them." She took a deep, unsteady breath. "Because it was all there. Jim's texts to you. I didn't want them to suspect you. That was why I was so against going back to Vulcanation. I didn't want them to find out the truth. So as soon as we landed, I snuck away so I could dismantle the ladder from the Foreman's Lookout before anyone else saw it. I climbed up fifty feet, got a million splinters, but I knew I had to present a compelling scenario with such assurance that they'd all be blind to the truth."

"What?"

She studied me with a soft smile.

"You know, Beatrice. You were there."

Chills ricocheted down my spine.

"I saw you. Coming back from the quarry." She squeezed

my hand. "You have nothing to feel guilty about. Whatever happened, I know you acted with a full heart. I never doubted you. And I never will."

All my blood drained into my feet. I was going to be sick.

"Jim loved you. But he didn't see you. He was incapable of that. You were the one to keep him propped up. You were his scaffolding. He could be riveting, and addictive. And you loved him, and we rarely see those we love as they are." She sighed, hunching her shoulders. "That's what killed me the most. Why I could never be your friend. Why I couldn't stay around you. You made me so mad, Bee."

She shook her head, staring at me, her face a wild pool of emotion barely contained.

"I've seen it before. It happened to my sister. She loved a boy, and that love made her put herself last and forget herself, and it killed her. Your love was that unquestioning. It made you do things that were dangerous. *That* ripped me up."

"What are you talking about, Martha?"

"*Nowhere Man*. Jim's musical? Everyone gushed about how brilliant it was. And it was. But it was strange, wasn't it, how suddenly after weeks of whining, being unable to write a single word, Jim had it all come together on the eve of his debut at Spring Vespers? Like magic?"

She stared at me, her face grave.

"You were the magic."

I was unable to speak. I felt as if a glaring light were suddenly shining into my eyes.

"You showed them to me the night of the snowstorm. Those

dream soundtracks. I never forgot them. I committed the words to heart. I recognized your voice immediately when Jim showed me what he'd written. 'You're my Sunday best, my new-car smell, / You're Château Margaux, no zinfandel.'" Martha shook her head. "Jim thought nothing of passing off your words as his own. Did he say he was just *borrowing* them? That he'd give you credit *later*? He swallowed everything around him, leaving nothing behind." She wrinkled her nose. "It's so funny. For such an energetic person, the space around him was always so cold. And anyway, his grand plans for himself always exceeded his *actual* talent."

She shrugged with a look of resignation. I felt a wave of hot emotion in my chest.

"Jim didn't steal the lyrics from me," I said. "I gave them to him. They were just sitting in a drawer in the dark, no use to anyone. I had to help him."

Martha surveyed me so intently, I felt light-headed.

"Everything I've done in this Neverworld," she said, "the good, the weird, the absurd, the exhausting, was for you. Pushing the discussion in a calculated direction. Asking you the pointed questions so I'd appear impartial. Distracting the others from seeing the rot that kept bubbling up around you all the time. Mold, breaking glass, tar, oil, tumbling trees, falling Lookout Towers— *God,* Bee, it was like trying to hide a typhoon swirling around you, all because of this secret you were hiding. That you were there that night."

She shook her head, biting her lip.

"I even spent a million hours talking to this kooky professor with scary facial hair and bad breath at Brown to learn the art of persuasion, to implant the idea in all of their heads that *you* had to go on, because you had to be the one to tell our story."

My mind was crawling stupidly over her words like a crab, trying to make them out.

What was she talking about? I had voted for Martha. Martha was going to live.

"I couldn't tell you what I was doing because you'd have tried to stop me. You'd have messed it all up. We had to get to the bottom of Jim's death for the vote, but you had to stay beyond blame. You had to remain Sister Bee." She shook her head. "I'm only telling you all this so you'll know. So you'll see. Because we all have our words tucked away in notebooks in drawers in the dark. You can't just give them away, Bee. They're yours. Like a fingerprint. Like your children. They are the light that shines your way. Without them, you'll be lost."

She reached out and gently tucked loose strands of hair behind my ears.

"Never, ever give away your words again."

Martha. *I was so wrong.*

"Anyway." She removed her glasses, folding them, carefully setting them on the seat beside her with a faint smile. "Chapter Seventy-Two. This is only the beginning."

She stood and, mumbling something that sounded like *breadcrumbs,* she dove into the water, kicking into the turquoise depths.

I sat there, shaken, unable to move.

So absolutely wrong.

I lurched to my feet, shading my eyes.

"Martha!"

There was no sign of her.

Whitley and Kipling, swimming a few yards away, turned in alarm.

"She was just here. Martha. I—I have to tell her. I have to let her know—" I was untying the skiff, grabbing the oars, crying as I steered the boat between the trees. "Martha!"

I jumped overboard, swam into the darkness, reached out into the empty cold.

When Whitley and Kip hauled me back into the boat, I was sobbing.

"She was just here. And now it's too late. Too late. Don't you realize? Martha. She's never coming back. I have to tell her. She's gone, and it's too late now to tell her—"

"Shhh," said Whitley, hugging me and wiping the tears from my cheeks. "It's all over now, Bee. Look around. It's almost gone."

———

Look around. It's almost gone.

If only someone had told me that before. About life. If only I had understood.

We didn't speak after that. We didn't need to. All we did was wrap ourselves in the blanket, and gaze out at the water.

Cannon was already somewhere else.

The sun was setting. It had turned the bold orange of children's paintings, and it was casting a warmth on our faces so gentle it seeped into us, filling every dark hole and lighting every corner. I'd felt this way before, back at Darrow on some ordinary Tuesday with my friends, when one of them said what I felt and life sharpened into focus, as it did sometimes. There was a momentary stillness, a sense of the eternal in the strands of our laughter like windblown ponytails, in the touch of our shoulders, side by side.

Something began to happen to me. Whether it was death or some other state in the mystery of all life, I didn't know. It pulled me to the bottom of the boat, leaving me staring up at the vast yellow sky. They had more time in their last wake, Kipling and Wit. But they would feel it eventually. I could see them crouched beside me, whispering words I couldn't hear, uncertain yet unafraid, their hands warm as they squeezed mine, waiting for what came next.

I would never let go of them. Never.

Then their faces dissolved into the darkening day, and I slipped away.

CHAPTER 26

I was floating in milky space.

Something hard was shoved down my throat. I heard footsteps.

"Good morning." A man was speaking. "How you holding up?"

There was a clattering noise. Someone was beside me.

"I know this is difficult. As I explained yesterday, we'll be taking this one step at a time. Her weaning parameters look very good. So I'm hoping to remove her breathing tube today. We need to see if she can follow commands."

There was a flurry of activity, hushed whispering. A hand touched my arm.

"Beatrice? Can you open your eyes for me?"

I blinked. All I could see were streaks of color.

"Oh, my God."

"Beatrice?"

"There. There she goes. . . ."

"Bumblebee?"

"Can you show me two fingers?"

Dizziness. I was floating in a swamp. I tried to lift my hand. My throat was on fire.

"What about your other hand? That's great. Wiggle your toes."

Someone was leaning over me. Suddenly a light beamed into my eyes, sending a hot purple pinball knocking around my skull.

I blinked again.

That was when I saw a TV on the wall. It was a morning talk show, the sound muted, the date at the bottom of the screen snapping into focus.

7:21 a.m. September 10.

I was alive.

——

As I fell back into the warm, watery darkness, my final conversation with Martha drifted through my head. It felt like she'd just left me moments ago. Her confession had turned me inside out. It was the secret I'd kept so deep inside my heart it had actually remained buried, out of sight, like a missing airplane that had vanished with such totality, some questioned whether the passengers had even existed.

Whitley hadn't realized how right she was.

When you think about it, we all killed Jim.

No one had ever questioned me—not my friends, not the police, not my parents. No one. Because I was the good one, Sister Bee.

I'm going to the quarry. Meet me.

In my dorm room, I listened to Jim's message over and over again, staring out the window at the empty lawn. I was so alone. I loved him. Yet I hated him. I hated how he could make me feel so alive, then invisible, as if he were a magician and I was the rabbit in his hat. I was desperate to see him, forgive him, to banish him from my thoughts. I wished he'd never seen anything rare in me. The prospect of being without him was too painful to imagine.

I jumped out of bed, threw off my pajamas, and slipped on the sexy lingerie I'd saved up for, the tight white jean shorts Jim liked, the white off-the-shoulder Gucci top borrowed from Whitley. I was going to sleep with him. It was a stupid decision, but it filled me with excitement, a concrete resolution I could hold on to like a towrope. I put on eyeliner and mascara, Whitley's red MAC lipstick. I pulled my hair out of its usual ponytail so it fell down my back. I pulled on my Converse, threw two candles into my backpack, yanked the comforter off my bed.

Then I went running out to Vulcan Quarry.

By a stroke of luck, I was so distracted by my decision to sleep with Jim that I left my phone on the sink in the bathroom. Later, I would gather that the detectives, pinging the cell towers on the night Jim died, saw that mine hadn't moved, providing me with an alibi. Yet if they had questioned me, I doubted they would have suspected I was lying. No one ever doubted anything I said.

And they should have.

When I arrived at the quarry it was 12:15. There was no sign of Jim. He hadn't arrived yet. The night was cool, the sky clear, stars bright. We always met at the base of the Foreman's Lookout and did the ascent on the ladder together. This time, I went first. I wanted to set everything up, to surprise him. I couldn't wait to see him, to forget it all, to go back to how things were in the beginning. I was scared too—scared to be with him again, scared of the doubt in my head. As I climbed, I noticed that some of the nails holding the ladder's wooden rungs were looser than usual. Others were actually missing, especially in the final few feet where you reached the hatch.

Halfway up the ladder I stopped, noticing not just that my hands were shaking, but that I had ripped my entire left shin without realizing it. It was bleeding, gruesome-looking. I looked like a skinned possum. I started climbing down again. I didn't want Jim to see me like this. I was lopsided, overtired. I was ugly, unlike Vida Joshua. Vida Joshua was a siren. I should go back to my dorm. That was the right thing, the safe thing.

I was almost on the ground when I stopped again. I was being a coward, meek, living so *pianissimo,* as Jim used to tell me. Why was I always so afraid of things happening to me? I began to climb up again—*Carpe noctem!* Whitley was always shrieking with her head back. Seize the night. Why couldn't I do it for once? When

I reached the landing, I noticed that some of the nails holding the ladder's wood rungs were rattling.

I lit the candles in the grimy room. I turned on the oil lamp on the old wood table where a hundred Darrow students had carved their initials. I spread out my comforter, undressed, and waited.

Soon I heard Jim. He was talking to himself, his words slurred.

I rolled to my feet, gathering the comforter around me. I crept to the landing, peering out.

He was halfway up the ladder. He was also drunk, swinging an arm out as he sang something. It was the lyrics to a new song in his musical, lyrics I had written.

" 'In the dark there grows a tree. / A castle tower shelters thee. When will I stop, when will I see? / There is no poison but for me.' "

Muttering, he began to climb again. I tiptoed back inside and reclined across the comforter. He'd be here within seconds. It was happening. The thought gave me a strange feeling of emptiness. I was making a mistake. It was obvious. I needed to stay away from Jim. I should be asleep in my room.

At that moment I heard a clanging noise. Jim was screaming.

I leapt to my feet. Three of the rungs by the landing had fallen away. Jim was barely holding on. He was straining to grab the next rung, but it was just out of reach. Gasping, he managed to swing his leg out so his foot rested on one of the crisscrossing beams supporting the tower legs.

"Bee?" He blinked up at me, sweat glinting on his forehead. "Oh, God, Bee. Thank God." He held out his hand. "Pull me up."

I froze. He began to shout, his face contorting.

"Beatrice! What's the matter with you? Pull me up! *Beatrice!*"

——

What happened in those four seconds?

I'll never know.

It was so fast. I saw Jim. Yet I couldn't move. I couldn't breathe.

I wished with all my heart I could say it was just panic, but it wasn't. It was something else too. A little cave inside my heart. Somehow I knew if I pulled him up I'd never be free of him. Maybe Martha was right. Maybe it was about the lyrics he'd taken from me, albums I'd slid in front of him after he'd been sobbing that he was a hack, that he'd never be as accomplished as his father, that it was all over, his dreams were done. I'd gone into my closet and handed him my collection of dream soundtracks, eleven books of lyrics and drawings I'd worked on all my life for no reason except they were the one place I could be myself. Maybe it was how he had taken them, sniffing as if I'd only handed him a pen when he knew what they were to me, what they had meant, and started copying my rhymes into his notebook. Maybe it was the question that if he could so easily take my words, would he take everything else?

My hesitation lasted only a moment. I sprang to life, racing toward him, wedging my feet in the landing door so they were secure, lying on my stomach, reaching to him.

I was too late.

He fell. His head smashed a wooden beam, his hat flying off. He hit the ground with dull thud.

He lay still, five stories below me, a streak of blood across his cheek.

The next minute was a dream. The realization of what had just happened got bulldozed dumbly around my disintegrating mind.

Jim's dead. Jim's dead. This isn't happening.

Madly I ran around the Foreman's Lookout, shivering, crying, blowing out candles, stuffing the comforter into my bag. I yanked on my clothes. I scrambled down the ladder four rungs at a time, barely making it around the gaping hole, threw myself into the grass.

I rolled to my feet, staring down at Jim.

Blood was oozing across the side of his face. His eyes were closed. He was dead. I was certain. I had to call the police. Yet, groping around in my backpack for my phone, I couldn't find it. Had I left it in the Lookout? Looking up, I realized I'd accidentally left the oil lamp burning. It was then that I saw headlights igniting the grass like wildfire. A car. It appeared, bouncing along the rutted road, a loose hubcap, radio blaring.

It was Mr. Joshua's beat-up red Nissan, the For Sale sign taped to the back window.

Vida Joshua. That was who I thought it was. What was she doing here? Had Jim meant to text her to meet him here, not me?

The question sent me retreating into the dark, sprinting back through the grass. I needed to go home. I needed my mom. I found the opening in the fence and struggled through.

Vida was going to find Jim and call an ambulance.

He would be fine. Everything was fine.

I don't remember sprinting back through the woods and across campus. The next thing I knew I was barreling up the steps to the fourth floor of my dorm, racing down the hall. That must have been when Martha saw me. She lived on my floor, studied in the corner common room. I hurried to my room and locked the door, stripping naked. Everyone says I'm the good one, the kind one, so that means I am, doesn't it? It means I always do the right thing.

I folded the La Perla underwear back into the tissue paper at the back of my drawer, returned Whitley's top to my closet. I found my phone where I'd left it on the bathroom sink. It was 1:02 a.m. No messages. My hands trembling, I managed to wipe the lipstick off, splash my face with cold water, yank the grass and leaves out of my hair.

The realization of what I was doing hit me like a slap in the face. What was I doing, not calling the police? I had to go to Jim. My love. I began to dial 911, but the conversation I was about to have with the dispatcher made me stop.

My boyfriend is lying dead in Vulcan Quarry. He fell. Please send an ambulance.

Are you there? Where are you?

I ran away. I was jealous of another girl. I was angry. I loved him. We'd had a fight.

Cannon. I needed Cannon, the problem solver. I ran across the courtyard and climbed the oak tree to his room on the third floor of Marlborough. I knocked on his window. No answer. I pulled it open. There was no one there.

Kipling. Kipling would help me. He had a tower room in Eldred. I climbed back down the tree, raced across campus, slipped in through the fire exit, up the back stairs. His room was empty too. When I ran along the gable to Whitley's dorm room and knocked on her window, she too was missing.

What was going on? Where was everyone?

Martha. Racing back to Creston, I could see her light on in the window on the fourth floor, but imagining her flat response as I confessed to her, weeping, frightened, sent me running straight back to my room, my heart scuttling around like a rodent in my chest.

I crawled into bed, staring at the ceiling. I kept telling myself to call my mom, but I couldn't move. Questions exploded in my head like grenades: If I'd never decided to surprise Jim, would he still be alive? Had he wanted to see Vida, not me? Had I loosened the rungs from climbing up and down and then up again? Where were my friends? Had Jim managed to call them for help, and were they with him right now, hearing all about what I'd done, that I'd let him fall and left him there? Had I killed Jim?

I had to go back to the quarry. From there I'd call the police. I climbed out of bed, yanked on jeans, a T-shirt, boots. I ran all the way out there again, petrified, certain Moses was going to catch me. When I arrived it was after four. My entire body shaking, I stepped to the spot under the Foreman's Lookout where the ladder was, and stopped.

Jim was gone.

There was no sign he'd ever been there.

No blood. A few blades of bent grass. Otherwise, there was nothing.

Vida had found him and taken him to the hospital. Or, by some miracle, he'd gotten up and walked away unscathed, which meant he loathed me now. They all did.

I returned to my room, staggered. All I wanted to do was die.

I wandered through the next day like a zombie. When I thought of the night before, the memories were distorted, as if I'd made them up. Had it actually happened? There was no sign of Jim. No one had seen him. Whitley, Kip, and Cannon all acted friendly but stiff. They said they'd been in their rooms all night. Martha claimed she'd slept in the library.

A day later, the news arrived: Jim had been found dead in the quarry lake.

It was impossible. I didn't understand. What had happened after I'd run away? What had Vida done to Jim? Why were my friends all lying? What were they afraid of?

To find answers, I'd gone to Wincroft.

And all along, Martha had known my secret. Martha had been cleaning up my every move, all the while protecting me.

How had I never seen it? How could I have been so blind?

——

When I opened my eyes, I was propped up in a hospital bed. The room was in sharp focus: pale yellow walls, counters and tabletops, an air conditioner, a vase of flowers, a teddy bear with a helium balloon proclaiming GET WELL SOON. In front of me sat a plate of hospital food, a pink cup with a straw.

There was no longer something lodged in my throat, though it felt scratchy and raw.

"She's awake," blurted my mom, turning from the window.

"My dear sweet Bumble," said my dad, stepping toward me.

They hurried over, peering anxiously at me. My mom was gripping a wad of Kleenex, her hair standing vertical in places from sleeping in a chair. My dad had more gray hair than I remembered.

"Don't try to talk," he said. "All is well. You're at Miriam Hospital in Providence. You were in a car accident, and you sustained a head injury. Bleeding on the surface of the brain. The doctors took care of it, and you're going to make a full recovery, okay, kiddo?"

I could tell my dad had instructed my mom not to talk very much, because she was nodding at everything he was saying, trying not to cry.

Just tell me my friends are still alive. They're recovering in rooms down the hall.

"You're going to rest," said my mom, squeezing my hand.

I looked past her across the room, where there was a framed print of a beach scene on the wall and a dry-erase board sign reading *Your nurse on duty is LAURIE.*

A bony teenager with a mop of blond hair was sitting in a chair by the door, staring at me. It took me a moment to realize it was Sleepy Sam, the British teenage boy I'd scooped ice cream alongside all summer at the Crow.

My mom followed my gaze. "You remember Sam."

"He's come here every day to read to you," said my dad.

Sam shuffled over.

"Really glad to see you open your eyes, Bee. Welcome back."

My dad clapped a hand on his shoulder. "Sam's a world-class dramatic reader. Who knew? He does all the different voices. Fifty characters? No sweat. He could have a big future on the West End."

It was then that I noticed the book under Sam's arm. The cover was silver with a collage of birdcages and steam trains, rosy-cheeked characters wearing top hats. *The legendary cult saga of future pasts. Present mysteries.*

The title sent a shock of adrenaline through me.

The Dark House of Elsewhere Bend.

"Good morning, Beatrice."

A silver-haired doctor in a white coat and green scrubs entered carrying a clipboard and a paper coffee cup. He was accompanied by an Asian woman, also wearing a white coat.

"Welcome back," he said. "Allow me to introduce myself. I'm one of your physicians. Dr. Miller. It is a pleasure to finally meet you."

He was leaning over me, shining a light into my eyes. When I looked past it to his face, I gasped.

I'd recognize him anywhere. He was and would forever be etched into my brain, floating in front of me whenever I closed my eyes for the rest of my life: those green, all-seeing eyes, the mahogany baritone, the elegant, exhausted manner suggestive of a retired ballet dancer whose every step held thousands of hours of rehearsal and a faint ache.

It couldn't be. It's impossible.

"When can she move to the rehab facility?" asked my mom.

"A few days. The weakness on the left side of her body and some of the short-term-memory difficulties should improve over time. But it can take months."

The Keeper.

He asked me to raise my arms, hold up three fingers, and bend my knees. He asked me if I knew what year it was, who the president of the United States was, my age. I was dizzy. I could hardly focus on anything he said, gaping as I was so incredulously at his face. He'd set down his paper cup on the tray in front of me. The tag on the tea bag dangled over the side.

He grabbed the cup, took a sip, turned on his heel. He whispered something to my parents as they moved after him to the door. Then he slipped out with the woman in tow, vanishing down the hall.

CHAPTER 27

My mom and dad had no choice but to tell me, even though I knew.

Kipling St. John.

Whitley Lansing.

Cannon Beecham.

Martha Ziegler.

They were dead.

I moved to the rehab facility and spent six weeks there, wandering the linoleum hallways with my soft-grip adjustable cane, practicing going up and down stairs and raising my left arm, which trembled and shuddered with a mind of its own. I snuck onto the public computer after dinner the first night I was there and read about it.

The accident was reported in the *Providence Journal,* the *Warwick Beacon,* and *USA Today.* All the articles used the same phrase: "shocking loss of young life." It also came up in a *Republican Nation* editorial about drunk driving and its prevalence in New England communities with a rising unemployment rate. Every story led with photos of Whitley, the textbook dead blond dream girl, then moved on to Cannon, Kipling, and Martha, always mentioning Martha's full scholarship to MIT. My name was mentioned at the very end, the name of the lone survivor, the lucky one.

Their Facebooks became memorials. I wasn't surprised. It had happened with Jim. Kids they barely knew at Darrow and friends from their hometowns posted messages like *my heart's broken* and *the world is empty now,* littered with prayer emojis, anonymous comments of *life is pain,* and GIFs of Heath Ledger.

I'd missed their funerals. I'd been in the hospital. So I read about them. All their hometown newspapers did follow-ups to the tragedy (because the initial articles had racked up hundreds of Shares and Likes), featuring photos of some red-eyed family member reading a poem in a church pulpit. The blown-up, framed picture of Kipling/Cannon/Martha/Whitley stared out from the easel beside them, their unwitting happiness and total lack of understanding of what was to come a powerful reminder that life, among many things, was all hairpin curves.

Linda Tolledo speaks during a service for her daughter, Whitley Lansing, who died in a car accident.

There was even an ongoing memorial of flowers, photos,

candles, and teddy bears being left on the side of the coastal road at the crash site. People took pictures of it and posted them with hashtags like #rip and #neverforget.

They never suffered, the police told my mom and dad. They all died on impact.

I survived because I hadn't been wearing my seat belt. I'd gotten tossed out, landing in a cluster of bushes, while the others were trapped in the car as it barreled down the ravine.

Little did anyone know the real reason that I'd survived: I had lived a century inside a second. I had died thousands of times, learned about and loved four people in a way few ever had the chance. I had called a place home where details such as life and death didn't matter, where what did matter were the trembling moments of connection in between.

And afterward, you felt nothing but awe for every second of your little life.

———

So began life outside the Neverworld.

It was different from what I remembered. *I* was different.

And it wasn't just the scar of a reverse question mark wrapping around my skull above my right ear. My hair hid the scar, but it was there if you looked for it, my tattoo, my memento. To outsiders I seemed confident, if a little solemn. I was less prone to biting my lip and tucking my hair behind my ears. I no longer worried whether people liked me, or whether I was pretty or had made a mistake. I wasn't afraid to eat in a crowded cafeteria at a table alone or talk to a cute boy I didn't know, or to sing karaoke, audition, give a speech. All the things people spend so much time worrying about in this world—the Neverworld had unchained me from all that. I was no longer in a hurry to fill silence. I could just let it sit forever like a bowl of fruit.

My parents' friends whispered, "Beatrice has really come out of her shell," and "You must be so relieved." They marveled when they heard the news that I had transferred to Boston College, was majoring in music theory and art history, working part-time at a video game company, volunteering at a nonprofit that had people read books at bedtime to foster children.

It was those kids I told about the Neverworld Wake.

I told no one else, not even my mom and dad. Somehow I knew that those children, with their wide eyes and knowledge of the dark, their kingdoms of morning and hide-and-seek, naptime, and snack, that they, of everyone, would understand. I told them I'd visited the secretest, wildest wrinkle in all the world. That one day, they might find themselves in one too, some lost dreamland between life and death, where past, present, and future are a jungle and hell can become heaven in the blink of an eye.

"How do we go there?" a girl whispered.

"If you're chosen, it'll find you. But the trick is not to be afraid. Because it isn't so different from this world after all."

Had the Neverworld been real? Or had it been a side effect of my injury, the *right-sided subdural hematoma requiring a craniotomy for evacuation,* eleven days passed in a coma, intubated and sedated. Sam had read me the book. One of my physicians looked like the Keeper. Had it all been in my head? Had my senses, as I slept, pulled details from the boisterous world in motion around me, spinning it into a reality that existed only for me?

Of course the Neverworld had been real, though I could never prove it.

I tried to. I tried to corroborate all the secrets. I discovered that while some things did check out—Mrs. Kahn did live down the road from Wincroft with her collection of snow globes; there was an exclusive marina called Davy Jones's Locker, a Ted Daisy who lived in Cincinnati, an Officer Channing at the Warwick police station who worked in traffic—others didn't. There was no mention of Estella Ornato on the Internet. Honey Love Fried Chicken had once existed, but it had been replaced with a Foot Locker the year before. The White Rabbit, the Black-Footed Sioux Carpet—there was no way of verifying them.

So many of the dots we had connected could not be connected here.

The only real evidence of the Neverworld's existence was time. It no longer ran in a straight line for me. Instead, now and then, it looped and lost its balance. An hour would pass in the blink of an eye. I'd sit down for a history lecture and my mind would wander so completely, the bell would ring and I'd realize in shock that everyone was packing up to leave, an entire class's worth of notes scribbled across the dry-erase board, which seconds earlier had been bare.

I'd look around, wondering if the Keeper was nearby, standing in a flower bed planting tulips or atop a ladder trimming ivy, because I recognized this out-of-body interruption for what it was: aftershocks of the Neverworld, instability, just as Martha had warned. My locomotive was skidding ever so slightly along the tracks.

I still thought of Jim. But he was no longer the ghost who haunted me. I saw him as a boy, beautiful and unsteady like the rest of us. I saw our time together closer to what it probably was—something between the wild imagining of love and the real thing. Sometimes in that shaky in-between we found each other and it was real. Other times it trembled and broke like a wild kite with too fragile a string. If Jim hadn't died, our love would have stopped and turned off the lights like the carousel in a traveling carnival, the music, played later, not as beautiful as I'd always thought. We would be barely remembered. In twenty years, we'd find each other on Facebook or whatever came after that, and we'd marvel at how ordinary we'd become, how all the glory we swore we'd seen in each other's eyes was gone.

I thought of my friends every day. Sometimes when I closed my eyes I could feel them beside me. I imagined where they were now. Because they were somewhere. And together. That I knew. I prayed that they were happy—or whatever lay beyond human happiness.

I think they were.

Mostly I thought of Martha, who she was and what she had done for me. There wasn't a moment of my life that I didn't owe to her. Sometimes it rendered me listless and sad, made me say no to the frat party, the Sunday-night pizza feast, the Spring Fling, and I'd hole up alone in my dorm, drawing or writing lyrics, left with the painful truth of it, how the people who change us are the ones we never saw clearly at all, not until they were gone.

I'd remember how Jim had insisted that one day I'd think with wonder: *I was friends with Martha Zeigler. That's how big she's gonna be.*

He had been right.

I shouldn't have lived. It should have been Martha. I was never the good one. I saw very little as it truly was. But that was what Martha taught me. We swear we see each other, but all we are ever able to make out is a tiny porthole view of an ocean. We think we remember the past as it was, but our memories are as fantastic and flimsy as dreams. It's so easy to hate the pretty one, worship the genius, love the rock star, trust the good girl.

That's never their only story.

We are all anthologies. We are each thousands of pages long, filled with fairy tales and poetry, mysteries and tragedy, forgotten stories in the back no one will ever read.

The most we can do is hold out our hands and help each other across the unknown. For in our held hands we find pathways through the dark, across jungles and cities, bridges suspended over the deepest caverns of this world. Your friends will walk with you, holding on with all their might, even when they're no longer there.

———

Two years after the accident, I published a dream soundtrack.

It was released by a little publishing house out of Minne-apolis called Brace Yourself Books. Not even they knew what to do with it. The market for an album soundtrack for a movie that doesn't exist is a pretty small one.

When I received the four printed albums from my publisher, though, I left school and boarded an Amtrak train bound for St. Louis. When I arrived, I took a bus to Winwood Falls, where I hiked a mile past pink brick mansions with shell fountains to a cemetery called Ardenwood. With a map I took the self-guided walking tour past mausoleums of famous writers and captains of industry, peeling off when I found a section for the new graves.

Whitley was up a stone path on a hill. Standing in front of her marble headstone made me cry, because the quote that Linda had chosen was from one of Jim's best songs, "Immortal She." The fact that she'd had the insight to comb Whitley's Instagram and find it meant that maybe I'd been wrong about her too. Maybe she'd understood her daughter all along.

She lives on, fireflies in my head.
I will not forget her when I am dead.
She is my memory, she is my song.
She is the road when the car is long gone.
She is the pillow on my bed.
She is my words, unsaid.
When the sun goes dark and the earth is bereft,
She'll live in the echo the silence left.

I set the little album by the flowers and walked away.

Next, I boarded another Amtrak, bound for New Orleans,

and then a bus with broken air-conditioning to Moss Bluff, a town with Spanish moss giving every street corner the shadowed scruff of a three-day beard. I walked the eight miles to Kipling's.

To my surprise, the house was just as he'd described it: a rambling white mansion of peeling paint, with a white peacock wandering the yard. I'd always thought he exaggerated his life, but in fact, he left out all sorts of colorful details, like the green Cadillac sitting in the middle of the driveway, weeds growing through the floor like hair overtaking old men's ears.

I left the album on the porch swing. When I looked back, I saw a bent-over gray-haired woman in a green housedress examining it. She looked after me, puzzled.

Then Los Angeles: two days on the train, barreling past deserts and strip malls and palm trees. I took a bus to Montecito, where I walked to Cannon's house, a cream-colored Victorian. I slipped the album into the mailbox and jogged down the steps as a car alarm sounded. A man across the street stopped watering his lawn to look at me.

Three days later, I arrived in Providence, Rhode Island. I had read seven mystery novels and twelve magazines, and was out of clean underwear, with a kink in my neck. I walked the final four miles feeling a strange sense of calm, arriving at Ziegler Auto Repair just after dusk.

There was no one in reception. Most of the lights were off. I stuck the album in the window next to a sign, COFFEE 99¢. As I was leaving, the door to the garage opened.

"Can I help you?"

I turned. It was Martha's dad. Though I had never met him, they had the same chin, the same thick glasses. He was wearing oil-streaked coveralls, wiping his hands on a rag.

I introduced myself, telling him I was an old friend of Martha's.

"Of course. Beatrice, right? That's so nice. It's not often I meet a friend of Martha's."

"I'm here because I made an album. Sort of. I wanted her to have it. It's a soundtrack for a movie that doesn't exist about four unlikely superheroes. They all have these hidden powers. Anyway, I wanted you to have a copy."

I held out the album, and he took it, turning it over. He put those thick glasses away and took out reading glasses, placing them on the end of his nose.

"Ah." He glanced up in surprise. "You dedicated it to Martha?"

I nodded.

"'To Martha. Who saw me and still believed.' How about that." He smiled at me, pointing toward reception. "You know, I got her posters up in the waiting room. She always had a vision of the world that lay beyond. Even when she was little. Nothing much scared Martha."

I let him show me her things, drawings she'd made as a child, a collection of paintings featuring an owl with purple feathers, blueprints of a winged invention she'd made. He showed me the work of Martha's older sister too, a girl named Jenny who had painted incredible canvases of oceans, hiding entire ink kingdoms and words inside the waves.

"Everything is on loan to us," he said, wiping tears from his eyes. "Even our children."

He offered me a root beer, but I refused, explaining that I had to go.

"Maybe I'll come back sometime," I said.

"Well, sure. You're always welcome."

I left him staring after me, turning the album over in his hands, doubtlessly sensing there was much more I hadn't told him.

Then I was on the bus, staring out the window at the darkened sky. At one point I saw a streak of orange light along the horizon, but it was only the track lights on the ceiling of the bus. The shimmering leaves of the passing branches seemed somehow electric and alive, more than usual, and though I wanted to believe it was some hidden world opening up for me again, I sat back against the seat and told myself the truth.

This time it was just the wind.

ACKNOWLEDGMENTS

I'd like to thank my editor, Beverly Horowitz, for shepherding me through my first adventure into the world of young adult books. From our first conversation three years ago through the many drafts, her wisdom, humor, and awake-all-night meticulousness were an education and an inspiration. I am also deeply indebted to my agent and friend, Binky Urban, for following me into uncharted territory, always providing unerring advice and insight.

I am especially grateful to the many creative thinkers at Delacorte Press who worked tirelessly on this book's behalf, especially Noreen Herits, John Adamo, Colleen Fellingham, Alison Kolani, Tamar Schwartz, and Rebecca Gudelis. Thanks also to Kate Medina and the team at Penguin Random House, whose commitment to writers and readers, no matter the trend, never fails to awe.

I would like to thank Felicity Blunt, Roxane Eduard, and Mairi Friesen-Escandell for introducing this book to readers abroad; Ron Bernstein for his film rights expertise; Brenda Cronin, Seth Rabinowitz, and Nicole Caruso, confidants and sounding boards; and Anne Pessl, first-draft champion, seer of all blind spots, and wonder-mom.

Most especially I wish to thank to my three Fates, David, Winter, and Avalon, whose vision of the world and reverence for all stories, great and small, are my daily joy.

Finally, I would like to thank every young reader who has ever approached me at a bookstore. It was you who whose passion for characters who empower and overcome inspired me to write this story.

ABOUT THE AUTHOR

MARISHA PESSL is the author of *Night Film* and *Special Topics in Calamity Physics,* her bestselling debut, which was awarded the Center for Fiction's First Novel Prize and selected as one of the Ten Best Books of the Year by the *New York Times Book Review.* She lives with her husband and two children in New York City. Visit Marisha online at MarishaPessl.com and on Facebook, and follow @marishapessl on Twitter and Instagram.